MW00960475

JANICE WHITEAKER

Take Me to Church, Book 1 of the Sinners and Saints series

Copyright 2023 by Janice Whiteaker.

All rights reserved. No part of this publication may be reproduced, stored in a retrieval system, or transmitted in any form or by any means electronic, mechanical, photocopying, recording, or otherwise without the prior written permission of the publisher and copyright owner except for the use of brief quotations in a book review.

First printing, 2023
Cover Image by Wander Aguiar
Cover Design by Janice Whiteaker

BLURB

One year ago I walked away from everything I knew and all the lies I'd been told.

For the first time in my life I was free from the constraints put on me by power hungry men who twist faith and devotion into fear and control.

All to feed their own egos.

Now my sister's ready to leave too, but the only one who can help me save her is a ghost from my past. One who's haunted my thoughts more than I'd like to admit.

Christian was my older brother's best friend. He saved me countless times when I was a little girl, protecting me from the wrath of my unpredictable father when everyone else in the house turned a blind eye.

Except Christian's no longer the lanky teenage boy from my memories.

He's older. Darker. Deadlier.

He's changed in ways I'm only beginning to understand. Ways that make me desperate for his touch. Ways that make me worry he still sees me as that little girl instead of the grown woman I've become.

But one thing hasn't changed.
Christian is still willing to do whatever it takes to keep me safe...
and he's more than ready to prove it.

This book features:

✔Age-Gap (10 years)
✔Brother's Best Friend (former)
✔Touch Her and Die (literally)
✔Dirty Talking Hero
✔No Cheating & No 3rd Act Breakup

TRIGGER WARNINGS

This book contains topics some readers might find difficult to read or hear about. These include spousal abuse, religious abuse, discussion of in-marriage rape, violence, and murder. Please consider skipping this story if you are sensitive to any of these subjects.

I

LYDIA

I SWALLOW HARD when I reach my destination, eyes going up, up, up as my stomach drops down, down, down.

I double-check the address texted to me by an unknown number, hoping it might have transferred incorrectly to the Maps app, but everything lines up, which means I'm right where I'm supposed to be.

And right where I'm supposed to be is apparently a dead-end road on the wrong side of Memphis.

The building in front of me is imposing and dark. It's three full stories high with gaping windows void of even a hint of light. The block exterior is painted a color so deep it might as well be black and the eerie edge of deterioration makes it seem almost sinister. It's the kind of place I'd normally cross the street to avoid passing.

Not tonight. Tonight I have to go inside and face the ghosts who haunt it. Nameless, faceless men who speak in whispers and codes, moving in the shadows of night, blurring the lines of good and evil as they take on the monsters of the world.

I hope they can slay one for me.

"*Hello?*"

The disembodied voice nearly stops my heart and I stumble back, scanning the dimly lit street for the source of the strangely pitched tone.

"Hello?" I hate how shaky my voice is. I've been through too much to show weakness now, so I clear my throat and straighten my spine. "Who's there?"

"*Hello?*"

I swallow hard when the single word repeats, thready and muddled. My eyes go back to the three-story structure looming over me. The face of it is lined in shadows that seem to move just when I start to blink, shifting around as I try to pin them in place.

Maybe the ghosts here are more literal than I initially thought.

The possibility of finding yet another flaw in the words my father spewed would normally intrigue me, but tonight I have more important things to worry about than the faults in his sermons.

I lift my chin, doing my best to brush off the odd sounding voice, and reach for the keypad fixed to the metal gate standing between me and my sister's safety. I attempt to punch in the code texted to me from the same unknown number that provided this address, but my hand is shaking so much I accidentally screw up and enter the wrong numbers. Dragging in a deep breath, I force myself to calm down yet again as I think of my sister and how much I know she's suffering.

Myra needs me to get it together. To prove I'm just as horrible as they all say I am.

"*Hello?*" The slightly screechy voice comes again, stealing any semblance of calm I managed to attain.

"Listen," I grit my teeth and clench my hand into a fist,

squeezing tight before stretching my fingers over the illumi-nated pad of numbers again, "I'm going to need you to stop being creepy for just a second so I can get this open." I slowly push my way through the code, letting out the air burning in my lungs as the lock flicks free. I take one more steadying breath before shoving the gate open and stepping inside what some might consider a courtyard.

If their standards for that sort of thing are very, very low.

It's barely deep enough to park a small car and completely overgrown. Ivy vines pile around the edges of the fence and foundation, clawing their way up the block and across the gutters. The front porch doesn't look much better. It's big, probably the same size as the entire yard, but just as rundown looking. The pillars and plank flooring are faded and peeling, and more than a few of the spindles are missing from the rails.

The place definitely looks haunted as hell.

"*Hello?*"

This time I ignore the voice. It hasn't responded to me yet, so there's no sense continuing to reply. That would be crazy.

I almost laugh because right now everything I'm doing seems crazy.

I'm alone in an industrial park on the outskirts of Memphis at midnight because a sketchy barfly told me the man who lives here can help me.

Can help my sister.

So, after nothing more than a handful of cryptic text messages offering a meeting time, location, and gate code, I'm here hoping to find that help instead of a homicidal maniac.

But maybe a homicidal maniac could be just as useful in this situation.

"*Hello*?"

I make my way up the narrow scrap of visible sidewalk leading to the crumbling steps, a little less phased by the repeated greeting than I was before, probably due to the fact that I'm more terrified of what awaits me on the other side of the door than what's lingering on this one. The steps feel sturdier than they look as I climb them, putting my focus on the door that might be the only thing left between me and the salvation my sister deserves.

A shadow moves, darting around in the corner of my vision, but at this point I'm almost getting used to the continued creepiness, so all I do is stop, waiting to see if it happens again. Something small slinks from the darkness, sliding across the porch before curling around my ankles. Wide, glowing eyes blink up at me. "*Hello*?"

The laugh that flies out of me is built of both nervousness and relief. "You're a freaking cat." I crouch down, scratching my ghostly friend behind one ear. "You scared the shit out of me, do you know that?"

"*Hello*?" The cat meows at me again, the odd sound just as otherworldly as the iridescent sheen the moonlight casts on its glossy black fur.

The lock on the door slides open, dragging my focus upward, along with the pace of my heart. I give the cat a final pet. "Wish me luck." Then I straighten and open the door, unsure exactly what I'm stepping into.

The interior of the building takes me by complete surprise. I fully anticipated the inside to match the outside, but it doesn't. At all.

Where the outside is dilapidated and foreboding, the inside is warm and, dare I say, welcoming.

Sure, the darkly painted walls mean it's almost as dim in here as it is outside, but there's nothing gloomy about what I'm looking at.

The floor is wide planked hardwood, stained a rich brown, and the stairs leading to the second floor are dramatic and sweeping. A large area rug cushions my steps as I quietly close the door behind me, not realizing my little friend has followed me in until he's circling my feet, back arched as he rubs against my bare legs.

"I hope you live here," I whisper. Letting stray animals into this guy's house probably won't make the best first impression, and I need this meeting to go well.

Especially since I'm asking him to bend the rules for me.

"Join me when you're ready." A deep, smooth voice carries out through the open door to my right.

I'm not sure how I expected the man I'm meeting to sound, but that wasn't it. Maybe under different circumstances I might consider the richly resonating tone sexy, but tonight it's only intimidating. The man waiting for me just through the door sounds confident. Powerful. Decisive. All good for my ultimate goal, but also nerve-wracking as hell as I prepare to meet him face-to-face and plead my case.

I glance at my reflection in the circular mirror positioned over a curved-leg table, taking a second to smooth down my freshly highlighted strands before straightening my shoulders and striding in, trying to look more confident than I am.

The room is an office. Large and masculine looking, with custom bookshelves built against the walls. Like the rest of the house, it's dark and shadowy, but it carries the same warmth the entryway did. The scent of leather and bourbon hangs in the air, making me glance down out of fear I spilled something on myself at work, but the jean shorts and T-shirt I'm wearing are fresh, pulled on before I rushed from The Cellar to get to this meeting.

"What can I help you with?"

I lift my eyes to the man sitting behind a large desk, swallowing hard at the sight of him. He's younger than I expected. Maybe only ten years older than I am, putting him in his early thirties. The line of his jaw is sharp and his nose is regally built, but barely crooked, as if it's been broken. The dark wave of his hair is thick and shiny.

In short, he's stupidly good looking. I shift on my feet, feeling even more uncertain I have what it takes to handle this situation. But I'm here. And this is my best shot at getting my sister the same kind of freedom I have.

He's not actually looking at me, which makes standing here a little easier. His dark eyes haven't left the computer screen to his right, scanning whatever he sees there as he waits for me to answer.

I swallow down the nerves climbing up my throat. He's just a man. A gorgeous one, admittedly, but still simply a man. And allowing men power over me is what brought us to this point, so it's time to suck it up. "My sister needs your help."

His gaze slowly drags to where I stand, leveling on me.

Most of my life I would have wilted under his stare. Shrank back, believing I needed to be smaller. Quieter. Sweeter. It's a difficult habit to break, one that has been ingrained in me since the day I was born, but I'm getting better at it. I lift my chin, meeting his oddly familiar hazel eyes. "Her husband's abusive. He's going to kill her if she doesn't get away from him."

He silently studies me as the seconds tick by. The need to tug at my clothing, to hide more of my body, to squirm under his scrutiny, crawls over my skin. But men no longer have power over me. Men no longer decide my fate and I am no longer responsible for theirs. So I wait, forcing myself to stay still. Forcing my eyes to hold his.

The hard set of his sharp jawline barely softens as his dark brows pinch together. "Lydia?"

I'm a little surprised he knows my name, though I probably shouldn't be. This man is supposed to have contacts all over Memphis and beyond. He's supposed to be able to help my sister get away from the man basically holding her hostage, so it shouldn't be difficult for him to find out who I am.

What confuses me though, is that he seems surprised. As if my identity is unexpected.

"Yes." I manage a nod. "That's my name."

He stares at me a second longer, the surprise on his handsome features morphing into something I want to say is disbelief. His broad frame suddenly shifts as he pushes to his feet. "Lydia Parks?"

My tongue fuses to the top of my mouth as I follow the long line of his body as it continues stretching higher. It seems like his voice isn't the only unexpected part of him.

This man is tall. Definitely taller than average. He's also one step beyond fit. Solid bands of muscle push and stretch at the black fabric of his T-shirt, fighting against the constraints of the shoulders and the sleeves. Every inch of him is toned and tight, built-up just past muscular and easing into bulky. Like his body is more for work than for show.

I force my focus back to his face, still fighting the rules of impropriety I was forced to live by up until a year ago.

That's when I see it.

The thin white line of a scar runs from his hairline to his eyebrow, cutting across the tanned skin of his forehead in an almost perfectly straight line that separates the dark hair of one brow in half.

I know someone with a scar like that, or at least I did, a long time and a whole different life ago. "Christian?"

I want to believe it's him, that the man in front of me is the same gangly boy I remember idolizing when I was little, but that would be impossible. Christian moved away years ago to be a preacher at a church in Georgia. Out carrying on the same misogynistic view my father is so fond of, eating up the life their way of thinking offers the men who keep it going.

The man's sinfully perfect lips slowly curve in a smile that probably sends women all over Memphis stumbling. "You remember me."

Oh shit.

It *is* Christian.

"Of course I remember you." The confession slips out, taking advantage of the shock loosening my lips.

Shock and a little awe.

I've imagined Christian as a man more times than I can count—and definitely more than I should admit—and not once did my brain come up with what's standing in front of me.

Which is probably a good thing.

My contact with the opposite sex was greatly limited growing up, especially once I hit puberty, so my isolated teenage brain didn't have many options to work with when the hormones started to hit.

But it had Christian. My older brother's best friend.

He was at my house more often than not for a few years, giving me plenty of memories to work with. Memories like the time he snuck me a snack after I was sent to bed without dinner for not bowing my head long enough during grace.

Or the time he hid me away when my father was on a rampage, looking for someone to belittle and degrade.

Or worse.

Unfortunately, it's also easy to conjure up other memories. Less factual ones. Ones my brain strung together late at night when I was in bed alone, lacking any sort of understanding of what exactly I was doing when I slipped my hand into my panties, pressing against the ache there as I thought about the boy from my memories.

The boy who is all grown up.

My skin heats with embarrassment as all those fantasies an innocent girl created come flooding back—sweet scenes of holding hands and closed mouth kisses I naïvely believed were in my future. But the thoughts take a turn as I stare down the man Christian has become. A man whose kisses are probably anything but sweet.

It's suddenly very hot.

His gaze skims down my body, quick and assessing, lingering just a second on the thin black line inked down the inside of my forearm. "What are you doing in Memphis?"

"I ran away." I blink, willing away the thoughts I should not be having. "I left a year ago."

Christian gives me an approving nod. "Good for you."

I glance around the office, forcing my eyes away from where he continues to study me, hoping I can get my wayward brain back on track. "I thought you went to Georgia to become a preacher."

Christian's expression hardens instantly, the clench of his jaw so tight I can see the muscle there twitch. "Is that what they said?"

I suddenly feel foolish. Like the past year hasn't taught me anything. "They lied."

"Of course they lied." Christian snorts out a bitter

sounding laugh. "That's what they do." He rounds the desk, dragging my attention away from the artwork lining the only space not eaten up by bookshelves or windows. "I'm glad you got away."

"Me too." One hand goes to my hair, smoothing it down as he continues to come closer. "I just wish I could've left sooner."

Maybe if I'd walked out when I first made the decision to leave I wouldn't be here begging for my sister's freedom. Maybe we both could have escaped. Started the lives we deserve to live instead of being trapped in an existence someone else decided for us.

Christian is quiet for a minute. His voice is low and soft when he asks, "What about Myra?"

"She's why I'm here." I move toward him, feeling confident about this meeting for the first time.

Christian knows me. Knows my family. Knows why I need to get my sister away from them.

"I need you to help her escape her husband." I dig into my purse, pulling out my phone and swiping the screen, flipping it his way so he can see the proof of just how much danger she's in. "This was two weeks ago."

Christian flinches at the image of Myra, her eye swollen and her lip bleeding. "That the first time?"

I shake my head. "Not even close."

She's had bruises more often than not since my father married her off to one of the most well-connected men in his congregation, leveraging his way into yet another powerful, wealthy family by using his own flesh and blood as currency.

I drop my arm and move closer. "He's awful. He locks her up for days at a time. He hits her. He starves her. He—" My voice cracks but I won't let that stop me from sharing the awful, horrible truth of what my sister and so many of my old friends face. "He rapes her." I practically spit it out, disgusted at how easily Matthias, and men like him, twist faith into a shield, thinking it will save them from the truth.

It won't. Not if I have anything to say about it.

"And you're sure she's ready to go?" Christian's skepticism dampens a little of my hope. "Because I need to hear it from her."

I deflate a little more.

The regular at the bar warned me Myra would have to tell them she wanted to leave herself, but I hoped that rule had a little flexibility. That the picture I showed him would be the unspoken words he needs to hear.

Because right now there's no way for Myra to tell Christian she wants to leave Matthias.

"I can't make that happen." My chin quivers the tiniest bit and I hate how weak it makes me feel. "Because I can't find her."

2

CHRISTIAN

LYDIA PARKS IS the last person I expected to walk into my house tonight.

Seeing her standing in my office, a freed woman, is a shock—

And a relief.

The little girl I remember following me around her family's house was always too sweet to be trapped in the life she was born into, but I knew the chances of her getting out of it were slim to none. Yet here she is, looking like she's left every part of that world behind her. The long skirts and high-neck shirts women are instructed to wear, out of modesty and to protect men from the sin of lust, have been replaced by cutoff shorts and a draping T-shirt exposing way more than the sinful line of her collarbone. Her long brown hair has been cut just below her shoulders and highlighted, racking up the misdeeds the world we came from would tally against her.

But I'm not here to notice how different, and grown-up, the little girl from my past has become. Lydia came to me for help, and I intend to do everything in my power to offer it to her.

But there are limits.

"Then we have to wait." I hate having to say this to her, but I do. "I can't offer Myra help until she tells me she wants it."

It's one of the few rules I live by. And as much as I wish I could break it for her, I can't. I know just how dangerous it is when a woman leaves a man only to go back again, and the likelihood of that happening is greater when she's not willing to look me in my face and tell me she's done.

Lydia comes closer, her big brown eyes pleading as they gaze up into mine. "She would tell you if she could, Christian. I promise." She reaches out to grip the front of my shirt in a bold move that surprises me. "She asked me for help. Begged me to get her away from him." Her hand twists tighter, like she thinks she can hold me hostage until I agree.

Most people would never try what she is. They're intimidated by me. Know what I'm capable of. But Lydia's seen me at my best. She only knows what I used to be before I was faced with the harsh reality of the way the world really works. I want to hold onto that the same way she's holding onto me so I cover her hand with mine, trying to provide a little comfort in a situation I know is breaking her heart. "I believe you, but saying that to you and saying that to me are two completely different things." It's easy to tell your friends and family you're done. They love you. They're less likely to hold it against you or judge you if you change your mind.

But me? Telling me means I'm showing up on your doorstep, ready to make whatever mess I have to in order to get you out of there safely. Telling me is final. Telling me means you want to get away by whatever means necessary and you won't be going back.

Lydia's hand squeezes tighter, managing to twist a few chest hairs into the bunch of cotton clenched in her fingers, but I welcome the pain. I deserve it.

Because I have to tell her no.

"You know what they're like, Christian. You know what happens to women who start to stand up to them." Her voice carries a surprising edge. One that stokes the fire of fury that feeds me.

"How do *you* know what they do?" The thought of any of the men from our shared past touching her makes my skin burn. "Which one of them hurt you?"

Her chin barely lifts, giving me a peek at the defiant nature responsible for carrying her to freedom. "Does it matter?"

"It matters to me." I remember hiding her away when things got out of control at her house. Sneaking her food when her dick of a father tried to punish her. I protected her then and I will sure as shit protect her now. "I want to know whose face I need to put my fist through."

Her eyes hold mine, hope springing back into their depths. "Does that mean you'll help me?"

"I never said I wouldn't help you, Lydia." She's killing me right now, but I know the kind of men we're dealing with here, and they are nothing like the ones I normally face. "But I need to hear it from Myra."

Normally, the woman who goes back to an abusive relationship is the one in danger, but this situation is different. If Myra leaves and then goes back, she won't be the only one at risk. Lydia will be as well. She'll be labeled as something even worse than she is now. Not just a sinner who turned away from God's word, but something evil trying to take others down the path to hell with her. She will never see her sister again. She won't be able to set foot in town, not without risking her own safety.

Most people don't understand how groups like this work. They don't see the darkness they hide behind their soft voices and carefully crafted images.

"Fine." Lydia lets go of my shirt, yanking her hand out from under mine and lifting it to wipe at her eyes as she steps back. "Thanks for nothing."

Even though she's angry, her voice is still sweet and soft, a testament to just how deep the teachings of Will Gardner and the cult he calls a church run.

"You know I want to get her out of there just as badly as you do, but I've seen what happens when women aren't really sure. When they go back." I don't try to temper the harshness that creeps into my words. I need her to understand why I can't give her what she wants, no matter how much I might want to. "You think she's getting hurt now, just imagine what it will be like if she leaves and then changes her mind."

"She won't change her mind." A little of the softness leaves Lydia's voice, replaced with a sharp certainty I wish I felt.

"I know you want to believe that, but most women who leave go back." It's a devastating statistic, one that turns my stomach. I wish it wasn't true and do everything in my power to bring that percentage down, but I can only accomplish so much.

"Whatever." Lydia turns from me, shoulders a little more slumped as she moves toward the door, pausing to glance back my way when she reaches it. "For what it's worth, I'm glad you didn't move to Georgia to become a preacher. I hated thinking you were one of them."

The second the words are out of her mouth, she's gone.

Footsteps moving quickly through the entry before the front door quietly closes behind her.

I groan, raking one hand through my hair as the bell signifying the gate latch opening chimes. "Fuck."

I hate when shit like this happens, but I especially hate that it's happening with Lydia. I should be able to help her. She should be able to rely on me. To trust me because I know exactly what she's dealing with. But I won't risk Myra getting hurt worse, and I sure as hell won't risk Lydia's safety. Especially since she's finally free of those fuckers who thought she belonged to them.

The security system chimes again as I slump into the chair behind my desk, grabbing the bottle of bourbon from the corner to add a few more fingers to the glass I've been nursing all night.

I've swallowed down half of it by the time Tate reaches the doorway. He leans against the frame, eyeing me as he crosses his arms. "Meeting went that good?"

"Worse." I swallow down another mouthful before staring into the glass. "It was someone I know." I pause before correcting. "Used to know."

The Lydia that came to see me tonight was nothing like the little girl I remember, and it has little to do with her being a fully grown woman.

A fact which also didn't escape me.

"Oh shit." Tate's arms drop as he straightens. "Who was it?"

I work my jaw from side to side, fighting my way through the bitterness and frustration that continue to linger. "Her older brother and I were best friends when I was a kid. I used to spend as much time at their house as I could because it was better than being at my own." I lift my eyes to meet his. "Which isn't saying much."

Families like Lydia's and mine live behind a mask. One they create to hide an ugly truth. A truth they will do anything to keep from coming out. That's why I can't help Myra until she calls me herself. No matter how much I want to.

Tate crosses the room and drops down onto the leather sofa along the wall. "Can we help her?"

I reach in my drawer and pull out another glass, sliding it his way because I know he's about to be as pissed off as I am. "No." I nudge the bottle of bourbon closer. "Lydia wants us to get her sister out, but she's been cut off."

The IGL has a method for dealing with women who step out of line. First they're threatened with eternal damnation. Next they're shunned. If she continues to act out, violence comes next, at the hand of the man tasked with running her life, be it father, brother, or husband. Sometimes all three.

If that's not enough to stop a woman from daring to think on her own, she's moved someplace off the grid under the guise of healing and holiness. They make it clear no one can help them. That if they don't fall back they will never have freedom again.

Most women crack easily. No one wants to be separated from their friends and family, so the technique is frequently effective. Hopefully it is this time too, because the only way we can do anything for Myra is if we can talk to her.

"Will you be okay handling it if we can go ahead?" Tate watches me as he pours himself a drink. "Simon and I can take the lead on this and you can step back if—"

"No." I clench my fist, a little too bothered by the thought of my best friends being the ones to help Lydia. Of them being the ones she looks to for protection.

My memories of her have always mattered to me more

24

than they should. Over the years I relied on them to remind me I wasn't always the ruthless man I've turned out to be.

But her memories of me obviously didn't sit the same. For years, Lydia thought I left without a second thought, choosing to stay in the fucked-up world that tried to break her, and that bothers me. Almost as much as it bothers me I can't go find Myra tonight and get her someplace safe. "I need to be a part of this if it happens."

I haven't been back to the little town in Arkansas where we grew up since I was thrown out in the middle of the night fifteen years ago. Sent away to survive on my own with nothing but a half-assed homeschool education and a complete lack of understanding on how the real world works.

Tate watches me a second longer, clearing his throat before shifting to a less touchy topic. "Simon called earlier. Said he was coming in early Friday so we could rehearse for the show this weekend."

"I'll believe it when I see it." Simon is notorious for rolling into town an hour before we're set to play.

Or an hour before we're set to knock heads together and pull a woman from a bad situation.

He grew up in the same sort of way I did and it's left him unwilling to put down real roots. To lose any of the freedom so many people take for granted.

"It sounded like it was a done deal. His job in West Virginia is finished and he's packing up to head back this way." Tate tips back a little of his bourbon, rocking his jaw from side to side as he rolls it around his mouth before swallowing. "Sometimes I wish I had his life. It might be nice to get away now and then."

I manage to chuckle at that. "You and I both know you would hate not having a consistent schedule." Tate is a creature of habit. Even more than I am. He gets up at the same time every day. Does his laundry on Sundays. Eats his lunch at noon. Hell, I'm pretty sure he even plans his shits.

"Don't act like you're not just as bad as I am." Tate's mouth curves in a slight smile. "I see your bedroom light go out at the same damn time every night."

In my younger days I might've been ashamed of my boring life, but that was back when I thought the only way to live was wild and free.

It's probably the same way Lydia's living now, stretching her wings after spending so many years being caged and controlled.

"I get up early." I take another sip of my bourbon, this one more sparing than the last few. "If I don't get enough sleep, it's a hell of a lot harder to haul piles of shit out to a dumpster."

Tate lifts his pointer from the rim of his glass and aims it at me. "That's why my business is better than yours. No heavy lifting."

His claim isn't entirely true, but most of the lifting Tate does is limited and aided by machinery. Fixing cars isn't clean or easy work, but it's not quite as back breakingly physical as the career I fell into.

"That's probably why you're getting soft around the middle." The jab is unfounded and we both know it. Tate is every bit as solid as I am, only he has to put in time at the gym while I get more than enough of a workout at my job.

Tate rubs one hand across the flat plane of his stomach, grinning at me. "It's all the potlucks my employees have."

"You better watch out. Someone might try to start poaching your staff." I shove away the last of my drink, deciding it's not worth suffering over tomorrow. "Hell, it might be me."

"Liar." Tate sets his own drink down, proving I'm not the only one making different decisions than they used to. "You know damn well they wouldn't come work for you anyway."

I scoff, feigning surprise. "Why the hell not? They'd get ten weeks paid vacation a year."

Tate's head falls back on a laugh. "You have to give them ten weeks off because of all the stuck-up old bitches they have to deal with."

I make a tsking sound. "The richest men in Memphis don't appreciate being called bitches."

Tate smirks. "I bet a few of them would pay extra for the women on your payroll to call them worse."

He's not wrong. Both our businesses are staffed mainly by the women we've helped over the years. Freeing them from a bad situation isn't enough to really make a difference in their lives. They need a way to support themselves and the children they often bring along. Residential demo and car repair might not be the most glamorous of professions, but they pay well and provide the stability these women are searching for.

Plus they know their bosses won't hit on them.

"I don't doubt that." I straighten, snagging my glass and Tate's. "And after what they've been through, a few of them might be willing to do it for free." I carry the glasses out of my office with Tate following behind me. "Speaking of time off, I've got the next few weeks free if you want me to help out at your place."

Tate, Simon, and I, along with most of the family we've managed to build ourselves, have taken over a dead-end street in an old industrial park on the outskirts of Memphis. In the past five years, we've managed to purchase every building on the block, renovating them one by one into the kinds of homes none of us ever dreamed we would have. Many of the houses are fully finished, but a few of us are dragging our feet.

Or maybe we just don't have the same motivation.

"I might take you up on that." Tate leans against the custom concrete counters in my kitchen as I load our glasses into the dishwasher. "I'm getting real tired of living in a construction zone."

"And probably real tired of inviting women over and not being able to make them breakfast." I close the appliance and switch it to run.

Tate rubs one hand along the back of his neck, looking oddly uncomfortable. "I don't do as much of that as I used to."

I lift a brow at him. "Probably because you ran through every available woman in town."

He scoffs. "Don't act like you've been a fucking monk." His gaze lingers, moving over my face. "It just isn't the same as it used to be." His next breath is deep and long, rushing out on a sigh that's just as substantial. "I've been thinking maybe I'm missing out, you know?"

I'm a little stunned by his admission, but maybe I shouldn't be. Because I've been feeling the same sort of way, and it makes me regret passing on that last swallow of bourbon.

"I do know."

3

LYDIA

I HANG UP the phone and groan. "That is the tenth call I've answered from someone wanting to know what time we're opening the doors tonight." I turn to Piper, my best friend and one of the bartenders filling the drinks I'll be delivering at The Cellar tonight. "I feel like it's a sign this is going to be a shit show."

Piper waves me off, looking unconcerned as she continues to get set up for our Saturday night shift at the bar where we met. "Nah. That's pretty normal for when these guys play." She gives me a wink. "And it means you're probably gonna make hella tips tonight."

I could definitely use the money, but I'm not in the mood to be the kind of pleasant that will earn me top dollar. Just because Christian won't help me save Myra doesn't mean I'm giving up, but after spending the week looking for a plan B, I'm feeling frustrated and sour.

Because it turns out my options are pretty slim.

Slim and expensive and a little scary.

"And, if you do a great job, maybe Stella will give you

more Saturday night shifts." Piper crouches down to double check the stock, doing her best to improve my foul mood with the promise of a more lucrative schedule. "This is the third time in five weeks Danielle has called off, so I'm pretty sure Stella's going to stop giving them to her."

A week ago I would've been thrilled at the possibility. I've been working at The Cellar since moving to Memphis, grateful anyone at all would give me a job since I had a limited education and even more limited life experience. Luckily, Stella, the owner, didn't bat an eye at my situation and hired me on.

Of course I get the least desirable shifts, but I still make more than enough to pay my half of the rent on the apartment Piper and I share, so I'm not complaining.

Piper straightens. "And I'd sure as hell rather have you here on Saturdays. At least I know you'll bust your ass as hard as I do." She jerks her head toward the back room. "Come help me bring up some backstock."

I follow her into the storage area of the historic building The Cellar occupies in downtown Memphis. The bar takes up the walk-out basement of the navy painted brick structure. A neon sign points down a cement staircase that leads to the front door from the street, giving the place a sort of retro, speakeasy vibe that appeals to both the visiting crowd and the natives. The upper floors have been renovated into the gorgeous loft Stella calls home. Seeing her success was mind-blowing when I first arrived in town. I was told my future was only about finding a husband and making babies and then taking care of them, so seeing a woman with her own life and her own money shocked me in the best possible way.

Gave me hope that I could do it too.

Not that I expect to ever be as successful as Stella. She's

built The Cellar into one of the best-known bars in town. She brings in the most popular local bands and hosts local events that bring in crowds even during my early shifts.

But I'm starting to suspect those crowds were nothing compared to what I'm about to see tonight.

Piper and I spend almost thirty minutes collecting everything we need to get through the night from the back room, stacking it all in empty boxes before organizing what remains on the shelves for the next person. By the time we're coming out, I can hear the scratchy sound of the speakers as the sound guy helps tonight's band get set up.

"Thank God they finally got here." Piper huffs out a breath as she pushes through the swinging door leading to the bar. "I was starting to get a little worried."

I carefully set down my load of boxes and go to work sliding the bottles into place. "What time do they normally get here?"

"These guys?" Piper rolls her eyes. "They pretty much get here whenever they want." She empties out her first box and slides it away. "But everyone puts up with it because of how many people they bring in."

I stack my empty box into hers. "Are they that good?" My musical knowledge is pretty limited. I spent the first twenty years of my life closed off from the outside world, listening to nothing but the holiest of Christian music. All of it was prescreened by the leaders of the IGL to ensure it met their strict standards. Of course I can listen to whatever I want now, but I've had more important things to focus on.

Things like getting an education and figuring out how to help my sister.

"Good doesn't even begin to describe them." Piper looks my way, her expression serious. "Just wait. The lead singer's voice will melt the panties right off your body."

I snort out a little laugh because the chances of that happening are slim to none. I've definitely educated myself more on the world of sex than I have music, but so far I haven't actually dipped my toe into the waters of physical intimacy. It's not as easy as I expected to move past the beliefs ingrained in me from the moment I was born, so I've decided my panties are better off staying on for a little while longer.

Especially since the only object of my fantasies shut me all the way down.

I understand Christian's point, but I'm still angry. Still frustrated. Still disappointed.

But tonight I need to shove all those feelings aside. Focus on what's important. Bust my butt and rake in all the money I can.

Because the only group I found willing to help me collect my sister charges a hefty fee. I guess that's the price you pay for the luxury of a no-questions-asked type of situation.

I finish emptying my last box and stack it with the rest, snagging them before heading straight back into the storage portion of the basement and carrying them to the spot we stack our recycling before hurrying back down the hall. My hand is on the door when I hear him. The lead singer's voice is smooth and deep, carrying just the hint of a ragged edge, adding interest and depth.

I push open the swinging door and step out, hoping to hear a little better.

Piper smirks at me from behind the bar. "Told you."

I scrunch my face up at her. "My panties are still firmly in place, thank you very much." It would take a whole lot more than just a great voice to make me consider crossing that bridge.

But that doesn't mean I don't want to get a look at the man connected to the ridiculously sensual tone carrying through the empty bar. I snag a rag from one of the buckets of bleach water behind the counter and wring it out. "I'm gonna go make sure all the tables are wiped down." It's a lame excuse, but Piper doesn't call me out on it. Probably because she's enjoying being right a little too much.

I start on the tables closest to the bar so it looks like I'm just going about my job, which I am. I do need to make sure the tables aren't sticky. I just probably don't need to wipe each and every one of them.

But that's what I do, creeping closer to the corner I need to see around to get my eyes on the stage. I work quickly but it still seems to take forever to reach the edge. When I step around the final hi-top, the stage comes into view. The second my gaze lands on the lead singer, the rag falls from my hand. All I can do is stare. Partially because I'm a little in shock and partially because I've always had a hard time keeping my focus off the man standing in front of me.

I thought Christian looked good when I saw him the other night, but that was nothing compared to what I'm seeing now. He is clearly in his element up on that stage, lips hovering a breath away from the microphone as his fingers stroke the guitar held tight to his body. The words coming out of his mouth are unlike any song I've ever heard.

This isn't music. This is more like vocal seduction.

At least what I would imagine seduction to be like.

Christian's eyes are closed as if he's completely immersed in the music, and for a second I close my eyes too, lured in by the sound of his voice. It's so familiar and yet so different, and the combination does things to me. Tingly, achy things. Things that make me imagine what it might be like if Christian touched me in all the ways the internet has shown me are possible.

Christian stops singing and the abrupt pause jolts me, sending my eyes flying open. They meet his across the room and we stare at each other. I feel like I've been caught doing something I shouldn't. Not because I was enjoying music I've been taught to believe is a gateway to sin and self-destruction, but because I'm now pretty sure I understand exactly what Piper was trying to tell me. My panties aren't necessarily dropping, but the thoughts I'm having about Christian are anything but holy.

"This is an interesting reaction." Piper moves in at my side, crossing her arms as she looks between me and Christian, smirking. "Seems like you two might know each other."

I force my eyes away from the stage, crouching down to grab the rag I dropped before spinning away. "I don't want to talk about it."

Piper chases after me, completely undaunted. "I can totally see that, but you know there is no way we aren't discussing whatever in the hell is happening." She sounds a little too excited right now and that only sends the heat of embarrassment creeping across my skin faster.

"Nothing is happening." Actually, something should have happened. I should have chucked my bleachy bar rag right at the center of Christian's face, called him an asshole, and gone back about my life.

Instead I stood there hypnotized by the sound of his voice and the imaginings of a little girl that were quickly turning into the fantasies of a woman.

"Lydia." Christian's tone is sharp and demanding behind me and I almost stop. I've been trained to jump when a man calls. Conditioned to act on their whims. But that stopped a year ago, and I have no intentions of starting back up.

I keep walking, shoving through the swinging door and into the dimly lit hall, doing my best to get away from both my friend and the man who let me down. I duck into an open doorway, leaning back against the wall and letting out a breath.

I've barely relaxed when I hear a body hit the swinging door, flinging it open so hard it bounces off the wall.

"*Lydia.*" The frustration in his voice sends me slinking deeper into the room, pressing tighter to the wall. I don't want to face him now because I'm really not sure what I'll say. I know I shouldn't be as mad as I am. I understand where he's coming from. But that doesn't change that he's refusing to help me when I need help the most.

Christian rushes into the room, big body blocking out the tiny bit of light filtering into the windowless space from the hall. His eyes find me too quickly, locking onto my ineffective hiding space. Again, we stare at each other. It seems to be a thing we do. Like we're still not quite sure we're seeing what we think we're seeing.

He is different but yet so much the same. Bigger, broader, but still focused and intense. Like there's so much more brewing beneath the surface. I've always been fascinated by him and apparently that's yet another thing that has not changed.

His gaze is sharp as it fixes on my face. "Why did you run from me?"

It's a complicated answer. One I still struggle with every day. "You know why."

I find a certain amount of comfort knowing Christian understands me. Understands the life I was forced to live.

Most people don't.

37

Most people can't grasp the extent of what went on in my childhood and teenage years. What would have happened in my adult life. Even when I try explaining it to someone, I can see in their face that they don't really believe what I'm saying is true. They can't imagine that I didn't watch television until I was twenty years old. That I'd never had fast food or worn jeans. That I didn't fully grasp the concept of the internet or how complicated cell phones could be.

The goal of the IGL was to keep me, and every other woman and girl in the church, as innocent and naïve as possible. It made us easy to manipulate and control.

And when that didn't work, they used fear. They took away any luxuries we did have one by one.

If that wasn't enough, they threatened. Yelled and screamed about hellfire and damnation. Eternal suffering and unbearable pain.

Then they resorted to violence, and that was where I drew the line.

That's also why my first instinct is to run. To hide.

Christian's nostrils barely flare as he moves closer. "Who put their hands on you, Lydia?" The voice that was so smooth and melodic seconds ago is now deep. Lethal. Hinting at a level of danger that makes my heart flutter just like it did when I was six years old and Christian came to my rescue. "I want names."

"You don't need names." I swallow hard, trying not to wilt under his scrutiny. "You know exactly how things work with them."

It was my father and brother's responsibility to keep my sister and me in line. They were the ones that stepped in when I started to walk too far outside the margins of where

I was supposed to be, taking my punishment for bad behavior into their own hands. Literally.

Christian's whole body is strung tight, like he's struggling to keep it together, and that only makes my heart beat faster. Makes those old, silly feelings I'm still harboring for him flare to life even though I know they're not real. They're just one more byproduct of the sheltered life I was forced to live.

"Everything okay?"

I nearly jump out of my skin at the unfamiliar voice.

Christian steps in front of me, blocking my view of the man now standing in the doorway. "Everything's fine."

I expect the man to leave, but he lingers. "Didn't seem like everything was fine when you fuckin' ran off." His words come in a slow drawl. "Who was that girl?"

He must not know I'm in here too. It almost makes me feel like I'm hearing a conversation that's not meant for me, but that's Christian's problem. He's the one who chased me in here.

"I don't want to talk about it." Christian's words are clipped and short. "I'll be out in a minute."

The guy I can't see doesn't immediately move, but eventually I can hear him shift around. "Don't take too long. We've got to finish the sound check before they open the doors."

Christian offers a jerky nod and the man slowly retreats, his steps unhurried as they drift away.

"Who was that?" I whisper, feeling like I need to stay quiet so the other guy doesn't know Christian basically lied to him. I now know it's not my job to protect men from themselves, but old habits die hard, and this is yet another one I'm still attempting to murder.

"The bass player." Christian moves away from me and for a second I think he's going to leave—going to give me room to breathe again before I have to go out and pretend like everything is fine.

But then he grabs the door and swings it shut, closing us into the little room, before turning that intense stare my way. "We need to talk."

4

CHRISTIAN

I KNEW OUR paths would cross again. I just didn't expect it to happen so soon.

I was hoping to give Lydia a little more time to cool off before I tracked her down and explained exactly why I couldn't help her just yet. But fate has forced me to show my hand early. Hopefully she's not as upset with me as it seems because I need her to listen objectively.

"If we go get Myra before she's ready, the chances of her going back are high." The space is cramped enough that my body barely brushes hers and the soft scent of her skin reaches my nose. Teasing me to distraction. I clear my throat, forcing myself to stay on topic even though all I want to do is inch closer. Breathe a little more of the sweet smell surrounding her. "And if she goes back her life will be ten times worse than it is now." Normally that's the extent of my concerns, and even that's plenty. But this time my fears go far beyond just Myra's safety and Lydia needs to know that. She needs to understand it's not just Myra that might suffer if this goes wrong. "And they will blame you. At the very least they will cut her off from you completely. You will never see her again."

"She won't go back." Lydia's sweet voice carries a level of certainty I need to feel too. "She's worried he's going to kill her. Women don't go back to someone they think is going to kill them."

I wish I still carried her same level of innocence. I wish I still believed that escape was possible for everyone. That each abused woman had the level of support it takes to break away.

But they don't. And when abuse is all you know, the task of leaving is daunting. Abusers make sure of that. They break you down. Snap off pieces until you're nothing. Until you're positive you can't exist on your own. Until you believe you don't deserve more. It's heartbreaking. It's frustrating.

But it's reality, and pretending it's not only gets people hurt.

And that could include Lydia.

"I know you believe that. And I want to believe it too." I shake my head, knowing I'm letting her down. "But I have to hear from her."

Lydia's nostrils flare and her eyes narrow. "I told you I can't find her. How in the hell am I supposed to have her tell you when I can't even call her?"

"I know it's hard but you have to be patient. Eventually she will be able to get in touch with you, and then we can move forward." I know how difficult it is to wait when someone you love is suffering, but we have to do it. It's simply not worth the risk.

Lydia lifts her chin, the tilt defiant as she stares me down. "Actually, I don't need your help anymore. I found someone willing to get her out right now."

I go still. "Who?" The kind of people willing to take a

woman from her home, no questions asked, are the same kind of people who are willing to do just about anything. They're not trying to rescue an abused woman or help save someone's life. That's not their goal.

Lydia lifts one shoulder in a shrug. "Does it matter? They said they'll get her and that's all I care about."

"That's fucking kidnapping, Lydia. Do you know what kind of people are willing to kidnap a person?" She's being reckless—risking her own safety—and I won't let that happen. I know just how many dangerous people lurk in this town, most of them by name, and there's no fucking way I'm letting a single one of them near her.

"I don't care who they are or what it costs as long as they get my sister out of there."

Now I'm really fucking pissed off. "What do you mean, what it costs?"

Lydia squares her shoulders, standing as tall as her slight frame will allow. "You know what? I'm done talking about this with you. You lost the right to have an opinion when you decided not to help me." She steps around me, yanking open the door and rushing down the hall, walking away like she thinks I won't chase her.

And I'm definitely fucking chasing her. She's not going to be able to get rid of me until I find out exactly how deep she is into whatever scheme she believes will save her sister.

"We're not done talking, Lydia." I chase her down the hall, moving fast enough to cut her off before blocking the door to the bar with my body. "Who have you been talking to?"

The list of people her arrival in my life is forcing me to deal with seems to grow more every time I see her. First her dad and brother, and now whoever the fuck wants to charge her to kidnap her sister. "Tell me who."

I know how to intimidate people. It's not difficult. I'm bigger than just about everybody and twice as mean. Add in that I spent more than a few years behaving badly all over Memphis, and most people know not to cross me.

But this tiny bit of a woman isn't scared of me in the slightest. Instead of giving me what I want she rolls her eyes. "Stop acting like this really matters to you."

The comment is a punch to my gut. "This does really matter to me."

Lydia stares me down, her voice surprisingly soft. "No, it doesn't. If it mattered you would help me."

I ignore the sudden urge to grab her and haul her out of this place. Lock her up until I find whoever she's talking to and make it clear their services are no longer needed.

But that's not an option—for a number of reasons—so I have to make her understand she's being unreasonable. That I know what I'm talking about and she should trust me. "Have you ever helped someone escape an abusive relationship?"

She scoffs, laughing lightly as she sweeps one arm from her head to her toe. "I got myself out of there, didn't I?"

"You know what I mean." I step in her way as she tries to move around me. "Getting away from a family is a lot easier than getting away from an abusive man."

Lydia's eyes lift to mine. "What makes you think those aren't the same thing?"

I open my mouth to argue before the words fully sink in.

Fuck.

She takes advantage of my reaction and quickly ducks around my side, disappearing through the swinging door behind me.

I rake one hand through my hair. Frustrated with myself. Frustrated with her.

And pissed as hell at whoever thinks they're taking her money.

I slam my way through the door, intending to chase her down again, but Tate is right there waiting for me.

"Where in the hell do you think you're going?" He grabs my arm and hauls me toward the stage. "We're already behind because Simon is as fucking full of shit as you said he was. We don't have time for you to go chasing after the first cute bartender you see."

"It's about time." Simon stands on the stage, arms outstretched. "What the fuck?"

I glance around, looking for Lydia, but there's no sign of her. "Where's she at?"

Tate leads me back up onto the stage. "Probably hiding from your crazy ass." He meets my eyes, expression serious. "You need to calm down."

Out of all the men I think of as brothers, Tate is the one I'm closest to. We've been inseparable since our paths crossed fifteen years ago and he knows me better than anyone else in this world. Well enough to know that right now I'm on the edge of doing something really fucking bad.

"Whatever it is, we will handle it later." He moves to his mic, grabbing his abandoned bass and slinging it over his shoulders. "Right now we've got a show to do." He adjusts the instrument across his chest. "And nobody's going anywhere until it's over."

He's right. As much as I'd like to hunt Lydia down and force her to talk to me, there's not really any rush. She's got a shift to work and I've got music to play. I can take this time to get my shit together so maybe I'll be a little less volatile the next time we talk.

And we will be talking.

I take my place at the front of the stage, strapping on my

own guitar before tipping my head at the guy manning the sound booth. We quickly run through our check, rushing since Simon made us late getting here and I ate up what little time we had trying to talk sense into Lydia. We finish up, barely making it backstage before the doors open and excited conversation fills the bar.

Normally this is the time I love most. The anticipation. The adrenaline. The excitement. But right now I can't focus on anything except for Lydia. The risk she's taken.

"You look like you're about to rearrange someone's jawbone." Simon tips back one of the bottles of water situated on the small table reserved for us. "Is that what we're doing when we leave here?"

I work my own jaw from side to side, trying to force away the tension clenching my teeth. "I don't know what we're doing then."

I'd like to say I'm not going to go out and start some shit — that I'm a better man than I used to be — but I'm not so sure that's true anymore. I've tried to be an upstanding citizen. To put my old ways behind me the same way so many of my brothers have. But right now I want to hurt someone. Specifically the someone trying to take advantage of a desperate woman. It reminds me of just how much I like to throw my fists around. Just how much I like to dole out the kind of punishment too many people in this world deserve.

Tate studies me as he takes another swig of his water. "She the girl from the other night?"

I force in a deep breath, knowing it won't help. "She is."

"What girl?" Simon looks between me and Tate. "You know I don't like being out of the fucking loop on shit."

I rub one hand down my face, suddenly exhausted. "She came to us for help with her sister." I keep my explanation as simple as I can. I don't want to dig into the situation with

Lydia right now. There's not enough time to explain it. "We grew up together."

Simon lifts a brow. "You grew up together?" He glances in the direction of the bar even though our view is blocked by blacked-out sheetrock. "Like hell you did. That girl's at least a decade younger than you are."

It's a reminder I probably need.

Ever since she showed up in my office I've been looking at Lydia as something besides the little girl she used to be, and that's a problem. For a whole host of reasons. "She has an older brother. He was my best friend growing up."

Jeremiah and I had been inseparable. Not that I'd know him if I saw him now.

At least he better hope I don't. Because if I do, he won't be able to run fast enough to get away from what he deserves.

"This mean we've got a hunt coming up?" Simon's lips pull into a slow grin. "I've been itching for a fight. Hopefully he's a live one."

"No." The word is bitter on my tongue. "Her sister's not in a position to reach out to us."

One of Simon's brows slowly lifts. "Not in a position to reach out to us?" His eyes narrow. "What in the hell does that mean?"

"It means they've figured out she's a flight risk and they're keeping her locked down." I hate the way this has to be. Wish there was something I could do to change the facts.

But there's not. I've fucking tried.

Simon rubs at the dark stubble peeking out across his jawline. "Such fucking bullshit." He stands, pacing around the small space as the noise outside ramps up. "Who the fuck do they think they are?"

He knows exactly who they think they are. They think

49

they're above it all. They think they are the righteous ones. They dish out promises of salvation and threats of damnation to feed their own wants and desires.

"I wish we could sit here all night and come up with ways to fuck those pricks over, but we've got a show to do. And if we're late, Stella is going to kick our asses." Tate cuts the conversation short with a reminder of why we're here.

Simon scowls. I know the rage he still holds close simmers just as hot as mine, and it makes me feel better that I'm not the only one pissed on Lydia's behalf. That I'm not the only one considering breaking the rules we made. "Let's get this over with." He walks straight out onto the stage, leaving Tate and me to follow him.

Simon's moodiness is one of the reasons he's such a great songwriter, but it's hell to deal with on a regular basis.

Tate puts his arm across my chest, stopping me from following Simon out. His gaze is serious as he levels it on me. "We're not going after her sister, Christian."

I scoff, a little surprised he thinks I'm the one who would try to bend the rule I'm responsible for creating. "No, we're not."

As much as I know it has to be that way, I still hate myself for saying it. Because I know Lydia doesn't understand why we can't just go drag Myra away. And I hope she never finds out.

I hope she never has to live with the knowledge that she's responsible for something horrific happening to someone she loves.

I protected her before and I'll do it again. Even if it means she hates me, I will make sure Lydia doesn't have to bear the same kind of burden my brothers and I do.

5

LYDIA

"HE HASN'T STOPPED staring at you all night." Piper smirks at me as she pours out the drink order for a group of women clustered around the bar. The glares they're shooting my way make it clear my best friend isn't the only one who's noticed the focus of Christian's attention.

I grab my loaded tray from the bar and balance it on one upturned palm. "You can't even see the stage from here."

"Don't need to." She winks at me. "You haven't stopped blushing since the show started."

"I'm not blushing." I try to will the heat from my face. "I'm hot. There's too many damn people in here and they're all freaking sweating." It's not a lie. The place is shoulder-to-shoulder and I've nearly spilled my tray more times than I can count. The entire night has been a mess of people bumping into me, completely blind to anything but the three men on the stage.

And I get it. They are pretty darn nice to look at.

The bass player is the clichéd tall, dark, and handsome, with the bluest eyes I think I've ever seen. The drummer is just as attractive, with long hair and a wild edge that I'm guessing most women lose their minds over.

But neither one of them has anything on Christian.

He stands at the front of the stage, commanding the crowd from behind his microphone. His voice is freaking amazing, but the way he sings is about more than how he sounds.

With every word—every line of lyrics—I feel like I'm drawn deeper into his soul. As if he's claimed the power to control my emotions. My perceptions.

My wants and my desires.

It's a little unnerving.

Not that the crowd of women clogging the bar seem to care. They appear to be more than happy to give Christian any amount of power he wants. Over their minds. Over their thoughts. And definitely over their bodies. I'm pretty sure there's at least three pairs of panties lying at his feet right now.

Not that I care. It doesn't bother me at all that any number of gorgeous women are throwing themselves at him. He'll probably even take one or two of them home tonight.

I ignore the ridiculous stab of jealousy poking at my insides. The man standing on that stage is not the one within my head. The one in my head is purely fictional. A complete fabrication I conjured up during my lonely nights to help me hold onto hope that one day I would have a different life. Sure, the man in my head might look like Christian, might sound like him, might even smell like him.

But it's not really him.

Because the fictional man in my mind would have absolutely done whatever it took to save Myra. He would have understood what I'm dealing with. He wouldn't have turned me down, forcing me to take desperate measures and spend every penny in my bank account to give my sister what I have.

Freedom. The ability to make her own choices. To live her own life. To get out from under the smothering blanket of control she's been saddled with.

I weave my way through the crowd, carefully avoiding drunk dancers and sloppy singers, delivering my drinks to their intended table. Once they're in place, I turn, accidentally stealing a glance at the stage as I go. Christian's eyes meet mine and my face prickles with heat, the flush I attempted to will away flaring back to life instantly.

I grit my teeth, embarrassed and frustrated at the same time.

Male attention doesn't usually affect me anymore. Not the way it did when I first moved to Memphis. Working at The Cellar offered me a crash course in how men and women interact in regular society. So even though I grew up in a situation where I wasn't allowed around boys my age without supervision, I've certainly more than made up for lost time. Rarely do I make it through a shift without being propositioned. Usually more than once. It's an expected occurrence that's easy to blow off and ignore.

But for some reason Christian's attention flusters me. Maybe it's because I spent so many years dreaming of what it would be like if our paths crossed again as adults. Wondering if he would still look at me like a little girl. A kid.

I guess now I have my answer, and that's probably what's got me so messed up. Because Christian absolutely does not look at me like I'm his friend's baby sister.

Just the thought of the way his eyes hang on my every move makes my belly do a little flip and warms parts of me that don't usually pay attention to things like this.

Piper gives me a knowing look when I return to the bar, but thankfully keeps her mouth shut. I don't really want to hear anything else about Christian or that his eyes find me every time I deliver drinks. Unfortunately, I know my reprieve will be short-lived. The second the doors close on the bar she's going to do way worse than offer me her opinions.

She's going to start asking questions. Questions I have no intention of answering.

So I focus on the reason I'm here, doing my best to make the most of the night even though it's become messier than I ever would have expected. I keep passing out drinks, pretending I'm not going to look at where Christian stands on the stage even though every single time I do. And by the end of my first Saturday night shift at The Cellar, I've raked in twice as much as I do on a normal shift.

Not that I will get to enjoy the extra money.

Every penny of it will be gone tomorrow when I meet with the sketchy guy who's promised he will go get Myra and bring her back to Memphis.

"Tonight was crazy." Piper wipes down the counters behind the bar as the bouncers clear the place out, making sure no one's lingering in the bathrooms or back hallways. Never in a million years would I have imagined how wandery drunk people can get, but we've found them literally everywhere. Passed out on bathroom floors. Propped up in the utility closets. Hell, one day we even found a guy laying in his own vomit underneath the stage.

Luckily, tonight's crowd was predominantly women, so even though it was crowded, things stayed pretty tame. I don't expect there to be any hidden surprises and hopefully we get out of here at a decent hour because I'm freaking exhausted.

"I'm kind of glad I didn't know how much money you guys make on a Saturday night." I dig through the front of my apron, pulling out my cash tips and stacking them into piles. "Ignorance is bliss, that's for sure."

Piper snorts. "The tips tonight weren't actually that good. Women don't tip us nearly as well as men do." Her expression turns thoughtful. "Of course, no one tried to grab my tits tonight either, so there's that."

"There's always tomorrow." I shoot her a grin, relieved that she didn't bring Christian up. "I wouldn't lose hope just yet."

"You definitely shouldn't lose hope." She snaps a towel in my direction, catching me on the hip with a gentle swat. "I'm pretty sure you could get whatever kind of action you wanted tonight."

I should have known my reprieve would be temporary. Piper has made it her personal mission to rid me of the pesky virginity hanging over my head like a cloud, reminding me I still haven't completely moved forward in my life. "I don't want any action tonight."

Piper stares at me, her jaw slack. "You're kidding, right?" She scoffs as if she can't believe what I'm claiming. "That guy has been eye fucking you all night. You should at least let him stick his tongue between your legs and see what else he can do with that mouth—"

Piper's eyes suddenly go wide, fixed on the spot just behind me.

I press my lips together, refusing to turn around. I already know who's behind me, and I am fairly confident he heard enough of Piper's words to know we were talking about him.

And not in a decent sort of way.

I quickly cash out the rest of my tips then rush past

Piper. I can feel Christian's eyes on me but I ignore his looming presence. I don't have time to deal with him right now.

Or ever, actually.

He didn't want to help me and that's fine, but there is no place in my life for him in any other capacity.

I bounce through the same swinging door I've used a million times tonight, quickly ducking into the employee lounge to grab my purse from my locker. An uncomfortable feeling sticks in my gut as I leave the room and find the hall outside empty. It's not disappointment.

It's *not*.

I shove the emotion down, crossing my arms over my chest as I go to the back of the building and let myself out the rear exit. I start to dig my keys out of my purse, fishing around a few seconds before I remember I carpooled with Piper, and drop my head back, squeezing my eyes closed as I groan in frustration. I cannot go back into that bar. Not when I know Christian is still inside.

"Something wrong?"

I freeze, my whole body going on alert as my eyes fly open to find a strange man watching me a little too closely. He's tall and lean with tattoos covering nearly every bit of visible skin.

And not the nice kind of tattoos.

The ones etched into his flesh look angry. Scary.

"I'm fine." I force on a smile, trying not to look like I'm completely panicked at the sight of him. "I just remembered I forgot something inside." I grip the metal handle of the door and yank as my heart rate picks up, planning to rush back inside because I would absolutely rather face down Christian right now than this guy and his leering expression. I don't like the way he's looking at me. And I sure as hell don't like that we're the only two in an isolated, empty parking lot right now.

But the door holds tight, fixed in place the second it closed behind me by the automatic lock Stella installed as a safety measure.

A safety measure that sure as heck isn't keeping me safe right now.

"You look a little worried." The man creeps closer, the way he's watching me making the hair on the back of my neck stand up. "No reason to be scared, sweetheart. You're the one who called me."

I'm not sure if I should feel relieved or even more concerned. This man isn't loitering around our parking lot late at night, looking for an easy target. He's here to find me. Because he's the man I stupidly asked to go get Myra, in a plan that no longer seems as viable as it once did.

I hold my pleasant expression, hoping it looks more genuine than it feels. "I think you have me confused with someone else. I didn't call you."

His lips pull back into what I'm guessing is a smile, revealing a line of gold-plated teeth. "You're definitely the one who called me, Lydia."

My throat clenches, making me gulp when I hear my name come out of his mouth.

"And I know we already negotiated a deal," his eyes slide down my body, "but I'm happy to revisit those terms if you want to keep some money in your pocket."

This is who offered to go get my sister? I almost laugh in spite of the terror shutting me down. I can only imagine the look on her husband's face when this guy kicks down the door and whisks her away.

But that is all I will be doing—imagining. Because I don't trust this guy around my sister. Not even a little bit.

"I am super sorry, but that whole situation has actually resolved itself and I won't be needing your help anymore." I shove on what I'm hoping looks like an apologetic smile. "But thank you so much for being willing to help me."

The man's expression hardens in the blink of an eye, the smile dissolving in an instant as his gaze narrows on me. "That's not how these deals work, little girl. Once they're made, payment is due whether you go through with it or not." His slitted stare fixes on me. "So are you payin' with cash or with cunt?"

I think I'm going to throw up.

If I give this man the money we agreed on, I'll have nothing left to use to actually save my sister. But I'm absolutely not fucking this guy, either. No matter how much it would piss my father off.

"You didn't tell me that was how this worked. If I'd known—"

"I don't have to tell you shit." He moves closer, taking up way too much space. "You're not the one who calls the shots. I am." His tongue slides across his lips as he steals even more of the gap between us. "And I'm thinking I'd rather take my payment in pussy."

Panic races through me. I didn't leave the life I had to end up getting raped anyway. I risked too much and sacrificed everything because no one was going to make me have sex I didn't want to have.

And that includes this motherfucker.

So even though it goes against every fiber of my being, I stand my ground. "I am not paying you. Not in money and definitely not in any other way."

"You're wrong, little girl." The man keeps coming until he's towering over me. Close enough I can smell the stink of stale cigarette smoke clinging to his baggy T-shirt and jeans. "And I don't have a problem taking what I'm owed."

It's taking everything I have, but I refuse to back down. Standing up to people, especially men, isn't in my nature thanks to an upbringing that left a lot to be desired, but I will do whatever it takes to make sure I can save Myra. I'm also willing to do whatever I can to save myself, so I lift my chin, look him straight in the eye and say, "Then you're going to have to take it. But I'm telling you right now, I will put up one hell of a fight."

His face splits in a sickening grin. "I don't think that's the deterrent you hope it is, little girl."

He lifts one hand like he's going to reach for me and I can't help but flinch.

But then he freezes, going completely still.

For a second I think he's realized what he's about to do is wrong. Reconsidered the possible ramifications of his actions. But then a smooth, deep voice cuts through the night air.

"You touch her and I promise it will be the last fucking thing you do, Rodney."

6

CHRISTIAN

GENERALLY WHEN DEALING with Rodney, or anyone else from the group of criminals who call themselves The Horsemen, I try not to show my hand, but I want this piece of shit to know exactly what he's risking if he continues to pursue Lydia and whatever he believes she owes him.

I've stepped into situations like this before where I had no connection to the woman involved. Where my actions were just about doing what was right. I know I should have made it seem like this was just another of those times, but I can't. Because it's not.

Not by a long shot.

I grab Lydia by the back of her shirt, fisting my hand in the fabric of her tank top before pulling her body behind mine, blocking her from Rodney's leering gaze.

I knew who was involved the second she told me she found someone willing to take her sister. The Horsemen's numbers have dwindled over the past few years, most of them managing to get themselves locked up or dead, but they're still lingering. Like a festering wound that won't heal.

And unfortunately, Rodney is the most infected of the

bunch. He's not simply a sociopath who doesn't care about anyone else but himself. He didn't just grow up locked into a system that drains children of empathy and hope. This guy would have been bad whether he grew up in foster care or with two rich as fuck parents who loved him and gave him everything he wanted. Hell, he might've ended up worse then.

Rodney's ugly face stretches into a smile. "Well look who it is." His smirk tells me he's just as pleased with this change of circumstance as he was with the possibility of forcing himself on Lydia. "The golden boy of Memphis."

Lydia edges closer to me, her small body pressing tight against my back as Rodney's focus fixes on me. I need to diffuse the situation, and I need to do it fast. So I decide to offer up something I know I shouldn't. "How much does she owe you?"

Rodney's brows lift slowly, cutting creases into the black lines tattooed across his forehead. "Are you trying to make a deal with me, Golden Boy?"

I knew he'd be surprised. My brothers and I have never dealt with The Horseman outside of intervening when they cross the line. Not even before we turned our lives around. But I want them to stay away from Lydia, and I'm willing to bend the rules to make that happen. "Give me a number."

I expect him to inflate it, and I don't care. It's just money. And I learned a long time ago that money doesn't buy me anything I really want.

But Rodney just gives me another slow smile. "You don't have what I want."

Lydia's hands latch onto my shirt as she gulps in a sharp breath.

"We both know you're not getting that, so you might as well get some cash." I keep my arms loose at my sides even though I want to reach back and comfort her, let Lydia know everything is going to be fine. But I've already given Rodney way too much ammunition. If he sees me put my hands on Lydia, he'll figure out she's much more than simply a random woman in distress. "How much?"

The smile slips from Rodney's face, mouth pressing into a disgusted scowl. "I don't want your fucking dirty money." He practically spits the words at me before leaning to give Lydia a long look. She presses tighter against me, as if she can hide away from his stare. "I'll be seeing you, little girl."

Rodney gives me another glare before turning away and crossing the lot, steps slow and unhurried.

Lydia doesn't move until he melts into the shadows, disappearing into the darkness from which he comes.

"What did he mean, he would be seeing me?" Lydia's voice is soft and shaky.

I turn to face her, finally allowing myself to rest my hands against her skin. I slide both palms up and down her bare arms, trying to soothe away the goosebumps raised along her skin. "I think you know what he meant."

Lydia's eyes go wide and for a second I see a hint of the little girl I used to know. The one that was always too sweet and too soft and too shy for the world she'd been born into.

But now she's found herself in another world. One that will chew her up and spit her out without a second thought. One that preys on the innocent. And even though she's no longer the same sheltered girl, Lydia is still clearly innocent to many of the evils in this world.

"I'm so sorry." She sniffs, shaking her head, eyes watery as they look up into mine. "I didn't know——"

"It's okay." I slide a strand of her soft brown hair behind one ear, trailing my fingers along the curve of her neck. I can't seem to stop touching her. I wish it was only because I want to comfort her, but it's not. "You couldn't have known."

There's a side of Memphis—and probably every other big city in the world—that people like to pretend doesn't exist. They want to believe every child grows up happy and safe and loved and becomes an upstanding and productive member of society. But that's not the way the world really works. Violence and neglect is a vicious cycle. One that's nearly impossible to escape.

That's why Tate, Simon, and I do what we do. To give at least a few of the women caught in that cycle a fighting chance.

Lydia's lower lip barely trembles and a thin line of unshed tears frames each eye. "What do I do?"

The way she's looking to me for help feeds the part of me that thrives on being needed. Wanted.

Trusted.

"You come home with me." I drag my thumb across the smooth skin of her shoulder, wondering what it might be like to have Lydia haunting the halls of my house. Filling it with her sweet scent. Her quiet laughter. "So I can keep you safe."

Lydia's head tips back in surprise. "I can't go home with you."

"You have to." Now that I've imagined what it would be like to have her close to me, there's no way it's not happening. "Rodney found you here, he will find you at home just as easily, Lydia. You're not safe anywhere you go."

Lydia's eyes move over my face, narrowing the tiniest bit. "But I'll be safe with you?"

I nod, wanting to convince her even though it's already a done deal in my mind. "Yes."

Rodney won't come near my house. The block my

brothers and I live on is nearly impenetrable. We own every building on the street and each one is equipped with a top-of-the-line security system.

In addition to a man willing to do unspeakable things to protect what's his.

Attempting to steal her from me would be a mistake.

The last one Rodney would make.

Lydia's head tips to one side. "Why will I be safe with you?" She continues to study me. "And how do you know Rodney?"

I open my mouth, ready to argue the connections she's clearly making, but the door at my back swings open and her bartending friend tumbles out, wild-eyed and breathing heavily. "Who in the hell was that creepy guy trying to talk to you?" She rushes forward, one hand outstretched as she scans the parking lot. "Is he gone?"

Lydia steps away from me, putting distance between us. "He was just trying to get some money." Her words are a distortion of the truth that comes a little too quickly and too easily, making me wonder if maybe Lydia isn't quite as sweet and innocent as she seems. "I told him I didn't have any and he left."

Her friend's searching gaze swings around, leveling on Lydia. "He believed you?" She's obviously skeptical of Lydia's story and it makes me feel a little better knowing at least her friend sees how dangerous this city can be.

Lydia shrugs, looking surprisingly calm considering what just happened. "I guess so."

Her friend huffs out a loud breath, shoulders slumping the tiniest bit as her outstretched hand drops to her side. "Damn. I thought I was gonna finally get to zap somebody in the nut sack."

My eyes drop to the small device clutched in her grip.

67

Shit. Maybe her friend is just as unaware of how bad this world can be as she is. I hold my hand out, palm up. "Give me the taser."

Her friend scoffs. "No way." She flips the safety on and slides the item into her pocket. "Get your own."

"Tasers are one of the most dangerous self-defense devices to carry." I wiggle my fingers, trying to encourage her to offer it up. "They're easy to take. If you use that on somebody stronger and faster than you, they'll yank it right out of your hands and use it against you."

Lydia's friend scoffs. "Do I look like an idiot?" She strides up to me, staring me down in a way most men won't. "I grew up in Memphis. I know how fucking dangerous this place is and I've taken more self-defense classes then you can count. So if a motherfucker wants to try and take away my stun gun," one hand flicks behind her body in a quick smooth motion, snapping free as the blade of a knife flicks open, "he's going to end up with more than just twenty-five thousand volts to his dick."

I look over the way she grips the blade, point coming out the bottom of her fist instead of the top, sharp edge directed back toward her arm. Most people grip a knife in the opposite direction. It's how they end up cutting themselves all up. But she's holding it in a manner that will allow her to inflict maximum damage while reducing risk to herself. I'm impressed.

I turn my focus to Lydia. "What about you?"

"I took a self-defense class with Piper." She glances at her friend. "But I need to take a few more."

"Lydia carries an alarm on her keychain so if something happens I can come find her and shock and stab." Piper's brows pinch together as her eyes move to Lydia's hands. "Where's your alarm?"

Lydia wilts. "On my keys at our apartment."

Piper's head tips back to the night sky as she groans. "God dammit." She straightens, frowning at Lydia. "When we get home we are ordering a ton more and I swear to God I'm hooking one to everything you own."

"She's not going home," I say with confidence. Piper's going to be on my side with this. She clearly knows firsthand how ill-equipped Lydia is to take care of herself in this world. "She needs to go somewhere safe."

Piper's eyes swing my way. "That's the lamest attempt any guy has ever made to try to get a woman to go home with him." She loops one arm through one of Lydia's, yanking her a few steps away. "At least pretend like you want to show her something cool or like you have a cute dog or something." She leads Lydia across the parking lot, headed straight for an aging SUV.

I cross my arms, keeping my eyes on Lydia as Piper loads her into the passenger's seat and pulls away, leaving me standing alone.

I could've argued. Filled Piper in on all the secrets her friend is keeping, making it clear they're both in way over their heads. But I'm pretty sure that would have earned me an electric current to the cock, and that is not how I want to end this night.

I wait until they're out of sight and then dig one hand into my pocket, fishing my cell phone free. I dial Tate's number and wait for him to answer.

"Where in the hell did you go?"

I scrub one hand down my face, suddenly more exhausted than I've been in a long time. "I'm out the back door. It locked behind me. Come let me in." I disconnect the call before he can ask anything else. I need every second to figure out what the hell I'm going to say.

Our night is about to get a whole hell of a lot longer.

The back door shoves open and Tate and Simon stare out at me. I shoulder past them, going back into the bar so we can finish loading up our equipment. "We probably need to make this a rush job."

I don't expect Rodney to immediately show up at Lydia's apartment, but that's the exact reason I want to be there as soon as possible. The man I thought was in my past is unpredictable, and his interest in Lydia was apparent. If he does wait, it won't be long.

Simon shoots me a smirk. "Why? You got plans?"

I focus on the task at hand, grabbing my guitar from its stand and sliding it into the velvet case. "Not just me."

I fill them in on what happened in the lot as we break down and load up, packing everything into the box truck we use to haul our equipment from gig to gig.

"I'm guessing you want to take the first shift." Simon tosses me the keys to his pickup. "Just don't get blood on the interior."

I tip my head at him, grateful for his offer. "Thanks."

Tate has been pretty quiet through my whole explanation and I'm not surprised when he hangs back as Simon climbs into the box truck's cab.

"You sure you want to dig into this again?"

We've clashed with Rodney and the rest of The Horseman in the past, but that was before. Back when we were still more similar to them than I'd like to admit. My brothers and I have come a long way since then. More than a few have settled down and gotten married. We've started businesses and families. Have homes and savings accounts. Our lives are completely different now. We have what we never believed would be ours and I wouldn't risk that for just anything.

But Lydia is different. She's always been different. She needs someone on her side. Someone looking out for her. That's why I couldn't stop myself from protecting her fifteen years ago and I can't stop myself from protecting her now.

"I'm not going to fucking feed her to the wolves."

And that's what it would be. Lydia's known bad men. The kind who believe access to a woman's body is their right simply because she's their wife. Men who think women are beneath them. Should be subservient. That they must obey. That they can never have the final say in anything that happens in their own lives because that is a right God bestowed upon only those with a dick swinging between their legs.

No matter how small it may be.

But Rodney is a different kind of bad. He doesn't hide his evil behind scripture or faith.

He doesn't hide it at all.

"I didn't say you need to let her deal with this alone." Tate moves closer, keeping his voice low. "But if you do this, you will drag us all in with you." He points to the center of his chest. "*I* don't mind. You know I'm with you every step of the way." He swings his arm in the direction of the box truck. "Simon too. We all agreed this was what we would fight for." Tate drops his arm to his side. "But everyone else didn't."

To be fair, we didn't give them the chance.

Tate, Simon, and I bonded from the start. Our pasts are similar and vastly different from the rest of the men we call our brothers. We didn't grow up wondering where our next meal would come from. We didn't watch our parents chase down their next high. We didn't move from rundown hotel to rundown hotel until the government stepped in under the guise of making our lives better, only to send us off to places so much worse.

But we did grow up afraid. We did grow up powerless to change our lives.

And we ended up in the same place. Alone on the streets. Cast out. Abandoned.

Alone.

"You don't have to tell them everything, but they deserve to at least know what's going on with Rodney." Tate meets my gaze. "And if this goes tits up, we're going to need all the help we can get."

7

LYDIA

"HAVE YOU HEARD anything from Myra?" Piper props one hip against the counter in our two-bedroom townhouse, scooping up a pile of cereal from the bowl she has balanced on one hand before shoving it into her mouth.

I shake my head. "Nothing." I drop my butt down to the second-hand couch where we spend our days off, binge watching Netflix, and go to work putting on my shoes. "Her phone just goes straight to voicemail, so I'm pretty sure it's turned off."

"I just don't get how there are still people living like that." Piper shovels in another bite of her afternoon breakfast. "Do they not know women have been able to vote since nineteen-twenty and equality is a fucking thing?"

I've explained my upbringing to Piper countless times, but she still can't seem to wrap her head around the fact there are still groups where women are treated as possessions. Manipulated into believing they have some sort of importance in the hierarchy of the saved.

But it's all bullshit.

Every bit of the rhetoric they spew is carefully crafted by

men who are terrified of women gaining any sort of power or strength. Men like my father. Men like Myra's husband—that one is especially ironic considering he's a district attorney and his career should be built on ensuring fairness.

"They know." I finish lacing up my Vans and stand. "They just don't care."

"It's not that they don't care, it's that they're pussies." Piper tips back her bowl, noisily sucking down the remaining milk. "They know an empowered woman wouldn't fuck them, so they've gotta figure out how to keep them suppressed." Her lip curls as she carries her bowl to the sink. "I'd like to give a few of them a good shot to the nut sack."

I'd like to let her. A few in particular. "Hopefully we can get our hands on my brother and father and Matthias and make all your dreams come true."

I keep telling myself Christian is right. Eventually they will loosen the chain they have Myra on. When that happens I know she will call me right away. Until then, I'm stuck.

Stuck waiting. Stuck worrying. Stuck feeling helpless.

I grab my purse, looping it across my chest. "I'm headed to work. I'll see you later."

Piper belches, wiping the back of one hand across her mouth. "Yup. I come in at six."

My heart skips a beat as I unlock the deadbolt on the door, hating she'll be here alone. It's been days since the incident at The Cellar, but I almost get more anxious as time goes on, like I'm waiting for the Jack-in-the-box to spring free. "Be careful."

I know Piper's the more capable of the two of us, but I still worry about her. Sometimes being a little too comfortable can be just as dangerous as being unprepared. And if she ends up hurt because of my bad decisions I'll never forgive myself.

Piper gives me a cocky grin, making it clear my concerns are not unfounded. "I'm always careful."

I hope it's the truth, but somehow, I doubt it.

I give her a wave before stepping out onto the stoop, closing and locking the door behind me because I don't trust her to do it. Part of me feels like she's almost hopeful something happens, and that's terrifying.

I scan the parking lot of our building as I move down the cement steps, looking for any sign of the guy from the other night, but I have no clue what kind of car he might drive. So unless I see his ugly, tattooed face, I wouldn't know if he was here or not.

All I know is it feels like someone is watching me. It's felt that way for four days now, and I can't shake the uncomfortable creep of awareness as it crawls across my skin. It makes me move a little faster to the door of my car. I don't fully breathe until I'm locked inside and the engine is started, because at least in my car I can get away. I might have to plow someone down to make it happen, but I think I could do it.

Probably.

The air-conditioning blasts as I head to work, but it doesn't even touch the sweat creeping across my hairline and making my pits sticky. Because that sweat doesn't have anything to do with the heat. That sweat is brewed of stress and panic.

I might have grown up sheltered and naive, but I'm no longer completely clueless about how the world really is. I know Rodney meant it when he said he would see me again. I also know he's probably enjoying that I'm losing my mind waiting for it to happen.

Unfortunately, he will just have to get in line, because I've got way worse things to lose my mind over. Like that I haven't heard from my sister in over two weeks.

I check my phone as I sit at a red light, just in case a text has come through. I know it hasn't, but I can't stop looking. I know Myra needs me. I know she's counting on me to get her out of there.

I can't let her down.

The creepy feeling I've been living with since leaving the bar Saturday night gets stronger and I slowly set my phone down, forcing myself not to shiver as the uncomfortable sensation pulls my skin into goosebumps. I glance at the car to my right, watching the middle-aged woman behind the wheel as she sings along with her music. I let out a breath, calming down just the tiniest bit as she puts on the performance of a lifetime.

I'm overreacting. I'm letting myself get caught up the way I did when I left home. It took me months to get over the fear of my father and brother coming to get me and drag me back. But until that point, I made myself sick worrying. Waiting. Watching for any sign of the boogeyman I feared.

Just like I'm doing now.

I force myself to take a deep breath, blowing it back out as a car slides into my peripheral vision and stops to my left. I glance that way, sure I'll see another normal person going about their normal day. But the man beside me does not look normal. His car is expensive. Black and sleek with leather interior.

But it's not what gets my attention.

The driver behind the wheel is stunningly handsome. Dark hair, chiseled jaw, expensive dress shirt unbuttoned at the neck to reveal tanned skin.

And something else.

The dark lines of a cheap tattoo peek from his collar, standing out like a blemish against the wealth surrounding it. His eyes slowly come my way, hanging for a second. Long enough to bring on a shiver I do my best to suppress.

It would make sense the man I tried to bargain with would have money, so maybe this is someone he knows. Someone he sent out to keep an eye on me. Track my movements so when he's ready to collect he'll know where I am.

The light changes and the man in the car acknowledges me with a nod before pulling away.

A car horn honks behind me, making me jump in my seat. I shake my head, gripping the steering wheel as I ease my foot on the gas.

I'm still freaking overreacting.

Rodney might have money, but not the kind of money the man beside me would need to have to own a car like that. Kidnapping might pay well, but not that well.

Especially when you're spending most of it tattooing your face.

The rest of the drive to the bar is uneventful and even the watched feeling starts to diminish. Hopefully I'm getting a grip on myself again and not just getting comfortable right in time for Rodney to jump out and snag me. Take the payment he clearly wanted.

I park as close to the back door of the bar as I can, scanning the lot before jumping out, one of the dozens of screaming keychains Piper's armed me with clutched tight in my hand. I quickly unlock the door and rush inside, yanking it closed beside me before letting out the air trapped in my lungs.

"That hot?" Stella looks me over from where she stands

in the hall, a box balanced in her arms. "You look like you're ready to melt into a puddle."

Somehow I manage what feels like a smile. "It's pretty warm." I quickly shove my keys and the screaming keychain in my purse, not wanting her to worry. "Luckily I get to work in the air conditioning."

She gives me a grin. "I'm glad you think working here is what makes you lucky." She jerks her head in the direction of her office. "Come on. Let's talk."

My stomach clenches, twisting into an even tighter knot than the one I've been steadily tying since Saturday night. "Okay."

I love Stella. Adore her, actually. She gave me a chance when I didn't expect anyone would, hiring on a completely clueless girl from the Bible Belt of Arkansas to serve up bourbon and beer. But she is so much I am starting to believe I will never be—confident, independent, decisive—and it intimidates me.

It also makes me a little sad.

When I left home, I thought I could become normal. That I would finally get to be the kind of woman I only caught glimpses of growing up. But after being on my own for a year, I'm starting to doubt that's possible.

I follow Stella into her cluttered office, a whole new fear climbing onto the backs of the ones I've been carrying. "What's up?"

"I wanted to ask you how Saturday night went." She sits down in the chair behind her desk, grabbing a handful of peanut M&M's and popping them into her mouth one by one as she stares at the computer screen. "The numbers look good, so hopefully you made a shitload of money."

I swallow hard at her mention of Saturday night. "It was good. Crowded, but good."

Stella gives me a knowing grin. "A whole lot different than a weeknight, huh?"

It was a whole lot different from any night I've ever had, but telling my boss about what happened out back is not something I want to do. I don't want her to look at me as a problem, and explaining I've brought a dangerous man to The Cellar would absolutely classify me as a problem.

"Different, but good." I smooth down my hair, falling back into old patterns of trying to look as perfect as possible so no one will see the truth. "It was nice to work a whole shift with Piper."

"I bet." She refocuses on her computer screen. "I heard you guys worked well together."

"I think because we're so close it's easy for us to know how to help each other." I do my best no matter who else is on schedule with me. But Piper and I can communicate with just a look, which makes it a whole heck of a lot easier when it's nearly impossible to hear each other over the sound of a band.

"Most friends don't work together that way." Stella leans back in her seat, gaze meeting mine. "I was actually a little worried the two of you might get distracted working the same shift, but it doesn't sound like that's a problem for you."

It hurts my feelings a little that Stella expected me to be less focused with Piper around. I've worked hard to show her she didn't make a mistake when she hired me, and now I've got yet another thing to worry about because I can't lose this job. Especially not now when I'm so close to having to take care of not just myself, but also Myra.

"I'm here to work, Stella. I would never slack off just because Piper was on the same shift as me."

Stella snorts. "I wasn't worried about *you*." She grins.

"Your roommate is a wildcard, but it seems like you kept her in line."

I don't like her thinking badly of Piper any better than her thinking badly of me, but at least she knows I'm here to be the best employee I can for her. "Piper is a really good bartender. She stays ahead of the line better than anybody else." Sure, she talks more and might be a little more easily distracted, but Piper can fill drink orders faster than anyone I have ever seen, so it all balances out.

"You're right, which is why I'm going to do some schedule shifting. I'm thinking the two of you are going to be my new Saturday night crew." Stella lifts a brow at me. "If that's okay with you."

I nod. "Sure. It's fine." It's better than fine if Piper is right and the tips are normally even better than what I earned this past Saturday. I'm still a little concerned I'll end up having to pay Rodney the price we agreed on, so every bit of money I can bring in will help.

"Awesome." Stella turns away from me, typing on her keyboard. "The new schedule should be up next week, so you'll finish out what's left of your regular hours and then move to your new schedule when it posts."

"Okay." I sit there a second longer, not recognizing I've been essentially dismissed. When Stella doesn't say anything else, I realize our meeting is over and stand up, feeling awkward as I silently retreat to the employee room.

Sliding my purse into my locker, I pull a freshly laundered apron from the hook inside the door and tie it around my waist as I make my way out onto the main floor, gearing myself up for a day full of fake smiles and distracted conversations. Normally I don't mind it. I know better than most people how to fake a smile and feign interest, but right now

I'm struggling to follow my own train of thought, let alone someone else's.

I push through the swinging door and greet Henry, the daytime bartender. He's old enough to be my dad but looks way younger than his fifty-five years. It serves him well when the ladies of Memphis cut out of their jobs early and meet for cocktails, as it seems many have done today. The bar is completely lined with women in expensive clothes sipping martinis and the occasional bourbon neat. I give him a wink before heading out to the floor to start rotating into the tables that will be mine for the day.

I only make it a few steps before my Vans squeak against the epoxy floor as I come to a full, abrupt stop.

The same man from the stoplight is sitting in the corner, sipping from a tumbler as he works on a laptop perched on the small table in front of him.

I can't move. Can't breathe. All I can do is stare as panic twists its way through my insides.

"Not too hard on the eyes, is he?" Candy, one of the wait-resses I usually work with, bumps into my side. "He specifically requested one of your tables, but I figured you wouldn't mind if I brought him his first round." She flicks her reddish hair behind one shoulder as she continues to gaze at the man. "I'm happy to take the table off your hands if you don't want it."

I would love for her to do that.

But I can't. Not because I want to serve him, but because I don't want him to know I'm scared. I've known a bully or two in my life and they thrive on fear. It feeds them in a way nothing else does, making them stronger.

And I'm not feeding any more of them.

"No, thanks. I've got it."

I try my best to look confident as I stride toward him,

refusing to look away when his eyes lift to meet mine. "Is there something I can help you with?" It's not exactly the confrontation I wish I could offer, but at least I don't smile when I say it.

He does though.

"Actually, yes." He lifts up his empty glass. "I'd like another."

I glance at the tumbler, but don't reach for it. "I'm not talking about your drink." I move closer, crossing my arms so I don't start to fidget. "Why are you following me?"

One of the man's dark brows slowly starts to lift and his lips follow along. "Christian will be happy to hear you're not nearly as clueless as we all thought."

8

CHRISTIAN

I CIRCLE THE Cellar's lot, looking for Damien's vehicle.
He was nice enough to offer to keep an eye on Lydia while I
crashed for a few hours, but I don't want to keep him away
from his family for any longer than absolutely necessary, so
I'm back in downtown Memphis before dinnertime, ready to
relieve him of his duty.

The only problem is it appears he's already relieved
himself of his duty.

The lot behind The Cellar is packed, but not a single
one of the cars belongs to Damien. Aggravation burns my
gut as I peel out onto a side street, scowling as I look for any
sign of his black Mercedes.

Ten minutes later, I finally find his shiny new car parked
in a public lot, empty. I whip into the spot next to him and
shut off the engine, doing my best to keep myself in check
until I know what's really going on.

Damien was supposed to be positioned near the back of
the bar, making sure Lydia stays safe as she comes and goes,
but maybe he couldn't get any closer than this and had to
come up with a plan B. I'll feel like an absolute shithead if

he's been sitting outside in this heat all day, especially if I stand here thinking he's a prick. Unfortunately, as I head toward the building, there's no sign of the man I consider my brother and the irritation biting at my heels flares to life.

Lydia's car was still in the back lot, but that doesn't mean shit. Rodney or one of his accomplices could have easily snatched her the second she walked out the door, dragging her off to God knows where.

I march down the stairs leading to The Cellar and yank open the door, ready to put my eyes on her before I lose my fucking mind. The air of the bar is cool and dark as I step inside, scanning the space for the familiar slender frame I'm already growing too attached to.

But it's not Lydia I see.

Damien shoots me a grin from where he sits in the corner, lifting two fingers in a salute style greeting.

It's still relatively early in the evening, so the bar isn't overly packed, but it's busy enough it takes me a minute to get to him. By the time I reach his side I'm seething. I thought not finding him in the back lot was a problem, but this is an absolute nightmare.

"What the fuck are you doing here?"

Damien ignores my question and instead motions at the bar around us. "This place is nice. Way bigger than it looks from the outside." He points to the stage I performed on a few nights ago. "And that is some high-end sound equipment. I bet the shows here are fantastic."

"They are." I slam the laptop in front of him closed and lean right into his face. "Too bad you aren't here to scout out ideas for your next club. You offered to keep an eye on Lydia. If I'd known you were going to literally park your ass right in front of her I wouldn't have taken you up on it."

Lydia has had men watching her every move her whole life. I don't want her to think I'm doing the same thing.

Because I'm not. This is different.

I'm just not sure she would see it that way.

Damien doesn't look bothered at all by my aggressiveness. If anything he looks amused. "I think your girl is a little more attentive than you realize." He leans back in his seat, taking a small sip from the tumbler in his hand. "She made me before we even got here."

I have a hard time believing that. Lydia's many things, but street-smart is not one of them. "That's not possible."

I've been watching her for days, switching off with Simon when I'm too tired to trust myself to stay awake. Not a single time did she come close to noticing either of us.

Damien looks me over, rocking his jaw from side to side. "If you really believe that you are seriously underestimating her."

I drag the chair across the table closer and drop into it, keeping my focus on his face. "She's not like the women around here. She doesn't understand how dangerous this place can be." I swipe one hand over my burning eyes. "Not that it would matter if she did." It's what's kept me close by since Rodney tried to snatch her from the bar. Lydia is too determined for her own good. Even if she did know someone was bad, it wouldn't stop her if she thought they could help her get Myra away.

"I think you're wrong." Damien hooks one arm over the back of his chair, angling his body in the seat. "I think she has a better idea of how fucked-up this world is than most people." He tips his head my way. "Just like you did."

I don't like how easily he compares us. The information I've offered my brothers about Lydia is limited. And it doesn't include our shared past. That would bring them too close to questioning how we reconnected and discovering the secret Simon, Tate, and I have been keeping from them.

"She might understand how fucked-up people can be, but she's not used to men who would just as soon slit your throat as they would walk away from you." She's used to men hiding behind suits and smiles, using twisted words to do their dirty work instead of fists and guns.

Damien tips his hands out in a halfhearted shrug. "All I know is she assumed I knew Rodney. That he'd sent me to follow her." One corner of his mouth turns up. "At least that's what she claimed when she confronted me."

I don't know if that makes me feel better or worse.

Damien is a big guy, bigger than me, but he's clean-cut and well dressed in a way I am not. He doesn't technically look as intimidating as Rodney, but learning she believed he was involved and still didn't back down is both impressive and terrifying.

"What did you tell her?" My plan was to fly under the radar. To watch over Lydia without her knowing I was there. I'm grown enough to know what I'm doing is crossing more than a few lines. And I don't want her to figure out that the difference between me and Rodney isn't as big as she thinks it is.

It's also not as big as my brothers think it is.

"What do you think I told her?" Damien downs the last of his drink before setting it on the table. "I told her the truth."

I'm not surprised.

It's one of many things that have changed dramatically over the past few years. Domestication definitely suits my brothers, but it has also made them more honest than I wish they were right now.

"Great." I rake one hand through my hair before scrubbing it down my face, trying to wipe away the lingering exhaustion I can't seem to shake. "I'm sure she was real fuckin' happy to hear that."

Damien grabs his computer and slides it into his work bag. "Actually, she didn't seem bothered by it all." He zips the laptop into place and stands up. "Not that I think it's tough to beat out being stalked by someone who's threatened to rape you, but she didn't seem to hate finding out you were the reason I was here."

Again, I'm not sure how relieved I should be. My interest in Lydia should be limited to only how I can help her and Myra. I should still be thinking of her as a kid. The little sister I never had.

I sure as shit shouldn't be toeing the line of obsession the way I am.

"Of course, my interpretation of the situation could be all wrong." Damien grabs his bag and gives me a wink. "My tab's in your name." He strides away, leaving me sitting alone at the table.

Alone with the knowledge Lydia now knows I've had eyes on her day and night.

"What can I get you, darlin'?" An unfamiliar waitress sidles up to my table, her drawl a little too pronounced to be completely real.

I twist in my chair, scanning the bar. "Where's the waitress that was here before?"

The woman's expression falls. "Lydia? Her shift's over. She's probably takin' the trash out before she goes." She inches in a little closer, and when she bends over, her ample tits test the boundaries of her low-cut shirt. "But I'm sure I can take care of you just as well as she did."

Shit.

I shove up from my chair, yanking a hundred-dollar bill

from my wallet and dropping it onto the table to settle Damien's tab, before I rush across the floor, ignoring the bartender's protest as I push through the swinging door into the employee-only portion of the building.

I want to smirk, but not until I have Lydia in my sights. Damien definitely read that situation wrong and I can't wait to rub it in his face. His wife Josie is sweet and soft, but she's still nothing like Lydia.

Lydia was raised to believe she *had* to be sweet. Quiet. Docile and easy going. If she was anything else she was punished. Threatened. Judged. So she learned to tell everyone exactly what they wanted to hear, men especially, even if it wasn't the truth. That means you can't take what she says or how she acts at face value.

I run down the hall, needing to get my eyes on her, knowing I'm probably overreacting. I shove the full weight of my body into the back door, flinging it open and stumbling out into the dusky light of the parking lot just in time to see a four-door Charger with tinted windows peeling across the blacktop.

Headed straight for where Lydia is hefting a pile of trash bags into a dumpster.

I don't have time to think it through. Don't have time to come up with any sort of real plan.

All I can do is react.

The car comes to a jerky stop a few feet from where Lydia stands. She spins to face it as the tires squeal against the asphalt, stumbling back as the driver's door opens and Rodney gets out, his jaw set, eyes narrowed and focused on her.

His intentions are clear.

He's come to collect what he thinks she owes him.

Lydia tumbles backward in her haste to put as much

space between them as possible, her ass hitting the ground hard as she goes down. Rodney pounces, lunging forward to grab her by the arms before hauling her to her feet.

He only makes it two steps toward the open door of his car before I'm on him. I swing hard, my fist connecting with the side of his head with enough force to jerk it in the opposite direction. The hit's hard enough to stun him and he releases Lydia. I shove her back, putting my body in his path because I know it's going to take more than one hit to end this.

Rodney's narrowed eyes snap to my face as he wipes a drop of blood from the corner of his mouth. "I thought you didn't play anymore, Preacher."

I grit my teeth at the name I haven't used in years, shaking my head at him. "I'm not fucking playing." I jerk my chin in the direction of his car. "Walk away."

Rodney huffs out a laugh. "I'm here for my due, so you're the one who needs to walk away." His dead eyes move past my shoulder to where Lydia stands. "Me and her have a deal and she's gotta pay up one way or another."

"You could've had your payment. You decided you didn't want it." I consider offering to pay whatever she agreed to again, but I know it's too late for that. He's already decided cash is not what he'll be collecting, and at this point there's no way he's backing down.

This only ends one of two ways. He gets what he wants or I do. Either way, one of us isn't making it out of this alive.

"I don't want money, Preacher." His eyes narrow on where Lydia hides behind me as he licks his lips. "Not anymore." He goes back to staring me down. "Now go back to your dirty little life pretending you're better than all the rest of us."

"Don't make this about me. You know damn well it's not." My brothers and I have worked hard to move forward in our lives. To be better than we were. To get away from the bullshit existence fate shoved us into. And I will do anything to keep from being dragged back.

Almost anything.

Rodney inches toward me. "But it's always been about you, hasn't it? You've always thought you were better than everybody, including the men who think they're your brothers." His disgust with me is apparent as he continues to close the gap between us. "That's why you got this little gig on the side behind their backs. You go around trying to save bitches from the lives they put themselves into so you can prove just how good of a man you are." He snorts. "And you won't even let your brothers help because you're the only one good enough. You and the other two just like you."

He's got my reasons for doing what I do all wrong, but I know damn well there's no way I'll convince him differently. I don't really care why he thinks I do it. But I do care what Lydia thinks, and right now he's putting all sorts of ideas in her head.

"And this bitch got herself right where she deserves to be." He motions at Lydia before turning to point at himself. "She came to me. She asked *me* for help, not you. So why don't you go back to your perfect fucking life with your perfect fucking business and leave me to mine."

My life isn't the only one he's twisting right now, and I might not care what he thinks of me, but I won't let him believe Lydia deserves the things he wants to do to her. "You're not touching her." I keep my eyes locked on his, making it clear I won't back down. That this won't end the way he wants it to. "So you can either take the money I'm offering you, or——"

"Or what?" He sneers. "What are you going to do, Preacher?" He shakes his head. "Nothing."

Rodney's hand juts out in the blink of an eye, fingers gripping Lydia's arm tight enough to leave a bruise as he yanks her toward him, sealing his fate.

And mine.

9

LYDIA

I'D ALREADY FIGURED out Christian and Rodney knew each other, but it's clear their connection is more than simply a passing familiarity. The bad blood between them is evident and making me more and more uneasy with each passing second.

The situation is going downhill fast, but I don't realize just how fast until Rodney reaches around Christian and grabs me, his grip so tight it hurts. The move catches me completely by surprise because I foolishly believed Christian was completely capable of keeping me utterly safe, the way he always did when I was little.

But this isn't about a missed dinner or a pissed off narcissist looking for someone to take his frustrations out on. The guy trying to drag me away is bad. Badder than bad. It's written all over his face. Literally.

I try to plant my feet, hoping to fight against his grip, but Rodney only pulls harder, the tips of his fingers digging painfully into my skin. Shockingly, I'm not worried he will actually get me into his car—I still believe Christian won't let that happen—but it's clear Rodney can do damage without actually getting me out of this parking lot.

I try again to resist, dragging my Vans against the blacktop as I use all my strength to tip my body away, wincing at the added strain it puts on my arm.

My plan miraculously works. Rodney's clamping grip releases, sending me careening back against the blacktop for a second time. I land hard on my already bruised ass, yelping at yet another round of pain.

"Lydia." Christian's tone is sharp enough to pull my focus his way despite the panic still frantically scrambling my thoughts. He jerks his chin toward Rodney's idling sedan. "Open the back door."

Years of following orders and the adrenaline shutting down my brain send me jumping to my feet to do as he says. I yank on the door, but it won't budge, so I pull harder, putting my full weight into it.

"You gotta unlock it, Sweetheart. Press the button inside the front door." Christian's directions carry a sense of urgency that makes me move as fast as I can.

I fumble with the automatic locks, accidentally re-locking everything before finally shoving the button in the right direction. The second I hear the locks click open I go back to the rear door, whipping it open.

"Good girl." Christian's praise is abrupt and unexpected. I'm used to men who bark out orders, knowing they'll be followed, and showing no appreciation when they are. "Now you need to step back."

Once again I do exactly as he tells me. But this time it's not purely out of reflex. This time I do it because I want to hear him tell me I've done something right again. I want to chase that feeling of acknowledgment and appreciation down.

At least I do until Christian pushes past me and drops Rodney's slumped body into the backseat, grabbing his legs and folding them into the opening before slamming the door.

Christian turns to face me, his face coming close to mine. "Lydia, I need you to look at me."

It takes everything I have to drag my focus away from what I think I just saw to meet Christian's gaze. "What's wrong with him?"

"That's not something you need to worry about." He shifts as I try to look at the car again, blocking my line of sight, forcing my eyes to stay on his. "I need you to tell me who watches the camera on the building."

I roll my eyes upward to focus on the security camera mounted above the back door of the bar.

"Piper saw you out here Saturday night. Is it the bartender who usually keeps an eye on the camera?" Christian's voice is shockingly calm and unbelievably gentle.

I swallow hard, fighting the nausea creeping up my throat. "Security watches it at night, but not during the day. We only have one bouncer on staff up until 8 o'clock."

"What about the recordings? Does somebody go back through those?" Christian's words are smooth and measured, like he's working hard to make sure I understand them.

I swallow again, fighting against the shaking settling into my limbs as adrenaline feeds into my veins. "No one looks at them unless there's a reason."

"Good. How long before they're recorded over?" Christian's left hand comes to my face, his thumb slowly dragging across my skin in a touch that's surprisingly soothing.

"I think it's on a twenty-four-hour loop." We've only needed the security footage once since I've worked at The

Cellar, and I remember Stella saying something about us barely making it since it had almost been twenty-four hours.

Christian's thumb continues to slowly slide against my cheek. "You're doing real good, Lydia." His eyes move over my face. "Take a deep breath." He breathes in with me, pursing his lips as he blows the breath back out again. "Good girl." He tips his head toward the car. "Now I need you to get in this car so we can get out of here."

I nod, the movement jerky. "Okay."

I was under no illusions I was as capable of handling a scary situation as Piper believes she is, but I sure as heck didn't think I would shut down the way I am right now. I feel completely numb as Christian leads me around the car, keeping the same hand that was on my face against my lower back as we go. He opens the door and carefully urges me inside, buckling me in before taking his place in the driver seat and pulling away.

I clench my hands into fists where they sit in my lap, fighting the urge to look into the back seat. I know what's there even if my brain isn't currently willing to acknowledge it.

"I've got a problem."

Christian's voice is flat beside me and I turn to see he has his phone pressed against his right ear. The skin of the hand holding it is stained with streaks of drying blood. "Rodney came back for Lydia. Tried to grab her in the parking lot after she got off work." His eyes slide my way before moving back out the windshield. "I handled it."

I hug my purse tight to my chest because the way he says it sounds final. Like the issue of Rodney has been eradicated completely.

Forever.

I slowly twist around, unable to breathe as I turn my

gaze to the back seat. My eyes meet Rodney's and my breath stutters at the way they seem to stare right through me, unblinking.

Unseeing.

"I need to call you back." Christian ends the call and drops his phone into his lap before reaching for me. His bloody hand hovers over the console a second before pulling back, fingers clenching into a fist. "You gotta keep breathing, Sweetheart." He turns at the next light, taking us onto the highway and away from downtown. "Everything's going to be okay, I promise, but you have to stay calm."

I would argue I'm being remarkably calm, but it's probably shock keeping me quiet, so arguing is also not going to happen. "He's dead."

I'm pointing out the obvious right now. Both of us know there's a dead guy in the backseat, so it's not really beneficial for anyone, but it still seems like it needs to be said. If for no other reason than for me to process the information.

Christian flexes his hand again, clenching it tight as he presses it against the console. "Rodney wasn't going to leave you alone until he got what he wanted, Lydia."

Even now, frozen in shock, I recognize how extreme he's making the situation sound. "Are you saying the only option was to kill him?"

"I'm saying not everyone was leaving that parking lot alive and I was willing to do whatever it took to make sure you were the one who walked away." Christian glances my way, expression uneasy. "You don't understand how men like him can be."

Don't I? My sister is currently being held captive by a man because he's willing to do whatever it takes to get what he wants from her. And what he wants from her is a sweet, quiet, unargumentative wife to do his laundry and his

101

cooking and his cleaning while bearing children for him to fuck up. She has unwanted sex forced on her daily. If she doesn't provide for her husband's urges, she's deemed responsible for any action he takes to sate his need. If those urges make him find his way into pornography or affairs, those sins don't belong to him.

They belong to her.

What Rodney wanted to do to me seems different, but it's really not. Even if he was probably only going to rape me once. And somehow I feel like Rodney is more than happy to claim his own sins. I glance into the back seat again, swallowing hard. Not so much anymore, it seems.

I try to face forward, to keep my eyes off the man who planned to do awful things to me, but I'm suddenly struggling in an unexpected way. I know I should be outraged Christian just murdered Rodney right in front of me. That he then shoved me into a car with a body and is now driving me and dead Rodney to God knows where.

But as I keep peeking back behind us there's only one thing I can think of. "If my sister tells you she wants away from her husband and he won't let her leave, would you kill him too?"

It was one of the reasons why I didn't mind if the person I found to help me rescue Myra was a little ruthless. Sure, Rodney looked terrifying and obviously had the bad behavior to back it up, but if he hadn't threatened to rape me...

I would've been a little hopeful he was capable of doing whatever it took to get my sister away from Matthias.

Maybe that makes me a bad person. Maybe it makes me a little ruthless too.

Or maybe it proves I'm just as selfish. Just as willing to do whatever it takes to get what I want.

At least what I want is to save someone else. It's the same difference I see in Christian. He only did what he did to save me. He would have walked away from Rodney. Tried his best to make that happen. Even offered to pay off my debt to settle the score.

So the only reason Rodney got hurt was because he wouldn't let it go. Wouldn't back down even when he knew what was on the line.

I shift a little in my seat, much more uncomfortable with this particular similarity we share.

Christian's jaw flexes as he stares out the windshield. "I don't want you to think this is who I am anymore, Lydia."

He's dodging my question, but I decide to let it go since it shows a little too much of who I might actually be. "Anymore? What does that mean?"

Christian deftly moves the car with the flow of traffic, sliding into open gaps between lanes as we cruise down the highway. "It means none of this should have happened."

Once again my eyes slide to the dead man in the backseat. "So you regret killing him?"

The muscles of Christian's jaw twitch and the tension across his shoulders grows tighter. "I didn't say that."

A little part of me, probably the sinful part my father claimed to always know was there, gets a little fluttery. "So you *don't* regret killing him."

Christian's nostrils flare as he glances my way, eyes returning to the road for a second before he finally responds. "He wanted to hurt you." His focus darts to me before once again jumping away. "And he wasn't getting his fucking hands on you."

It's yet another thing I should find horrifying—a man being killed because of me—but instead makes me feel oddly safe and a little light in my belly.

But in all truth, it's no more my fault Rodney is dead than it was my friend Rebecca's fault when her husband was arrested for trying to meet up with an underage girl. Both made their own decisions and faced the consequences of their actions.

Of course, the men of the church placed the blame squarely on Rebecca's shoulders, claiming her lack of willingness to meet her husband's physical needs was to blame. But that's not where the blame really lies.

And the fault here doesn't lie with me.

I look into the back seat again, meeting Rodney's dead eyes. "So what do we do now?"

Christian eases on to the next exit ramp, maneuvering us into an area of Memphis close to the one I visited earlier this week. "*We* don't do anything." He turns at the base of the ramp, intently focused on the road. "This isn't something you worry about. I'll handle it."

"How am I not supposed to worry about it?" A little of the upset I know I should be feeling finally starts to rear its head. I motion around the car. "I'm currently sitting in a dead guy's car leaving all sorts of evidence everywhere." I collect the pile of my hair and clutch it in one hand. "My DNA is probably all over. I shed like crazy."

"I will take care of it." Christian's voice is firm and unyielding and I know I shouldn't just let him make this decision, no matter how much I want to.

"So now you get to be in charge of my life?" I force myself to fight him. To stand up for myself the way Piper or Stella would. That's why I escaped my old life, right? So I could do what I wanted and no one would ever make decisions for me again.

But Christian's reaction to my argument is nothing like I've experienced before. Instead of getting pissed, he suddenly looks tired. "That's not what I meant." He rubs his clean hand, the only one he's touched me with, against his eyes, scrubbing hard. "I'm not trying to be in charge of your life, this just isn't something you should be involved with. It will put you in danger if—"

I laugh, sounding a little bit unhinged as the shock seems to wear off. "Are you trying to say I'm not already in danger?" I stab one finger at the dead guy in the backseat. "Because I'm pretty sure Rodney told at least a few people what his plans were and the second he doesn't show up at wherever he's supposed to be next, they're going to come looking for me."

The reality of what I'm saying sinks in a little and I almost want to cry. If I was in this mess on my own I probably *would* cry. Hell, I'd probably be curled up in the fetal position on the floorboard sobbing until I threw up.

But I'm not alone. Christian is here at my side.

And I'm not doing this for myself. I'm doing it to save Myra. Because I promised her I would do whatever it took to get her away from them.

It's starting to seem like I really meant it.

That realization smothers down the tears and replaces them with the same sense of determination I felt when I decided to leave my family and their fucked-up beliefs behind. I take a shaky breath and repeat the question I asked earlier. "So, what do we do now?"

Christian glances at me again, resignation joining the exhaustion etched into his features. "Now, we figure out how to make this go away and keep you safe."

I sit up a little straighter, feeling like I'm in control of my own fate for the first time. Like maybe I can finally tackle everything in front of me.

Up until now, so much still felt like it was being dictated

by the men in my past. The jobs I could get were limited because of my education. My ability to make friends was subpar because I didn't understand other people my age or the way the world really worked. Even clothes and hair were a struggle, leaving me caught in a confusing place where I didn't know who I was or what I wanted.

I wanted so much to break free, but it wasn't as simple as I expected.

And then Myra called, looking for help. Forcing me to tackle yet another thing I was completely unprepared for.

But in this moment I feel like I can do it.

Because the man next to me is on my side. He won't let me fall and he won't let me fail.

I meet Christian's eyes as he eases through the heavy metal gate of what appears to be a warehouse. "Okay."

10

CHRISTIAN

I PULL UP to one of the bay doors as it lifts, easing Rodney's sedan into the warehouse my family owns and shutting off the engine as the door slides back down—hopefully before anyone has spotted the car.

Coming here puts my entire family at risk. We've all worked so hard to get away from what we used to be and now I'm dragging us right back. But I don't have any other options. I can't deal with Rodney or his car on my own. Especially not if Lydia insists on being a part of it, which it appears she does.

Cody, my brother and the man in charge of the warehouse, walks up the side of the car, tucking a pen behind one ear, a clipboard clutched in his hands. He reaches the open window and leans down, holding my gaze a second before his eyes move to the woman in the passenger's seat. He gives her a grin. "Looks like you've had one hell of a day."

Lydia's brows lift, her eyes moving from Cody to me and then back again. "You could say that."

Cody glances into the back seat before straightening and

pulling open my door. "Why don't you get your girl set up in the office? Damien will be here in a few minutes with Niko. I'll come get you when they pull in."

I don't correct his assumption that Lydia is mine. I don't want to admit I've put everything we have on the line for a woman I'm not currently attached to. It's the same reason my brothers don't know about what Simon, Tate, and I do in our free time. Breaking our rules for family is one thing.

Breaking them for strangers is another.

Normally, the secret I keep doesn't bother me. I know what I'm doing matters. Changes lives. But Cody's reaction to what I just drove into his warehouse is dragging up the guilt I usually manage to avoid.

I offer him a nod because I can't manage much else. "I really appreciate it."

Cody slaps me on the shoulder, seeming like his normal, laid-back self even though I've just delivered him a dead man in a car that needs to be dismantled. "No worries. We'll get it handled."

I return his shoulder slap, reminding myself I would do the same thing if he showed up and needed my help. No questions asked. "Thanks."

I turn to help Lydia from the car, but she's already out, her purse clutched close as she scans the large storage space. "What is this place?"

"Just a warehouse. We offer temporary storage options to businesses." Cody continues to act like this is just any other day.

He thumbs over one shoulder in the direction of his office. "You can go hang out in the air conditioning. Watch some TV."

Lydia shifts on her feet, expression uncertain as she looks between me and my brother. "No thanks. I'll stay here."

Cody shrugs her rejection off. "No problem. If you change your mind, you know where it is." He tips his head toward the back of the building. "I've got some inventory to check while we wait for extra hands. I'll be back in a few."

I watch his back as he strides away, the guilt in my gut digging deeper. Cody's one of us that has the most to lose. A pretty wife he adores. A son and little girl who follow him around the renovated firehouse he calls home. My inability to come up with a better way of handling Rodney could ruin it all.

Lydia taps me on the shoulder, dragging my focus away from just how much I may have royally fucked up. She lifts her brows like she's waiting for something.

"What's wrong?" I automatically rest my clean palm on her back, intending to guide her away from the car. "Did you change your mind? You want to go stay in the office?" I sound hopeful and I am. I don't want her here to see just what I'm capable of.

The things I can do.

Lydia shakes her head at me, mouth pressing into a frown. "I'm not going to change my mind." She turns to the car, lips flattening even more. "This is my fault. The least I can do is—"

"This isn't your fault." I reach up with the hand clean enough to touch her, sliding my fingers through the softness of her hair as I tuck it behind one ear. "I should have known you wouldn't just stop looking for help when I told you no." I saw how upset she was. The panic. The fear. The desperation. "I should have known you wouldn't stop until Myra was safe."

Lydia almost seems to smile, her expression surprisingly soft. "How could you have known? The last time you saw me I was a little girl who was afraid of everything."

I slide my fingers down the length of her hair, unable to stop myself from continuing to touch her. "I've gotta admit I never would have expected to be here like this." I tip my head toward her. "With you."

Lydia's lower lip pinches between her teeth and I swear her cheeks barely pink up. "That doesn't surprise me." She glances down. "It's probably hard to think of me as anything besides the little girl who followed you around all the time."

Not as hard as it should be.

I give her hair a gentle tug, bringing her focus back to me. "You still seem to be following me around."

Lydia's jaw drops in mock outrage. "You've been literally following me everywhere for four days, so I'm pretty sure I'm not the one who's the issue this time."

I'm not surprised to discover Damien spilled all my secrets. He's always been the most social and charming of my brothers, and having a family of his own and walking the straight and narrow has only made it worse. He's completely comfortable with his life now that there's nothing to hide and assumes none of us have any secrets we want to keep either.

But some of us do. Some of us are still lingering at the edges of our old world, keeping one foot in even as we pretend it's behind us.

"I didn't want you to get hurt." I sigh, wishing so much of this could be different. "I knew Rodney would come after you and I wanted to make sure someone was there when he did."

Lydia studies me for a minute and I can almost see the gears working in her head. "What if it wasn't you that was there when he showed up?" Her eyes lock onto my face, watching me intently. "What if Damien was the one who was there?" Her eyes shift to the car before coming back to me. "Would we still be here?"

Part of me was clinging to the hope Lydia was as sweet and innocent and naïve as I initially expected, but it's seeming more and more like Damien is at least a little right. Like maybe Lydia is more comfortable in this world than I thought. "Possibly." I feel a little bad outing Damien like this, but he didn't seem to feel too guilty doing it to me. "Except his clothes would cost more to replace than mine."

Lydia's eyes slowly drag down my front, fixing on the half dry circle of blood soaked into the fabric of my black T-shirt. "Oh my God." Her hands go to the hem, yanking it free of my jeans to drag it up my chest. "Are you hurt?"

Her warm touch slides across my abs, skimming against my skin as she searches for the injury she believes created the stain.

I should tell her I'm fine. That the source of the blood is stuffed into the backseat of the car about to be shredded. But I can't bring myself to stop her. "I don't know."

Lydia continues to search my middle, making unhappy sounds as she worries over me. Her concern is just as addicting as her touch, and I hold my breath, soaking up every second.

"I can't tell what's yours and what's not." She looks around the warehouse. "Where's the bathroom?"

Again, I should tell her I'm fine. That the only injury I'm currently facing is to my conscience. Instead, I point toward the office. "Over there."

Lydia keeps her hand fisted in my shirt, using the hold to lead me into Cody's office. The door to the adjoining private bathroom is open and she hauls me inside, closing the door behind us before she drops her purse to the floor and faces me. "Arms up."

I immediately do what she says, drawn in by her sudden bossiness as much as the feel of her hands on my skin.

Lydia drags my shirt over my head, dropping it to the floor and kicking it away before turning to switch on the faucet. "I'm guessing this is an everyday thing for you? That's why you're being so nonchalant about it?"

The guilty part of me wants to lie to her, to hold back the truth of what I've become since she last saw me, but there's no hiding it from her now. "It's not an everyday thing anymore."

Lydia turns back to face me with a stack of dampened paper towels clutched in one hand and goes to work clearing away the blood on my skin. "Anymore? What does that mean?"

I hold still as she fusses over me, letting her clean my skin. "It means things like this used to happen a little more regularly than they do now."

Lydia turns back to the sink, chucking the first round of paper towels before grabbing another. Her expression is thoughtful as she comes back, movements slower as she continues stroking the damp towels across my stomach. "How much more regularly?"

I lift one shoulder in a small shrug, careful not to move too much in case it makes her decide to stop touching me. "Not every day, but often enough you won't have to worry about anyone finding Rodney and connecting him to you."

Lydia chucks the rest of the paper towels into the trash and I hold my breath, knowing judgment is coming.

There's plenty of supposed sins that are easy to move past. Modesty. Cussing. Drinking.

But most people still get stuck up on murder. No matter how deserved it was.

Lydia rolls her lips inward, eyes still focused on my stomach. The tips of her fingers inch toward me, barely tracing along the lines of my abs. "Thank you."

"You shouldn't be thanking me. Not now that you've seen what I've become." Maybe that's part of why I was so excited to see her again. Because Lydia might still see me the way I used to be. Before the world changed me.

Lydia's eyes lift to mine, her brows pinched together as she continues sliding her fingers against me in a whisper of a touch. "What have you become?"

I tip my head toward the main portion of the warehouse. I don't want to remind her but I have to. She deserves to see the truth. "You watched me kill a man, Lydia."

She rubs her lips together, easing in a little closer, the drag of her fingers against my skin firmer. "I watched you kill a man who was planning to rape me." Her eyes meet mine as she flattens her palms against my chest. "You protected me because you're still the same as you've always been."

I want her to be right, but there's no denying the years have changed me. Built me into the kind of man who knows how to clean up every kind of mess, because he's made more than a few of them.

I grit my teeth as her hands slide higher and the soft curve of her body presses closer. "You're making me out to be better than I am." Deep down I still want her to see me the way she used to, to look at me for help and protection, but the reality is I can't always give it to her. That's part of what brought us here. "I can't help you get Myra, remember?"

As expected, the reminder changes everything between us in the blink of an eye.

Lydia's hands fall to her sides, the warmth of her touch

abandoning my body as her expression hardens. "You can help me get Myra, you just won't."

This time I see it completely. The flash of anger. The flicker of defiance that tells me, in spite of everything that's happened, she's not finished trying to save her sister. Lydia might be just as sweet and soft as she ever was, but there's a strength to her that is impossible to deny.

And it's going to be one hell of a problem.

I open my mouth to argue with her, to start laying out all the reasons she needs to believe me when I say we have to wait, but someone starts banging on the bathroom door. Lydia gives me one final glare before turning to yank the door open.

Damien and Levi stand outside the door. Levi's expression is serious, but Damien just smirks at me as he tosses in a fresh T-shirt.

"Excuse me." Lydia shoulders past them, head down as she escapes the office.

Levi watches her go before turning back to face me. "Who in the hell is that?"

"That's who Rodney tried to kidnap." I shake out the shirt Damien brought, pulling it over my head before grabbing the one from the floor and shoving it into a fresh trash bag, wincing a little at the metallic scent of the blood soaked into it.

Levi looks me over as I scrub my hands in the sink. "I guess that explains why he ended up dead."

"It's not like that." I finally offer up the truth since it's going to come out anyway. "We knew each other when we were kids, that's all."

Levi stares at me like he doesn't believe shit I'm saying and Damien just continues to smirk.

Like Lydia, I shove my way past them, stalking into the

warehouse where Tate is standing with Cody, looking over the car we now have to dismantle.

I glance around as I cross the large space. "Where did Lydia go?"

Tate turns, brows going up as he shakes his head. "I haven't seen her."

"She just walked out of the office five seconds ago. How have you not seen her?" I turn back to where Damien and Levi stand in the doorway of the office. Levi shrugs and Damien just keeps fucking grinning at me.

"God dammit." I take off for the closest exit, pushing my way out into the evening air. To my relief, Lydia stands on the other side of the chain-link fence surrounding the property, staring at her phone.

An unfamiliar car turns onto the street and I race for the fencing, scaling it instead of wasting time going for the gate. She yelps as I drop down beside her, jumping back with wide eyes as the car pulls to a stop. "What are you doing?"

I haul her against me, using my body to block hers from whoever is inside that car. "What am I doing? What the fuck are you doing?"

Lydia pushes at me, wiggling loose of my grip. "I'm going home. I called an Uber."

I'm used to dealing with my brother's wives. Women who are more than happy to scream in your face and don't give a shit what you think of them. Women who will straight up tell you they're going to be a pain in the ass. And right now, I wish Lydia was a little more like them because it would be a hell of a lot easier to keep her safe.

"Cancel it. You're not going home." I grab her phone, closing out the Uber app before shoving it in my pocket and turning to the car idling beside us. I yank open the door, making the man behind the wheel jump. "She changed her mind. She doesn't need a ride."

To his credit, the terrified man doesn't pull away. He slowly points to Lydia. "She's gotta be the one to tell me that."

I grit my teeth even though I appreciate what he's doing. I take a step back, holding my hands out. "The choice is yours."

It's not, but right now she needs to think it is. She can leave in that car, but I will follow her.

Lydia glances at the open door, and for a second I think she's going to get in. But then her eyes meet mine. "If I'm not going to my apartment then where am I going?"

She's too damn smart for my own good.

I keep my eyes on hers as I offer up the option I hope she picks voluntarily. I'm not looking forward to her reaction if I have to take drastic measures. "Home with me."

II

LYDIA

I STUDY CHRISTIAN as I weigh my options, but somehow I'm not so sure they actually exist. "Do I really get a choice?"

Christian's expression is intense and unwavering. "Don't make me answer that."

I know I should be bothered by all of this, and I am. Just probably not in the way most people would be.

I know what it's like to finally be free from people who want to control you. Oppress you. My sister deserves that and I love her enough I'm willing to do anything to give it to her. Did I expect anything would include participating in a murder?

I wish I could say no, but from the very beginning I've prepared myself for the possibility someone might not make it out of this alive. Of course, I always expected that someone would be her husband, but Rodney didn't rank much higher on my 'worthy of continuing to breathe' chart than Matthias, so I'm struggling to feel too terrible about what happened. Especially since I'm sure he wouldn't have felt too terrible about what he was planning to do to me.

"Fine." I turn to the driver and give him a smile. "I'm going to stay. I'm really sorry."

Christian steps in beside me, flicking a one-hundred-dollar bill onto the seat. "Don't feel too sorry."

The driver snatches the money up like he expects Christian to take it back. "I'll hang out in the area for a little bit in case you change your mind."

Christian huffs out a loud sigh, like he's bothered that this guy is still trying to look out for me. He digs back into his wallet and pulls another hundred free, dropping it in the same spot he did the first before turning toward the building. "Come on. We've got work to do."

I hold my breath, waiting to see if he'll climb back over the fence, but he goes to the gate, looking slightly more civilized as he gets it open and holds it, waiting for me to go in.

And I'm more than a little disappointed I don't get to watch him scale the staggering height. I missed it last time and I wouldn't mind the opportunity to witness him racing to get to my side firsthand. Just to add a little more ammunition to my fantasy-based Christian arsenal.

Which now includes his willingness to do *anything* to keep me safe, a development that does tricky things to me. Things that make me ache in ways I've been too scared to explore on my own.

I bite my lip, ignoring the poorly timed throb between my thighs as I follow him into the fenced lot. The second the gate is closed and latched behind me, his hand is on the small of my back, urging me toward the door. "You can't just walk out of buildings alone like that, Lydia. Not until we really know how much danger you're in."

"Okay." I agree because that's what I do. It's simpler and less scary than arguing.

"See, you say that, but I feel like you'll go and do whatever you want the second I turn my back." He stops at the door and turns to me, looking frustrated, but not necessarily angry. "I get that you want to make your own decisions and do what you want to do, but can you at least be obvious about it?"

I'm a little taken aback by the request. "You want me to tell you when I'm gonna do what I want instead of what you want?" I shake my head. "Why would I do that?"

Being defiant in the household I grew up in was dangerous, but being openly defiant would have been more than a hazard to my health. The only reason I was able to escape was because no one saw it coming. They never expected sweet, quiet, agreeable Lydia to bolt the second they tried to marry her off.

Christian closes his eyes, blowing out a breath as he props his hands onto his hips. "I get it. I promise I do." He lifts his lids and focuses on me. "And I want you to have complete power over your own life." His head barely tilts to one side. "Just as soon as I get all this straightened out."

"So until then you want me to come live with you so you can boss me around?" I press one hand to my stomach as a lightning bolt of excitement zaps through. It's a little embarrassing. And frustrating. I should be doing everything in my power to have complete autonomy, not imagining Christian making ragged demands I'm a little too eager to follow.

But Christian shakes his head at me, voice low and deep. "I would never boss you around, Lydia. Never." His eyes pin me in place, his intense focus on me making my belly flip a little. "But I will do whatever it takes to keep you safe. And if it means I have to hunt you down when you take off, then that's what I'll do."

The possibility is oddly appealing. I left my family, my home, my life because I wasn't safe. Not a single decision was my own and the people making them for me only wanted to use me for their own gain. I was being bartered off to a man old enough to be my father because of the connections he could provide my actual father in his bid to take his own beliefs and power to the next level.

I expected them to hunt me down when I left. Without me as a pawn, my father was left with no bargaining chips on the table. No way to make his dream of controlling more than just his congregation and family a reality. The thought of him trying to find me made me sick to my stomach and had me watching my back for months.

But Christian hunting me down gives me a completely different feeling. One I don't quite know how to unpack.

"I know that's not what you want to hear, but you deserve to know the truth." There's a surprising amount of softness in his voice, as if he doesn't like admitting what will happen if I go against what he wants. "Until this is all handled, I go everywhere you go."

I drop my eyes, skimming down his body, and it takes everything I have not to clench my fingers at the memory of how his skin felt beneath them. I've come a long way from the virginal girl who moved to Memphis with a complete lack of understanding about how sex worked, but I'm still fully aware of how little I actually know. Touching Christian in the bathroom, imagining the opportunities physical contact with him would present, made that perfectly clear when I had no idea how to show him what I wanted.

How to get from point A to point B.

I shove both hands in the pockets of my shorts, trying to get my brain back on track. "Don't you have a job?"

"I own a demolition business, but we're off for the next three weeks. Until then, you're stuck with me."

"And I have to stay at your house?" The tingling ache

between my legs intensifies at the thought of being so close to him.

Christian's nostrils barely flare, his gaze still locked onto my face. "That's right."

I should be put out, but I'm not. I am, however, a little worried. "What about Piper? Is she safe?"

"We'll make sure she is." Christian sounds confident—like he's got everything completely under control—and it eases a little of the fear I have for my friend.

But only a little. I'm not sure Christian understands just how much of an undertaking keeping Piper safe will be.

"Are you going to have someone follow her, the same way you were following me?" I shake my head. "Because I'm not sure that's a great idea. We should probably tell her what's going on." I don't think Christian would be thrilled if one of his friends ends up with a taser to their privates, and that's exactly what will happen if Piper figures out they're tailing her.

"No." Christian's response is immediate and abrupt. "No one else can know about what's going on."

That's probably technically the best course of action, but he doesn't know Piper the way I do. Calling her a loose cannon is the understatement of all understatements. But I'm not one to argue. Even now, despite knowing I should at least try. So I just nod, pretending to go along with what he's saying even though I'm not so sure I will.

I glance up as the heavy metal gate barricading the lot slides open and a familiar vehicle pulls in. "Is that my car?"

"We can't leave it at the bar." He tips his head at the stranger behind the wheel as my little four-door pulls past us into the warehouse. A second car follows close behind, this one unfamiliar though I'm pretty sure I know who it belongs to.

"That's what you drive?" I look over the bright blue, sporty hatchback, a little surprised by what I'm seeing.

"They don't offer much in a stick shift anymore." Christian's explanation doesn't come close to touching on the reasons it's not at all what I expect.

"I thought you own a construction company." I continue staring at the cute, but impractical, vehicle.

"Demolition." Christian's hand gently clasps around my arm, leading me into the still open bay of the warehouse. "And did you think I drove my work truck everywhere?"

"Yeah. I kinda did." I can't fathom paying two car payments. The one I have is tough enough to make, and it's small by most people's standards.

The man driving Christian's car climbs out and tosses the keys his way. "We took the long way here, just to be safe."

Christian nods, jaw tense. "Good." He tips his head at the man who's almost as covered in tattoos as Rodney. "Lydia, this is Evan. Evan, Lydia."

Evan gives me a wide smile. "Nice to meet you."

I'm a little surprised at how happy he seems given the circumstances bringing him here. Actually all the men who've shown up have been shockingly laid back about the dead guy in the car. "Nice to meet you too."

The man behind the wheel of my car is the next one out, and he looks decidedly less friendly than Evan as he frowns at Christian. "You need to take that in and have Tate look it over. It's listing to the left, there's a tick in the engine, and I'm pretty sure most of the tires are bald."

My stomach clenches. It sounds like he's trying to point out that I'm clearly not keeping up as well on everything as I should be. Like he can't believe how incompetent I am as a human. It's something I'm all too used to hearing, and was one of the primary reasons I left Arkansas.

I don't like being chastised for being human.

"She's had a lot going on, man." Christian snatches my keys away from the giant, frowning guy. "Cut her some fucking slack. A tick in the engine is the last thing she's worried about right now."

The mountain of a man turns a little sheepish at Christian's reprimand looking my way as he scrubs the back of his neck with one huge hand. "I didn't mean it that way. I just meant you need to take care of your girl better than you are."

Oh.

Oh.

The realization he was lecturing Christian, not me, makes me feel a little better, but clearly he's misreading this whole situation. I shake my head, not wanting Christian to be upset his friends are obviously getting the wrong idea. "We're not together." I shift on my feet, suddenly very uncomfortable. "We're just—"

I pause, struggling to come up with a simple explanation for what we are, but come up empty. So I just stand there, feeling awkward and out of place.

Like usual.

"Lydia and I go way back." Christian continues to scowl at the huge guy. "And Tate is taking her car with him." Christian tosses my keys to the base player I remember from The Cellar.

"Umm..." I glance at Tate, struggling to put myself in the middle of the conversation. "...I need my car to get to work."

Christian turns to me, expression flat. "No, you don't."

I bristle, but do my best not to show any outward reaction. "I have to go to work. I have bills to pay. And once my sister gets here, I have to support her until she gets on her feet." I keep my words calm and soft so hopefully they don't piss anyone off. I know what happens when a woman tries to stand up for herself to a group of men, and I don't really feel like hearing how terrible I am for having thoughts, feelings, and opinions.

Christian glances at the men standing around the warehouse, carrying on casual conversations like there isn't a dead guy bleeding all over the backseat of the car. He comes closer, resting one hand on my back as he moves me away from the group. His voice is low in my ear as we walk. "You're still going to work, Lydia. I'm not trying to take over your life, I swear." He stops walking but doesn't take his hand off my body. "But I know how to keep you safe, so you've got to trust me."

Trust is a tricky thing for me. I'm not sure I've ever trusted anyone in my entire life. My mom drank the Kool-Aid and one hundred percent believes my father should make every decision right down to the way she wears her hair. And it was clear from an early age my best interests were the last thing my father ever considered.

I do trust Myra, but also understand the kind of person she is. She's passive and shy and broken down, and her decisions and actions will always be tainted by that.

Just like mine.

"I know it's hard." Christian's hand falls from my body as he glances toward the car we drove into the warehouse. "Especially considering everything that happened tonight."

Rationally I know I should be looking at him differently right now. And I am, but not in the way most people would. Because now I have proof Christian will literally do whatever it takes to keep me safe—something I can't say for anyone else in my life.

"Okay."

One of Christian's brows slowly angles up. "Is that bullshit? Are you just pretending to agree with me because you know it's what I want to hear?" He shakes his head, expression turning dark and a little threatening. "Because you can't just walk out of places alone anymore. You can't be sweet to my face knowing you're going to turn around and do the exact opposite of what you tell me."

I can, but I'm not going to point that out. Christian might think he wants me to tell him exactly what I think and what I want, but he doesn't. Not really. Men like sweet, agreeable women. And I don't think that just because I was raised in a cult, force-fed that belief every waking minute of my life. I think that because I've seen it in action, even in the real world.

If I'm having a bad day, and acting a little less friendly, my tips are lower. Every. Single. Time.

When I'm happy and sweet and full of smiles, the money goes up. It's bullshit, but that's just the way it is.

I can't count the number of times I've heard I should smile more. How many men have told me I shouldn't look so sad, when they have no idea what the reality of my life is... That I'm terrified for my sister's safety, and what she's going through never leaves my mind.

They don't realize, or more likely don't care, that my smiles are an act. A calculated and carefully curated facade, because I understand how they work and what they can accomplish.

So I do it now. I smile. "It's really fine."

I expect Christian to be happy he's getting what he wants—what all men want—but that dark, foreboding look on his face only intensifies as he crowds closer. "Don't lie to me, Lydia."

My smile barely falters and not because I'm scared.

When Christian is being careful with me, he's every bit the way I remember him. But when he's looking at me the way he is now, it's clear I don't know him nearly as well as I think. Because right now he's looking at me the way I imagine the wolf looked at Little Red Riding Hood.

Like he's more than willing to chase me down if I run. Like no matter how hard I try, there's no escaping him. He will find me. Always.

I don't hate the thought, but the rest of the story is a little trickier. Especially since the wolf was out to eat Little Red Riding Hood.

Except—

My thighs clench together involuntarily as my sheltered brain plays catch up, quickly filling in a much more debaucherous story. One that's even more appealing than the thought of Christian hunting me down to keep me safe.

I can't stop the strangled sound I make as visions of Christian's mouth, hot and hungry between my thighs, embed themselves in my brain.

Christian closes his eyes, tipping his head back as he takes a deep breath. "I know you hate this, and I wish there was another way." His head drops and his eyes level on me once again. "But there's not."

I swallow, hoping to form coherent words as heat thrums through my body, building into a pulse that throbs in my nipples and pussy. "It's okay. I promise."

This time I mean it, because now that I'm really thinking about it, maybe Little Red Riding Hood didn't have it so bad after all.

Especially if her wolf was anything like Christian.

12

CHRISTIAN

MY HOUSE IS as quiet and dark as ever as I walk in through the back door. Everything inside is the same. The kitchen I painstakingly built using refurbished cabinetry my company removed from a five million dollar home last year. The adjoining great room, with its large sectional and big screen television. The slightly creaky reclaimed oak flooring and the lingering scent of cut wood and polyurethane from the refinished hutch I added along the back wall a few weeks ago.

Coming home tonight shouldn't be any different than the hundreds of times I've done it before.

But it is.

Because tonight, for the first time, I'm not coming home alone.

"So this is where you live too?" Lydia comes into the space behind me, scanning the rooms as I flip on lights.

I nod, watching as she inspects the home I've painstakingly assembled over the past three years, wondering if she sees it the same way I do.

Lydia tucks her chin, lifting her brows as her eyes find

their way back to my face. "So you just give strange people your home address and the code to your gate?" Her eyes drift away, slowly moving around the kitchen. "Aren't you worried someone will come in and do something awful?"

I remain silent because I'm not sure I want to rehash tonight's events by explaining just how unworried I am about that possibility.

When Lydia's eyes jump back to mine, it becomes clear she didn't need reminding. "Yeah. I guess not.

I flip the deadbolt on the back door and engage the security system, not because I'm concerned someone will come in and try to get me. Right now I'm equally worried one of Rodney's cohorts will try to get at Lydia in retaliation, and that Lydia's willingness to be here with me isn't as genuine as she's claiming it is. I don't want to be yet another man she thinks she has to placate.

"The bedrooms are on the second floor." I grab the suitcase we quickly packed at her apartment, rolling it down the hall.

As I haul it off the floor when we reach the stairs, the lightness of the luggage bothers me just as much as the sparseness of her belongings did while I waited for her to collect them. Lydia's closet was practically empty, and most of the items in it looked like work clothes. She owns three pairs of shoes. About as many pairs of jeans and shorts. The majority of her wardrobe was shirts, probably because those are cheap and easy to rotate through.

It's clear she hasn't spent much of the money she's made working at The Cellar, which has got to be a decent amount. She's cute and sweet and exactly the kind of woman an inebriated man loves to throw tips at in the hope it will earn him a little attention.

Lydia's obvious scrimping and saving makes me think

she's been planning to save her sister from the beginning, living on as little as possible knowing she'd have to help Myra get on her feet. It's not surprising—as the two youngest of their family, with only older brothers, they were always close—but I hate she's done without the way she has.

"Your house is really nice." Lydia quietly follows me up the stairs, carrying her purse and the bag containing her toiletries. "Have you lived here long?"

"Probably longer than I should have." I reach the top of the stairs and pause, hoping she sees my home the same way I do. I need something to work in my favor right now.

Lydia has had a fucking nightmare of a day. She's also probably looking at me through different eyes now that she knows what I'm capable of, and I'm still not quite sure exactly how much her opinion of me has changed. The possibility that she figured out I'm no longer what she thought bothers me.

But the fact that she's under my roof soothes a little of that worry. It gives me time to fix whatever damage was done tonight.

While she sleeps in my bed.

"My brothers and I own all the buildings on the street." I lead her to the right and reach out to open the door, pushing it wide before flipping on the lights. "I bought this place a few years ago and moved right in even though it wasn't technically habitable."

Lydia walks in behind me, but her feet come to a screeching halt as her eyes widen on the room in front of her.

It's the reaction I was hoping for. I've put a lot of effort into my home, channeling shit I didn't want to deal with into blood and sweat as I reused, repurposed, and rebuilt everything I could get my hands on, turning the basic block building into the kind of home I never expected to have.

"Wow." Lydia's jaw is slack as she takes another step across the reclaimed wood floor, eyes searching the soaring ceilings. "This is amazing."

I keep walking, going straight to the large walk-in closet instead of soaking up her praise the way I want to. "I end up with a lot of high-quality stuff through my business, and instead of just throwing it all away, I figured I might as well put it to good use."

The finishings of my house would have cost a fortune if I had to buy them outright, but the majority of the stuff was destined for a landfill. The only cost I have in it is the effort it took to make sure it was reusable as my team removed it from the upscale homes I specialize in servicing.

Lydia takes another step, gaze bouncing from the floor to the lights to the brick stacked along the main wall. "You definitely put it to good use." She bends, reaching out to barely drag the tips of her fingers along the large bed dominating the space. "Did you make this?"

I jerk my chin down in a nod, feeling a little uncomfortable at sharing something I didn't expect to feel so personal. My brothers have all seen my home, but they're the only ones, and I feel oddly exposed as Lydia moves around the space.

"This definitely makes me a little more embarrassed of my bedroom." She chews her lower lip, eyes avoiding mine.

I suddenly feel like a jackass. I didn't bring her here to make her feel like her life was something to feel bad about. "Your room isn't anything to be ashamed of, Lydia. You should have seen where I lived when I first left Arkansas."

It's something I haven't thought of in years, and don't

necessarily want to think about now, but I also want her to see how well she's doing.

Lydia faces me, expression open and expectant as she waits for me to offer even more of myself. Not of who I am now, but who I once was.

"When they first kicked me out, I was barely old enough to get a job." I set her suitcase in the closet, abandoning it there before stuffing both hands into the pockets of my jeans. "And all the jobs I could get paid barely enough to survive. So I did what I had to do."

Lydia's hands clench at the purse strap across her chest. "What did you have to do?"

My jaw clenches, trying to keep in the truth of how differently our paths played out. But she's already seen the worst of what I can do, so hiding this seems pointless. "Sold drugs. Stole." I shift on my feet, wondering if this was how my brothers felt when they confessed their sins. "Whatever made enough money to put me up in a cheap motel for the night."

Lydia stares at me a second, brows pinched together, lips pressed into a tight frown. The bag of toiletries clenched in her hand slowly drops to the floor as she unwinds her purse and lets it fall beside it. "Were you completely on your own?"

"Not for long." It was a blessing and a curse how quickly I crossed paths with Tate and Simon. We were able to lean on each other, but we also fed each other's anger. "I met Tate and Simon a few months after my dad kicked me out and we ended up sticking together since we were all in the same boat. A boat that would have sunk quickly if we didn't figure out how to take care of ourselves."

Lydia slowly moves toward me, her presence in my bedroom somehow less bizarre than it should be after all these years. "What about all the guys who showed up at the warehouse to help you? When did you meet them?"

"A year or two after I came to Memphis, Simon met this old man who said he could help us. Called himself King. Said he was building an empire." King's opinion of himself was inflated—something I clearly see now that I'm older—but at the time he knew all the right things to say to three boys looking for what they'd lost.

Family. Security. Safety.

Technically, King provided all that, it just came at a cost. A cost my brothers and I eventually decided was too high.

"King?" Lydia's brows slowly creep up her forehead as she continues coming closer. "What's he like?"

"Dead." Of all the parts of my past I don't like to discuss, King might top the list. Admitting how easily he took advantage of me, used me, is humiliating. I should have seen him for what he was right away. Recognized he was no better than the power-hungry men in my past.

Lydia nods, her eyes wide and guileless as she stops directly in front of me. "Is that a good thing?"

I return her nod. "A very good thing."

King's death brought my brothers and me a level of freedom we never expected to have. It broke so many of the ties restricting us, making it possible to build a new life on a fresh foundation. One we created ourselves.

Lydia watches me a second longer, her lower lip pinching between her teeth. "Did you kill him?" Her tone isn't accusatory, simply curious.

It's unexpected.

"No." I shake my head. "His daughter did."

Lydia presses her lips tight together, flattening them out, her eyes dropping between us. "Will you think badly of me if I say I don't blame her?"

My head tips back in surprise. "No." Her question catches me a little off guard initially, but the longer it sinks in, the more I get where she's coming from. "I know most people wouldn't understand how you feel about your father, but I do."

Lydia shakes her head at me, her smile sad. "No you don't." She sighs, looking sad. "I know we lived in the same world, but being a man in that world and being a woman in that world are two completely different things."

I don't know what to say because it's true. I may have been thrown out for speaking out against the fucked-up way they were, but no one there ever told me what to wear. What to say. How to behave. If anything, I was raised to believe I was above just about everyone else in the world. Holier. A chosen one.

I was raised to believe I would be in charge of every-thing in my own life, but also the life of the family I would be the head of. I would decide where we lived. Where we went and what we did.

Lydia was raised believing she was less than me, less than any man. They don't come right out and say that, of course. They have a carefully curated dialogue to hide the truth of what they think. Calling a sweet and submissive woman a precious and priceless gift from God. Saying she was gifted to be a blessing to those around her. Offering whatever bullshit they believe will make women like Lydia and Myra shut up and be grateful for the lot they've been given.

"I'm glad you got away." I start to reach for her but stop. I scrubbed my hands at the warehouse, but I'm not clean enough to touch her.

I might never be.

The realization backs me up a step, moving my feet

toward the door. "I know you're tired. I'll let you get settled in." I pause, giving Lydia one last look. "I'll be down the hall if you need me." I duck out into the hall, pulling the door closed behind me and taking a deep breath.

I wish I could say I didn't know exactly what I was doing when I brought Lydia here, but I did. I wanted to keep her close. I wanted to know she was safe. That she was taken care of.

I also liked the idea of her being exactly where she's about to be. In my bed.

Knowing Lydia's soft body is about to be curled against my sheets sends my feet down the hall, putting as much distance between us as possible. I thought I could handle having her here, but maybe I can't. I expected having her close to me would be enough. Knowing she was safe would soothe the uncomfortable feeling I've been struggling to rectify, but it's only getting worse.

Because she's still not close enough. I want more.

I want her.

Not just in my bed. Not just under my body.

Not just in my home.

I want her to be mine. And I want it with an intensity that takes me by complete surprise.

So I don't stop moving as I pass into the spare bedroom, rounding the large bed and heading for the bathroom. I need a shower and I need sleep. Something to hit the reset button and get my brain back on the right track. A track that's focused on keeping Lydia safe instead of getting her into my bed. Into my life.

I strip off my clothes, chucking them in the trash can instead of the laundry hamper. Tomorrow I'll leave them in a dumpster somewhere on the other side of town, along with anything else that might connect me to Rodney.

Tonight was a messy night, so even the shirt Damien brought me is ruined.

I switch on the shower and climb under the spray before it has a chance to heat up, ignoring the cold sting of the water against my skin as I scrub away the remnants of what should be the worst day I've had in a long fucking time. I've put my whole family in danger. Dragged us back into the life we worked so hard to get out of.

And the fucked-up thing is, I would do it all over again. Even after fifteen years, the need to keep Lydia safe is impossible to ignore.

Maybe worse.

Before I was simply a kid trying to protect another kid— my best friend's little sister. Someone too small to take care of themselves. My motives are no longer the same. And as much as I want to continue trying to deny it, I can't.

Maybe it's desperation after seeing my brothers so goddamned happy and wanting it for myself. Maybe it's because Lydia's the only spark of happiness I remember in my past. Or maybe it's because of who she's become. The strength I know it took for her to walk away and start over. The determination I see when she talks about saving Myra. The sweetness she still retains, even after everything she's been through.

Whatever it is, I no longer look at Lydia as a little girl. Haven't since she showed up on my front porch, all grown up and everything I always hoped she would become. And now I want her for myself. I want to be the one she looks to for protection. For safety.

For more.

I haven't touched a woman in almost a year. The fast fucks and hookups that use to sate me no longer carry any appeal. That's probably why I can't get the thought of Lydia in my bed out of my head. Why I can't help but envision her naked body as she steps into my shower, running her hands over all that soft skin as she gets ready to sleep on my sheets.

It's definitely why my own hand moves to grip my straining dick, fisting it tight as I let myself imagine, just for a second, how it might feel to sink into Lydia's warm, willing body. To show her real men don't want a woman who simply accepts sex as a duty. A task they must withstand for the sake of salvation.

But maybe Lydia already knows.

The possibility of another man with his hands on her sends jealousy streaking through my already tense body—fists my hand tighter as I pump into it, angry.

Whoever's touched her, I know I could do better. I could make her forget there was ever anyone but me.

I could be all she wants.

That thought pushes me over the edge, spurting against the tile, imagining my mouth between her thighs as they lock around my head.

The door to the bathroom bangs open, and the shower curtain whips to one side.

Lydia's caught me red-handed, literally. But she doesn't seem to notice.

Her skin is flushed, eyes wide as she shoves her cell phone in my direction. "Myra wants to talk to you."

13

LYDIA

I SHOVE THE phone closer to Christian, desperate for him to take it before something happens and Myra has to hang up. Unfortunately, I've definitely caught him off guard and he stares at me in shock for what feels like an eternity as water continues to run down his naked body.

I do everything possible to keep my eyes on his face. To keep them from drifting down the solid wall of his chest, past the cut of his obliques to where his hand covers his dick. I fail, and that's when it registers that his hand isn't there in an attempt to retain some semblance of modesty.

It's gripping the still slightly erect length of him.

I swallow hard. I've interrupted much more than a shower.

I force my eyes to the ceiling, hating myself just a little bit for being so easily distracted from my sister's needs, and feeling guilty about wanting to linger on the thought of what was happening when I walked in. "Please talk to her. She'll tell you what you need to hear."

Christian carefully takes the phone from me with the

hand not on his dick, steps back from the water, and presses it to his ear. "Myra?"

His eyes meet mine as he listens, the hand I am trying so hard not to consider shutting off the spray before he steps out. Enormously big, utterly nude, and completely soaking wet, his movement sends me stepping back to avoid ending up pressed against him.

I want to hold my ground, just to see what might happen, but I can't. Not when I'm so close to having everything I need to get my sister safe.

"Do you know where you are?" Christian snags a towel from the rack, wrapping it around his waist without bothering to dry himself off first.

"Is it a new property he purchased?" He tucks the phone against one broad shoulder and wedges the end of the towel into place before walking past me into the bedroom. I trail behind him, twisting my hands together. Hopefully Myra has enough information about where she is for him to track her down.

"How long did it take you to get there?" Christian stands at the foot of the bed, looking calm and confident and in control—so many things I've never felt—and for the first time I really feel like this might happen. Getting Myra out of Arkansas has weighed heavily on my shoulders, and knowing I was her only hope of escaping was terrifying.

But now it's not just me. Now I have help. Help from someone completely capable of doing whatever it takes to get her out of there.

Whatever it takes.

"Myra?" Christian's eyes meet mine. "Myra? Are you still there?" He pulls my phone from his ear and looks at the screen, lips pressing into a frown. "The call dropped."

146

My throat goes tight. "No. She had to hang up because he was back." I close my eyes against the burn of tears because I know what will happen if she was caught on the phone. I can't focus on that. I can't let myself get dragged down by what I know she's going through because I'll start to spiral. "Did you get what you needed?"

"Yes." Christian's voice is very close and very soft. "She said she wants out."

I let out a shuddering breath that sits somewhere between relief and regret as I open my eyes and find him standing directly in front of me. "I told you."

"I believed you." His hand lifts to trace along the side of my face. "But I had to be sure she meant it. I knew you'd never forgive yourself if she changed her mind and something happened."

Maybe it's because we're standing so close. Maybe it's because my own emotions are so raw. Whatever the reason, I see something I haven't noticed before. The sadness in Christian's eyes. The regret.

It makes me think of a person I'd all but forgotten. "What happened to your sister?"

Like me, Christian is the youngest of his family. And considering the church that controlled our lives believed birth control was a sin and that truly godly women were always available to meet their husband's needs, being the youngest meant you could be well over a decade younger than your oldest sibling. Christian is ten years older than I am, which probably means there are more than twenty between me and his older sister. She was married and a mother before I was even born. The only reason she was ever on my radar was because she was connected to Christian. When he left, I soaked up every tidbit of information remotely pertaining to him, including any and all gossip concerning his family.

It's embarrassing to think about how much I thought of him. Some might call it an obsession. But I knew so few people back then, boys especially, and even fewer that I actually had any interest in. So I clung to his memory. Held it, and anything pertaining to it, close.

But then she left too.

Christian's expression tightens, the sadness I suspected earlier blooming across his handsome features. "She didn't really mean it when she said she was ready to leave."

My stomach clenches as a chill moves through me, settling around the tightening in my gut. "But she did leave. They told us she'd been—"

They told us she'd been possessed by the devil. That he turned her away from the light of God. I was young and innocent enough to believe that meant she'd cut her hair and put on a pair of jeans before walking away from the same miserable existence I wanted to leave.

But now I know it's not that easy. Especially when you've already been married off. Like my sister has. Like Christian's sister had.

"You helped her get out and she went back." The discomfort in my stomach only intensifies, sending it sinking so fast I need something to hang on to. I reach for Christian, hands falling against the warmth of his chest.

His eyes hold mine as he slowly nods.

I think I might throw up.

When I left the IGL, I hated how clueless I was. How naïve. How sheltered. But right now it's difficult not to want a little of that back. To wish that, at least in this specific situation, I was still just as clueless as I was before.

I step forward, closing what little space is left between us as I grab onto him, arms threading around his waist, holding tight as the reality of his situation and mine crashes down.

"I'm so sorry, Christian." I close my eyes, wanting to comfort him, needing to comfort myself as I bury my face against his neck, wishing I could block it all out. "It's not your fault."

Christian is stiff against me for a second, but then his arms slowly wrap around my body, his skin still slightly damp and tacky from the shower I interrupted as he presses my body against his. "Does that mean you won't feel responsible if something happens to Myra?"

The ache in my middle twists tighter because I know what he's trying to tell me. That even though Myra has met his criteria—has told him she's ready to go—there's still the chance she might return.

And the consequences could be deadly.

"She's ready to go. I promise." I can't think about what he's trying to make me understand. It's too scary for me and makes me ache too much for him. "She won't go back. I know she won't."

Christian's hand slides down my hair in a gentle caress. "I would have said the same thing about Rebecca. It's the only life they know, Lydia. Walking away isn't easy, even when someone is ready to help you along the way."

I take a steadying breath, standing a little taller as I lean back to look him in the eyes. "I did it." And if I did it, so can Myra.

So *will* Myra.

The hard line of Christian's mouth barely softens, lifting at one corner as the hand in my hair slides to my face,

149

stroking across my skin. "Not everyone is as brave as you are, Lydia."

I stand perfectly still as he continues to touch me. The brush of his fingers moves across my face, tracing my cheekbone, my jaw line, my lips. It's soothing and almost hypnotizing and drags free a confession I don't mean to make. "I'm not brave. I'm scared all the time."

Christian's eyes focus on where he touches me, following the path of his calloused caress. "Being brave doesn't mean you're not scared. It means you keep going anyway." His mouth flattens again. "Do you know how many people could have handled what happened today the way you did?" He barely shakes his head, eyes lifting to mine. "Not many."

"I didn't handle anything. I just stood there while Rodney tried to take me." Embarrassment and guilt make my skin hot. "If it hadn't been for you—" I swallow hard, but it doesn't have anything to do with worry over what might have happened. I'm just starting to notice all of me is pressed against all of Christian.

All of practically naked Christian.

I swallow hard as my nipples start to feel tight where they're pressed against his bare chest, the sensation building more with each passing second. "If it hadn't been for you I would be somewhere very different right now." It's a statement that encompasses more than just what happened today.

I always assumed my youthful fascination with Christian was primarily due to my lack of other viable options, but it's starting to seem like maybe that wasn't the only reason he was never far from my mind. I have plenty of options now, and I still can't seem to stop thinking about him.

Maybe it wasn't just the way he looked or what he did

that made me so fascinated with him. Maybe it was simply that his existence gave me hope.

Christian has always been different. Even as a little girl I recognized he wasn't like the other boys—the other men. He didn't treat me like an object to be possessed. Like I was less. Like I was simply there to serve him and the rest of the population lucky enough to be born with a penis.

He always treated me like I should be protected. Like I was valuable. Like I mattered.

And while so much of him has changed, that hasn't.

"I won't ever let anything happen to you, Lydia." Christian's face is so close to mine I can feel the warmth of his breath. "I promise."

"I know." I lean in a little more, wanting more. Of what, I'm not sure I'm willing to admit. Yet. "You've always kept me safe."

Christian's mouth hovers over mine, barely a breath away, and the ache in my nipples expands, spreading to lower, just as neglected, parts of my body. I want him to kiss me. Touch me. Show me all the things I'm too scared to discover for myself.

But suddenly Christian's whole body stiffens. His hands drop away from my skin and he takes a step back.

The separation feels more than merely physical.

My cheeks flame even as the throb in my body intensifies, protesting the loss of contact. I've clearly said or done the wrong thing. I'm not sure what exactly, but there's no denying Christian's reaction.

"You should go to bed." His eyes won't meet mine. "It's been a long day and we have a lot to do tomorrow."

I should be thrilled. Relieved Myra will finally be safe. Finally be free. But the disappointment of Christian backing away from me tanks any happiness I try to scrounge up.

"Okay." I want to ask him what I said or did that was so wrong he pulled away from me, but I can't make myself do it. So I leave, hugging myself as I go back down the hall to the room he dumped me in earlier. It's beautiful, and I'm grateful, but his sudden rejection stings.

Maybe I'm still just like a little sister to him. Maybe I'm too young. Maybe I'm still too naïve and sheltered to be the kind of woman he would have any sort of interest in.

I close the door to his room, and this is definitely his room, and strip out of the clothes I've been wearing for more hours than I can count. After carefully folding and stacking them on the chair in the corner, I drift into the bathroom to take a quick shower. The room is just as gorgeous as the rest of the house, decked out with a vanity that looks like an antique dresser Christian repurposed, and the most beautiful glass tiles I've ever seen. They're a dark pearly black with swirls of color that conjure images of the universe I didn't know existed until a year ago.

I quickly scrub down and rinse off, pausing just a second to appreciate how thick and fluffy the towels are before pulling on a fresh pair of panties and my nightshirt. Once I brush my teeth, I turn off the lights and slip under covers that smell just like him.

I jerk upright, startled out of a slumber I don't remember falling into, confident I heard something.

Rodney's friends have found me. Or worse, my father is finally coming to drag me back.

My sleep fogged brain begins to panic, my heart racing as I flip back the covers and bolt. I fling open the door and race down the hall toward the only person who has ever truly made me feel safe, rushing into the bedroom Christian is using. I can't think straight. Can't process what I should and shouldn't do. The only thought I have is to hide. To be quiet.

So I slip under the covers beside him, curling close as I squeeze my eyes shut, shaking with fear just like I used to as a little girl.

Only this time I don't have to be afraid alone.

"Lydia?" Christian's voice is rough with sleep as he stirs beside me. "What's wrong?"

I'm quiet for just a second. Long enough for it to register that the sound I heard might not have been as real as I thought. The fear clawing at my skin gives way to embarrassment. "I—" Humiliation clamps my lips together, sealing off the explanation I'm trying to offer.

"Come here." Christian pulls me close, arms holding me tight as he tucks my body against his. "Everything's going to be okay. I promise."

My throat goes tight as I blink away tears that should probably be for the man I watched die today.

They aren't.

And maybe that makes me just as evil as my father believes I am. Maybe there's so much sin on my skin that I'll never be able to wash it away.

The possibility doesn't bother me as much as it used to. Especially now that I've seen what sinners are really like. I've never been able to count on anyone the way Christian can obviously count on the men he calls his brothers. They will literally move bodies for him without the link of blood tying them together.

Well…

Maybe they have plenty of blood between them. Spilled instead of shared.

I take a shaky breath. "Can I tell you something?"

Christian rests his hand against the back of my head, cradling it in his palm. "You can tell me anything."

I look up at him, barely able to make out his features in the darkness of the room. "If the opportunity comes up, I'm okay with you killing my sister's husband too."

14

CHRISTIAN

WAKING UP WITH a hard-on isn't usually an issue. Not that it doesn't happen, there's just never anyone else around to witness it. Not over the last year anyway.

But even before then, any witnesses knew what they were getting into, and normally appreciated the events following it.

That's not the case this morning.

As far as I know, Lydia's never touched a dick, let alone had one shoved against her ass as she sleeps. And even though she's the one who found her way into my bed, the situation feels all kinds of inappropriate. I carefully roll to my back, stifling a groan as I peel myself away from the warmth and softness of her body. The loss of pressure and contact makes the ache in my cock worse and I lie still for a moment, trying to figure out some way to rub one out before she wakes up.

Suddenly Lydia pulls in a deep breath and rolls toward me. She slings one bare leg across my body, planting her thigh right against the line of my suffering dick, before letting out a content sounding sigh.

She has me pinned in place, making it next to impossible to escape without waking her, which would give her an up-close-and-personal experience with the struggle I've got going on.

Because this isn't just your run-of-the-mill morning wood. This is tied directly to the dream preceding it. A dream involving the same sweet thighs that are all but wrapped around me now.

Lydia takes another deep breath, the kind that tells me she's not sliding back into sleep but rousing from it. I don't have much longer before she'll be fully awake, and aware that there's something prodding at the tempting curve of her thigh.

Slowly working one hand under the covers, I carefully wrap my fingers around the soft skin just above her knee. I gently start to lift her leg away from my body, trying to work just enough room to slide away. No longer pinned in place, my dick rises and follows the warmth of her body, continuing to press against her inner thigh. I've almost got enough clearance when Lydia makes a soft sound, instantly heating my blood and sending what's left of it racing south.

She wiggles beside me, inching a little closer until every bit of her is pressed against my side, including the object of my most recent dream's obsession.

She makes another breathy, whimpery noise and then does something that stops me in my tracks.

The first time she grinds against my thigh I think it's simply her trying to get closer. Maybe she's caught in the throes of the same kind of nightmare that brought her to my bed in the first place, and she's simply seeking comfort and safety.

But then it happens again, and this time there's no mistaking the needy way she rubs her cotton covered pussy against me. I clench my teeth, trying to ignore the damp heat of her cunt as she finds a rhythm, unknowingly using my body as she dreams about God knows who.

Lydia's been in Memphis for a year. That's plenty of time to lose more than a little of her innocence. Hell, maybe she has a boyfriend who's shown her all the things the IGL never wanted her to know. The possibility stabs at me, a knife of unreasonable jealousy that keeps cutting.

Until—

"*Christian.*" My name passes through her lips on a hushed whisper, soft and sweet, and the best fucking thing I've ever heard.

And also the worst since I know she didn't mean for me to hear it. Lydia's dreams should be her own, so even though knowing I'm a part of them turns my already suffering cock to stone, I have to stay the course.

I hook my foot over the edge of the mattress, intending to use it to pull myself to the edge. But the second my body starts to shift away from hers, Lydia holds me tighter, her body locked around mine. "Don't go."

Her words are louder this time and less slurred with sleep. Clear enough I can almost make myself believe she's awake.

But she's not. The long length of her lashes rests against her cheeks, trapping her in a dream I wish I could see.

I try again to detangle myself from her, knowing there aren't many men in their right mind who would do what I'm doing. Which is a shame. But again, I barely shift before Lydia's foot hooks around my leg, pinning her body back against me.

"Christian, I need—" She makes a frustrated sound as she continues fighting for the friction she's seeking.

I know what she needs, and I wish like hell I could give it

to her, but that won't happen. Not now. Not until I know she really means—

Lydia's eyes flutter open, her blown out pupils locking straight on my face. She inhales sharply, throat working as she swallows hard. I expect her to be angry. Pissed I've let things get this far. At the very least embarrassed and shy.

But she doesn't pull away from me. Doesn't glare at me in accusation. The pink tip of her tongue darts across her lower lip before she pinches it between her teeth and rolls her hips, making another one of those unbearable sounds that test my sanity and my willpower.

"Lydia." I grit my teeth as she rubs into me again. "What are you doing?"

"I don't know." The admission is just as soft and sweet as she is. "You want me to stop?"

I should. I should send her back down the hall to the safety of my room, far enough away I won't be tempted to touch her. But if yesterday proved anything, it's that I'm not as good of a man as I pretend I am.

"What I want is for you to take your panties off so I can feel how wet you get when you dream of me."

Lydia makes a sharp little squeak of surprise but doesn't ask how I know I was the subject of whatever blessed fantasy her mind worked up.

I hold my breath, waiting silently to see if I've crossed the line, even though I'm sure I have.

The question is, will Lydia cross it with me.

A few heartbeats later, I have my answer. The hand gripping my middle slowly slides away and her fingers dip into the waistband of the simple cotton panties around her hips. She drags them down her legs, kicking them away before going still beside me. "I don't know what I should do now."

"Now you do whatever makes you feel good." I still

won't touch her unless she asks me to. If she just wants to continue using me, that's fine. But if she wants more, I'm more than ready to accommodate.

"I don't know what makes me feel good." Lydia pinches her lower lip between her teeth, lids hanging heavy as her eyes rest on my chest, refusing to lift any higher.

I reach out to slide one hand through her hair, pushing it back and curling it behind one ear. I can't not touch her right now, but if she wants anything more than the most chaste of contact, she will have to ask.

And I hope like hell she does.

"That's a damn shame. You deserve to feel good." I lean in and rest my lips against the top of her head, breathing in the sweet scent of her as I try to calm my rapidly fraying control. "You deserve to know it's okay to take what you need."

I know what she's been taught—what every woman in the IGL has been taught—that sex is something they provide, not something they experience. A woman who seeks sexual satisfaction is considered wanton. Loose. A creator of lust and sin.

Lydia whimpers again. The sound is pure frustration and probably the result of a lifetime of neglecting her body's needs. "There's never been anyone to take from." Lydia shifts around, rubbing her legs together in an attempt to find relief from an ache I desperately want to take care of for her.

"Then you give it to yourself." I lower my voice, shifting until my lips brush against her ear. "It's okay to make yourself feel good, Lydia. I promise."

As much as I want to touch her, I want to offer her liberation more. Freedom from the confines of a belief built on bullshit and male domination.

Lydia shakes her head. "I can't."

She sounds defeated. Broken.

I fucking hate it. I hate that she's never been given power over her own body. That she's been taught her primary purpose is pleasing men and her own happiness and satisfaction should be secondary, or worse, nonexistent.

"You can." I trace along her jaw and down the slope of her neck. "There's nothing to be ashamed of."

I almost point out she caught me doing the same exact thing last night, but that might open a can of worms I'm not yet ready to dig into. Not when I'd so much rather focus on her.

"I'm not ashamed." She's restless beside me and the constant brush of her body against mine is driving me absolutely fucking insane. "I'm scared."

The admission offers a possibility I never considered. After a lifetime of being told how to feel about sex and all the ways it could send a person to hell, even my own perspective was a little fucked up. And I had been taught sex was my right. Something I would have access to whenever I wanted.

But Lydia, and the rest of the women like her, were taught it was their burden to bear. She's had to come to terms with not just one complete change in her way of thinking about sex, but two.

"What are you afraid of?" I stroke down the bare skin of her arm, following a path from her shoulder to her wrist. "Are you afraid you'll like it?"

She shakes her head again, but this time her eyes meet mine. "I'm afraid I won't." She carefully rests one of her hands against my side, barely touching me. "I'm afraid they ruined me and I will always see it the way they said I should."

I didn't think it was possible for me to hate her father and the rest of the men in the IGL any more than I already do, but I was wrong. If they were in front of me right now, every single one of them would meet the same fate as Rodney, explaining their untimely demise to whatever maker they believe in.

"That won't happen." I don't have much faith left, but what little I retain I am willing to put into Lydia. Somehow she's managed to stay her same, sweet self while escaping a life that wouldn't serve her. Not only that, she's doing whatever it takes to offer her sister the same opportunity by standing up to the same men she was conditioned to bow down to.

"It might." Lydia takes a shaky breath. "I'm scared it will."

"You were scared of leaving and you still did it." I slide my fingers past her wrist, lacing them between hers. "You were scared of Rodney, but still hired him to save your sister."

"And you saw how that turned out." The hand on my side inches across my stomach with a touch so soft it almost tickles. "I would be raped and dead if you hadn't been there for me."

"Then you should trust me." I use my hold on her hand to shift it under the blankets. "I was there for you then and I'll be there for you now." I press my fingers against the back of hers as I urge them between her thighs. "Do you trust me, Lydia?"

"Yes." The word rushes out on a breath as our stacked fingers push deeper into the seam of her legs.

"Then let me help you. Let me show you there's nothing to be afraid of."

Lydia shudders as I work our combined touch against

163

her body, blindly seeking out the swell of her clit without the luxury of feeling it myself. I pause, waiting for her agreement, but instead of words, Lydia drapes her leg across mine, opening up her body.

And that's good enough for me.

I slick our joined fingers through the heat of her soaked folds. I can't stop the groan that rips free as her wetness coats my skin. "I didn't know how bad you needed this."

Lydia's breath stutters as my fingers move along her slit, no longer directing her touch, but taking control.

"Have you been aching, sweetheart?" I tease around the hard swell of her clit with a careful touch, not wanting to offer too much, too soon.

Lydia's hips work in tiny thrusts as I make gentle strokes intended to offer an introduction that is long overdue. "Please, Christian. I need—" Her lips clamp shut, sealing off any demands she might have made. Another strangled sound of frustration punctuates the dig of her fingers into my skin.

"Relax. I know what you need." And I'm a fucking asshole for being so willing to give it to her, but I can't seem to stop myself.

Lydia whimpers again, but her grip on my body softens.

"Good girl." I nip at the skin just below her ear as I continue working her clit in soft passes. "Let me take care of you."

I want to drag this moment out, but it's a selfish desire. One I'm sure would be for my own enjoyment only. And I want Lydia to know I will always put her first. That she can always come to me knowing I will give her everything she wants and needs.

So I tease her faster, cock leaking against the stretch of my underwear as my fingers glide against her wet cunt. The leg she has thrown over me jerks, clenching tight a second before she comes, silent except for the ragged sound of her breath as she clings to me, hand gripping my wrist as if she thinks I'll pull away. Leave her wanting more.

How wrong she is.

It's taken everything I have to keep my hands off Lydia, but now? Now that I've seen how desperate she is to be touched?

I'll make sure mine is the only one she ever wants.

15

LYDIA

I DON'T KNOW how to act right now.

I'm squirming in my seat—the same seat Christian was in the night I came to ask him for help—feeling like both of the other men in the room know exactly what I did this morning. The urge to wallow in shame is strong.

The bass player and drummer from Christian's band showed up early this morning, their arrival sending me rushing from his bed to the one I was supposed to be sleeping in.

But I didn't stay there long.

Christian came to collect me, acting like everything was completely normal. Like his hands hadn't been on my most sensitive area mere minutes before.

And now I'm here, behind his desk, doing my best to pretend my whole world hasn't changed with a few, well-placed flicks of his fingers.

The guilty, repentant woman I was raised to be feels like his friends are looking at me. Judging me. It's ridiculous considering they both showed up at the warehouse last night to help Christian dispose of a body and a car. I can't imagine they would judge me for anything.

"So, what's the plan?" The drummer from Sinners and Saints is seated on the large leather sofa, his feet kicked up on the table in front of it. "We gonna go in guns blazing?"

Christian barely stiffens where he stands close beside me. "No guns."

The drummer, I think his name is Simon, scoffs. "It's a fuckin' figure of speech, man." He tips back a long sip from the giant foam coffee cup clutched in his huge hand. "I didn't mean literal guns."

"We need to do this as quietly as possible." Christian glances my way. "If anyone sees Lydia in town they'll know what she's there for."

Tate, the bass guitarist and the one who took my car from the warehouse last night, lifts his brows. "In town? Does that mean we don't know exactly where we're going?"

Christian shakes his head. "When I talked to Myra last night she wasn't completely sure where she was. Only that it was less than twenty minutes from her house."

Simon turns his cool gaze on me and for a second I panic, thinking he can see right through the calm, collected façade I'm trying my best to keep up. But instead of chastising me for rubbing myself all over Christian this morning, he keeps to the topic at hand. "Do you have any idea where she might be, Lydia?"

I'm used to men talking over me. Around me. Like I'm not even there. Being included in the conversation hasn't ever been a normal or expected part of my life. And I'm surprised at how nice it feels.

"I know there are a few properties they call retreats where they take people who aren't following the principles so they can find their way back to righteousness." I glance at

Christian, unsure if it's okay for me to continue. He barely nods at me and I take that as encouragement. "But I've never been to any of them."

Simon's lips lift at the corners as his brows jump in an expression that almost looks surprised. "So you managed to leave right out from under their noses?" A grin splits his face, taking him from intimidating and a little scary to surprisingly handsome. "Smart girl. Well done."

Praise is another thing I haven't had much of in my life. Wanting it was a sin; good behavior the expectation. And just like being included in the discussion, Simon's words feel good. Soothe a little of my worry.

"Lydia did do an amazing job of getting herself out, but unfortunately that may make our job a little harder. Now they know what she's capable of, and I'm willing to bet they fully expect her to come for Myra." Christian leans against the desk I'm seated behind, propping himself up on the surface while staying close to me. Close enough he has to twist to face the two men across the room. "I don't expect anyone in town to remember me, but it is a possibility, so it's probably best if I keep a low profile too."

Simon glances at where Tate sits on the couch beside him. "I guess that leaves me and you to do the dirty work."

Christian shakes his head again. "Not you." His gaze drags down Simon. "You'll stick out in that little town and they'll know you're up to something." He turns to Tate, the more clean-cut of his bandmates. "You think you're up to the task of figuring out where she's at?"

Tate looks undaunted, shoulders squared, jaw set. "Absolutely I am."

"Good." Christian stands up. "Let's go then."

I blink, not certain I heard him correctly. "We're going now?"

169

Everyone in the room pauses and this time they're definitely looking at me, but not with the judgment I expected earlier. They look surprised.

Christian turns to me. "Do you think we should wait?"

Again, all eyes are on me, waiting for me to make the call. I've never been in charge of anything before and it's shocking to me how heady the feeling is. Especially being in charge of not just one, but what I suspect to be *three*, dangerous men.

Unfortunately, being forceful is not something I will ever accomplish easily, so I offer the same sweet smile I always do. "We can go now. That's fine."

I expect Christian and his friends to jump on my agreement, it's what they wanted after all. But none of them moves a muscle. Christian studies me closely. "We don't go unless you tell us it's a good idea, Lydia. You know these people better than we do, and if you say we need to wait, then we wait."

"Oh." I look from Christian to Simon to Tate, expecting to see irritation on their faces. Frustration that I'm not decisive. That their lives are put on hold, even if just momentarily, because of me. But no one looks bothered at all. They seem just like they always do. Intense, a little bit scary, but calm and in control.

"We're going to go grab something to eat in the kitchen." Tate taps Simon on the arm, tipping his head toward the door before walking out and closing it behind them, leaving me alone with Christian.

Christian's eyes have stayed on me the whole time, like he's trying to find something I'm pretty sure is not there. Or maybe he has regrets. Maybe he feels like I pressured him to touch me. He was essentially cornered in his bed when I all but threw myself at him.

I drop my eyes to the floor. "I'm really sorry about—"

"If you're about to apologize for what happened this morning then you can shut your mouth."

My eyes spring to his as my jaw goes slack. I've never heard Christian sound so sharp before and it catches me by surprise. "I just—"

He leans forward, bracing his hands on the arms of the chair as he leans down to line his eyes up with mine. "You just, what?"

I know he doesn't want me to apologize, he made that very clear, but I don't know what else to do right now. There's tension in the air between us and the only way I can think to alleviate that is to claim regret and offer remorse in the hope it will lighten his mood. "I just know that maybe I put you in an uncomfortable position and—"

"And what uncomfortable position was that?" Christian's voice drops low. "Because there was nothing uncomfortable about the feel of your soaked pussy against my skin."

Air rushes into my lungs and I gasp like the good church girl I used to be. But it's not shock that has my whole body clenching tight. Instead, it's that same ache he so easily identified this morning. The one I've never been brave enough to ease on my own.

"Is that what you think made me uncomfortable, Lydia?" Christian lowers to the floor, dropping to his knees as his broad body pushes mine apart. "Or did you think I was uncomfortable because I wished it was my mouth on your cunt instead?"

I'm suddenly very grateful for the rush of air my body claimed a second ago, because right now I can't seem to remember how to breathe. "That's what you wished?"

The specifics of sex are still relatively new to me, which is embarrassing to admit as a twenty-one-year-old woman, but they liked to keep us innocent in the church, that way we never knew what we were missing.

Of course, I know now. There's really no way to escape a sexual education once you have access to the Internet. And while certain aspects initially shocked me, they also intrigued me. The specific act he's addressing in particular.

"It is." Christian's hands skim up my bare legs, sliding over the bend of my knees before teasing under the hem of the single sundress I own. The one I pulled on hoping to look pretty enough he wouldn't have regrets. "Has anyone done that to you before?"

I shake my head because I'm confident it would be impossible to form words.

"I want to say that's a shame, but I have to admit I like the thought of being the first man to taste you." Christian's touch slides higher, the tips of his fingers sliding into the waistband of my panties. "Can I taste you, Lydia?"

Oh boy. I still feel like I should say no. Like I should be scandalized by my current situation. I know my father would be.

But I'm not.

And somehow that makes my blood rush through my veins even faster. I'm finally really breaking away from all those ridiculous rules and controlling double standards. And that desire for real freedom sends an answer rushing from my mouth. "Yes."

I should be a little worried Tate or Simon might come back to the office and see what we're doing. But I trust Christian, and I don't think he would ever put me in a position like that. Actually, I would be willing to bet every penny I have on it. Not that it would be very many pennies, but still.

Even though I trust Christian, I can't help but glance at

the door. When my gaze jumps back to his, his eyes are fixed on my face. He slowly pushes to his feet, striding to the door before quietly flipping the lock and turning back to me. My body clenches as he comes closer, expecting him to pick right back up where he left off. Instead, he passes me by, moving to the window, watching me as he twists the blinds closed.

Then he drops to the floor in front of me again. Big body pressing between my legs.

"Thank you."

Christian's hands rest against my skin as they curve around my thighs, shoving my dress up to my waist. "That wasn't for you. That was for me." He snags my panties, dragging them down as he leans back, snapping them free of my feet before tucking them into his pocket. "So I don't have to kill someone for looking at you like this."

I barely have time to react to his startlingly strong words before he hooks his hands behind my knees and shoves them up and wide, rocking me back in the seat as his mouth locks onto my most private part.

I had expectations for what this might feel like, but none of them come close to the hungry way Christian laps at me. The sensation is hot and wet and almost unbearable.

Almost.

The shock of what's happening keeps my eyes glued to the sight of Christian as his tongue glides over my sensitive flesh. I can't look away as his lips lock around my clit, gently sucking in a steady pulse that makes my legs jerk against his hold.

I grip the arms of the chair, holding on with everything I have as the tension in my body winds tighter and tighter. Each stroke of his tongue feels so good it almost hurts, both easing and amplifying the steady throb-like ache at my core.

I should hold still, avoid doing anything to give him a reason to stop, but it's impossible. I end up rocking against his face the same way I did his hand this morning, desperate for relief. Relief only he has ever offered.

Suddenly, everything snaps, breaking apart in a wave that seizes my whole body, possessing it completely. I have no control over the jerking of my limbs as I shudder against his still stroking tongue, riding out a sensation teetering on the edge of overwhelming, until my whole body goes limp, slumping into a pile of boneless satisfaction.

After only two orgasms, I'm starting to grasp why I was kept in the dark about their existence. Once you've experienced them, it would be next to impossible not to want more.

To expect more.

And the men of the IGL don't like women to have expectations.

Christian's mouth slides to the inside of my thigh, leaving hot, wet kisses as he slides his tongue and teeth against my skin, sucking hard enough to leave a mark where no one else will see it. "So fucking sweet."

Someone knocks on the door and I jolt, grabbing at my dress.

Christian's face twists into a scowl. "Stay here."

He stands up, pulling my panties from his pocket. For a second I think he's going to offer them back, but instead he uses them to wipe the glistening skin of his face as he walks to the door. By the time he opens the lock, the pale pink cotton is back in his pocket, leaving me sitting slippery and sated behind his desk as he and Tate have a hushed conversation through the tiny gap Christian allows.

"Calm down." Christian grips the handle of the door tighter. "We'll go right now."

Christian closes the door, but leaves it unlocked, before coming back and holding one hand out to me. "It sounds like we have to make a stop on our way to Arkansas."

I slip my palm against his, letting him pull me up from the chair. "Where are we going?"

Lacing his fingers between mine, he leads me back to the door of his office. "Your apartment."

"Did I forget to pack something?" Last night was a blur, and it wouldn't surprise me to find out I left something vital behind in my rush.

"No." Christian pauses, gaze steady as it meets mine. "One of Rodney's friends paid your friend Piper a visit this morning."

16

CHRISTIAN

TATE STANDS IN front of me as we wait for Piper to come to the door. Lydia called her on our way over, but after nearly a minute on their doorstep it seems like her room-mate is still a little skittish after having a strange man attempt to beat down her door.

"Who is it?" The voice on the other side is surprisingly strong.

"We're Lydia's friends. Open the door." Tate's tone carries the same hint of irritation we're all feeling. This is an unexpected detour we weren't planning on making, and we're all itchy to get on the road.

Because we know what's at stake. And right now Myra isn't the only one in danger.

Thankfully we had eyes on the townhouse just in case. A well-timed call to the cops kept Piper from getting hurt and my brothers and I from getting any more tangled with Rodney's group than we already are.

"Give her a break. She's having a shit day." I glance back at where Lydia's locked in my car, frowning since I wouldn't let her be the one to collect Piper. I know she's safe, but being away from her when one of Rodney's men was just here has my skin feeling itchy. Even with Simon parked right next to her. "If you're an ass she'll take even longer to let us in."

Tate's head swivels my way. "Someone just tried to kick in her door. She should be running out of this place."

"You obviously haven't met her." I intend to explain what happened behind the bar, but the door suddenly yanks open a few inches, held in place by the security chain. A hand shoves out the gap at crotch level, the crackling of the stun gun gripped in it sending Tate stumbling back against me.

"What the fuck?" He kicks, acting purely on reflex, knocking the weapon away and sending it tumbling across the cement stoop. "Are you fucking crazy?"

Piper yanks her arm back into the apartment, howling in pain as Tate shoves his foot between the door and frame.

"Christ." Tate scrubs one hand down his face before turning to me. "Go get the bolt cutters."

Piper makes a distressed sounding squeak as she fumbles with the chain. "What in the hell is wrong with you?" She flips it free and steps out, the wrist Tate kicked cradled against her middle, glare full of accusation as it cuts into Tate. "You can't just go around kicking people." She shoves against him as she moves toward the stun gun.

He snatches it up before she can grab it, switching it off and tucking it into his pocket as her jaw drops open in shock. "You fucking stuck twenty thousand volts in my crotch. You should be glad all I did was kick you." He moves into the apartment, gripping Piper's elbow and dragging her along with him. "Get your shit so we can go."

Piper plants her feet and yanks free of his hold. "I don't

know who in the hell you think you are, but if you think you can act like this because of how you look, then—"

"How I look?" Tate snorts. "What the fuck is that supposed to mean?"

Piper motions at him, waving the hand Tate didn't kick up and down his frame. "I mean the way you look." She winces again, her uninjured hand coming back to cradle the one still held against her chest.

"Fucking hell." Tate rolls his eyes toward the ceiling as he spins away, stalking to the kitchen and returning with a bag of frozen peas. Piper barely shrinks back, gaze wary as he crowds her. "Let me look at it."

"It's fine." Her words snap out and I'm not sure if it's because of anger or pain.

"It's not fine." Tate scowls at Piper as he holds one hand out. "Show me."

Piper scoffs. "You're the reason it looks the way it does." She snatches away the peas and presses them to her wrist.

"I'm the reason?" Tate shakes his head. "Sorry, Sugar, but this is your fault."

Piper's focus jumps to me. "Is he serious right now?" She turns back to Tate, brows pinching together. "I can't tell if you're serious."

I'm willing to admit Tate isn't handling the situation in the best way, which is unusual for him, but right now we don't have time for whatever is going on between them. "We'll talk about it on the way." I tip my head toward the staircase leading to the second floor. "You need to go pack your bags. It's not safe for you to stay here."

Piper looks me up and down, her eyes narrowing as she stands a little taller. "How do I know it's safe to go with you?"

I sigh, pinching the bridge of my nose as I try to relax. I

was hoping this would be a smoother interaction than it's turning out to be. Honestly, based on what little I know about the tiny scrap of a woman in front of me, I should've known better. I turn to the door, leaning out to scan the parking lot before waving Simon in. Lydia's talked to Piper, but maybe she needs to make this whole situation, and its gravity, a little more clear.

As Simon leads Lydia up to the townhouse she shares with Piper, I go down the steps to plant myself on the sidewalk, watching for any sign Rodney's friend is lingering, waiting for another opportunity to strike. Lydia's eyes meet mine as she passes and a hint of color pinks her cheeks, telling me I'm not the only one struggling to stay focused this morning.

I follow behind her, waiting until she's in the apartment before catching Tate's attention and thumbing over my shoulder. "We need to wait outside." I want Lydia to feel like she can say whatever she wants. Piper needs to know she's not being coerced in any way. It's the only way we'll be able to get her out of here willingly.

I've been in the business of a lot of things, but dragging an unwilling woman from her home isn't one of them.

I close the door, leaning against it as I wait. Simon looks between me and Tate. "What the fuck is going on?"

"She tried to tase me in the fucking nut sack, that's what's going on." Tate's normally relaxed expression is tight and tense as he crosses his arms and leans against the building. "Then she wants to act like we're the ones to be worried about."

Simon slowly smiles. "Come on. You gotta be a little impressed with a woman who's not afraid to stand up for herself."

"I'd be a hell of a lot more impressed if she didn't come

for my balls." Tate's frown deepens as he pulls out his cell phone and checks the time. "We need to go. We've got a long drive ahead of us and if they find out Myra called Lydia last night, shit could be going downhill for her really fast."

I know Tate is frustrated. We all have our reasons for doing what we do, and he understands exactly how much a delay can cost. The same way I understand what can happen when a woman goes back after walking away. But letting our own personal experiences and losses affect our actions will only make things worse. "Just relax. Lydia wants to get there even more than we do. She knows Piper. She knows what will get her moving."

The door at my back suddenly unlatches and I drop into the apartment, falling right on my ass against the ceramic tile at the entry. Piper glares down at me, looking no less pissed off than she did when Lydia walked in. "Why in the hell would you lean against the door you know we're coming out of?"

Someone snorts and I don't have to look to know it was Simon. He's always had a thing for women who walk a little on the wild side. I wouldn't mind placing bets on how long it'll take him to fall in love with Piper.

Hell, it might have already happened.

"Oh my gosh." Lydia rushes to my side, gripping my arm as she attempts to help me up. "Are you okay?" She looks me over as I stand, almost like she expects me to have sustained a major injury. "Does anything hurt?"

I don't hate the way she's worried about me. It's the second time her hands have fluttered over my body, checking me out as she makes little, unhappy sounds in her throat.

"I'm fine." I rest one hand on her lower back, pulling

her close as I look pointedly at the bag Piper's carrying. "Are we ready to go?"

"Where exactly are we going?" Piper grabs her purse, wincing a little before switching hands.

"We're going to the town I grew up in." Lydia chews her lower lip, watching Piper. "We're going to get Myra."

Piper uses her good hand to sling her purse across her body, staring at me in disbelief, like I'm the one who's dragging this out. "Why didn't you fucking tell me that was what we were doing?" She bumps past me, going straight out the door. "Let's go liberate Myra." She pauses, looking from side to side. "Where's my car?"

"We took care of it for you." Simon gazes at Piper like she's the best thing he's ever seen. "It's someplace safe so you won't have to worry about anything bad happening to it while you're gone."

Piper's skin pales the tiniest bit. "Those guys would fuck with my car?"

"It's not what they would prefer to fuck with, but when there aren't any other opportunities, they take what they can get." Keeping Lydia close, I move toward the cobalt blue two-door I drive when I'm not working, open the passenger's door, and urge her in.

Piper stops short. "I have to cram into the backseat?"

I point at the expensive SUV in the next spot over. "You're riding with Tate."

Simon's hands go out as he scoffs. "Why the fuck is she riding with Tate?"

I knew he was going to be pissed but he's going to have to get over it. "Lydia and I stay together because there's the chance we'll be recognized. You look like a fuckin' delinquent, and if they see Piper with you, we lose the ability to use her in any capacity."

Piper perks up a little bit. "Does that mean I get to help bust Myra out?"

"You and Tate are the only two who will be able to move around town without standing out." I've been trying to come up with a way for us to figure out where Myra is. Our best option is to have someone right under their noses, listening in. And while I know Tate is capable, a single, unknown man is only slightly less conspicuous than Simon would be.

"I can just about guarantee one of us will stand out." Tate glowers at Piper.

Piper's eyes narrow. "What the fuck is that supposed to mean?"

Tate barks out a laugh. "Are you serious?" He shoves one hand in her direction. "You can't keep your mouth shut for two seconds. No way will you be able to pull off being a subservient woman."

"Is that what you like?" Piper squares up to Tate. "Women who keep their mouths shut?"

Tate doesn't back down. "I like women who aren't complete—"

Piper's eyes widen before he can finish speaking. "You better not be about to call me a bitch, pretty boy."

"I was about to call you a psychopath." Tate looks to me, expression baffled. "You can't seriously think she's capable of doing what we need to do."

"She can." Lydia gets to her feet. "I can teach her on the trip." She goes to Piper's side. "Tate's windows are tinted. We'll sit in the back of the SUV. No one will see me." She moves toward Tate's Jeep, dragging Piper along. "We're all staying at the same hotel anyway, and it's far enough away our chances of passing anyone who would recognize me are slim."

Simon shoots me a smirk. "Makes sense." He backs toward his truck. "Send me that address. I'll take the lead."

I watch as Lydia climbs into the back of Tate's SUV, my jaw aching from being clenched so tight. I don't like being separated from her. Between Rodney's accomplices obviously having her on their radar and knowing this trip back to where we both grew up will be difficult, I want to be close. Right there in case she needs me.

"It'll be okay." Lydia holds my gaze, one hand on the handle of the door. "Piper really doesn't know exactly how she has to act. And we need her. The only way this will work is if I have time to explain it to her."

She's right. But I still hate it.

"Fine." I cross to where she sits in the seat, wedging my body as close as I can get, one hand cupping her chin. "Call me if you need me."

Lydia nods, her breathing barely speeding up at my touch.

I stroke my thumb across her lower lip, tracing the line of the mouth I haven't yet claimed. The realization makes my skin burn, but right now there's too many eyes on us.

I want that moment to be all mine.

So I pull my hand from her skin and buckle her in before turning my glare on Tate. "Be careful."

Tate nods, expression serious, but I could swear the corners of his lips twitch as I close Lydia into his SUV.

I turn to slam the passenger door of my car, calling over one shoulder as I go, "I've got the rear." I fall into the driver's seat and send Tate and Simon the location of the hotel we'll be staying at before starting the engine and falling into line.

THE TINY TOWN in Arkansas where Lydia and I were born and raised is about three hours away, and traffic is light, so it's barely midafternoon when we arrive. Tate goes in, claiming all three of the rooms I rented in his name before coming out to distribute key cards. Lydia watches quietly as he hands one to me, another to Simon, and keeps the last one for himself.

Piper is less quiet.

"Where's my key card?"

I open my mouth, but Tate beats me to the explanation. "You'll be staying with your husband, wife. We've got to be extra careful, and seeing a married woman coming and going from a different hotel room than her husband would raise the eyebrows of anyone who might be watching."

Piper glances at Lydia, flipping her long hair back behind one shoulder. "Fine."

I'm a little surprised at how easily she agrees.

Piper must notice my shock because she smirks. "See? I told you I could be sweet."

Her definition of sweet and my definition of sweet are still clearly worlds apart, but she's definitely come a long way in a short amount of time. "I'm sure Myra will appreciate the effort."

The reminder of why we're here seems to sober her and the smile slips from her face. "Do you think we're going to find her?"

"There's only so many places she can be." It's not technically an answer, mainly because I don't want to give her one. The truth is, we might not find Myra. Her marriage connects Lydia's father to the most powerful family affiliated with the IGL. He's not going to let that go easily. Especially since he's already had the shame of one daughter rejecting the husband he chose.

Piper's eyes narrow on me, and for a second I think she's going to call me out on the non-answer I gave her. But then her focus moves to Lydia and her expression softens. "Then I guess we'll just have to find all those places."

She turns to Tate, all the feigned sweetness filtering from her features. "And if any of those jackasses are there when we find her, you better take my stun gun to somebody's junk or we're getting a divorce."

17

LYDIA

IT FEELS EVEN stranger to be in the town I once called home than I expected.

I always knew I would be back, for this exact reason, but part of me was afraid to hope it would be so soon. I also expected to come alone. But right now I'm glad it's not just me. Christian's right. The second anyone from the church sees me, they'll know what I'm up to, and any hope I have of getting Myra out of here will be gone.

So, as much as I hate it, it seems like I am essentially relegated to my hotel room.

A hotel room I will apparently be sharing with Christian.

He passes me the key card as we reach the door, waiting as I swipe it across the sensor. The latch flips open and I go in, holding it wide as he follows behind me carrying our bags. The room is as nice as can be expected, given we're basically in the middle of nowhere, with a desk, a mini fridge and microwave, and a king-sized bed with bleached white sheets.

A bed I can't seem to stop staring at.

Christian sets my bag down, looking the space over before going back to the door, his own bag still slung over one shoulder. "I'll be right down the hall if you need me."

"What?" I face him. "Where are you going?" I might have been a little surprised we would be sharing a room, but I certainly wasn't disappointed by the possibility. "I thought you were staying here with me."

Christian pauses, eyes dark as they move over my face. "Is that what you thought?"

I start to respond but stop. Maybe I've read too much into things. I sometimes forget how different I am from everyone else. That most people my age are significantly more casual about physical connections than I will probably ever be. Maybe what happened between Christian and me isn't a big deal by his standards. Maybe I'm simply another woman who crossed his path. Maybe the hope that I was just as special to him as he was to me is as ridiculous as every other fantasy I've had about him.

"I guess I don't really know what to think right now." I force on the smile I always wear to hide what's underneath. "It's been kind of a crazy day."

Christian studies me a second longer and then suddenly he's coming my way, closing the distance between us in a few long strides. My breath catches as the front of his body goes against mine and he leans down, the tip of his nose tracing alongside mine. "You've waited a long time to be able to make your own decisions, Lydia. I'm not about to take that away from you." He's so close the warmth of his breath slides across my face. "If you want me in your bed, you'll have to be the one to bring me there."

I swallow hard. I'm not sure how I feel about that. On one hand I appreciate that Christian knows how important it is for me to feel like I have some say in my own life. On the other hand, I have no clue how to get a man into my bed. Especially not a man like Christian.

"But—"

Christian shakes his head. "No buts. That's the way it has to be." His hand comes up to trace against my cheek in a whisper of a touch. "I have no problem taking the lead, but that's a right you have to grant me."

The possibility brings an amazing amount of relief. I've struggled to make decisions since moving to Memphis. From my hair to my clothes to my body, I've stumbled over every choice I've made. It's embarrassing. Frustrating. So much more difficult than I expected. And it makes me feel like a failure.

But Christian taking the lead would solve all my problems, at least as far as this particular situation is concerned. Technically I'm still making the choice—controlling my destiny—but Christian will be the driving force.

I swallow hard, struggling even to voice this tiniest of desires. "I want you to take the lead."

Christian's gaze fixes on my face. "Are you sure about that?"

I nod because asking for that one little thing was already almost too much.

Christian's head tips, eyes barely narrowing as he continues to study me. "I'm not so sure you're as ready as you think."

What?

I lean back, more than a little surprised. "Then why did you offer it?"

"Because I'm greedy. Because I want everything I can get from you, Lydia." He inches closer to me, suddenly seeming every bit as dangerous as I know he is. "I want to feed my cock into your hot little mouth and watch you suck me as I come down your throat. I want to lick your clit until your cunt is so wet I can hear the sounds it makes while I fuck you." He leans in a little more. "I want to bend you over my desk and smack that sweet little ass until it's pretty and pink and you're begging me to fill you up."

I wait for him to say more, drunk on all the salacious words coming out of his sinfully seductive mouth.

But a familiar sound steals my attention.

I turn to where my purse sits on the bed as the source of the vibrating buzz registers. I race to my bag on wobbly legs, still absolutely affected by all Christian said, but now also flushing from the dump of adrenaline suddenly pouring into my veins. I yank the phone free, swiping across the screen as fast as I can before pressing it to my ear. "Myra?"

"I need you to come get me, Lyd. Right now. Please, please, *please* tell me you're here."

"I'm here." I grab my purse and go for the door. "Where are you?"

"Do you remember the old tree that fell down when we were little? The one we used to walk across and pretend it would take us into a different world?"

"Yes." The memory makes my chest ache. It's so hard to imagine us as little girls, already aware enough of the futures waiting for us. Futures we dreamed of escaping.

"I'm there, but I know they're going to be looking for me soon. You've got to hurry."

"I'm on my way now. We'll be there as fast as we can."

I hear someone yelling in the background, but the sound is distant enough that I hope they haven't already found Myra's hiding place. "Just stay hidden and be very quiet."

"I have to hang up now and turn my phone off so they can't ping it."

"Okay. I'm coming. I love—" The call disconnecting

cuts me off. For a second I just stand there, devastated by the possibility these might be the last words I have with my sister and I wasn't even able to finish telling her I love her.

"We've gotta move, Sweetheart." Christian grips my arm, the touch firm and steadying as he leads me out into the hall, rapping four times on the door of the room right next to ours before going straight to the elevator. Simon rushes from the room and follows behind us, jumping in the second the doors open and punching the floor for Tate and Piper's room. We're silent as we hurry down the hall, summoning them with the same four strike knock he used on Simon's door.

The muffled sound of voices on the other side of the door stops at the interruption and a second later Tate stares out at us. No one says anything, but he turns to where Piper stands in the middle of the room, looking ready to commit murder. "It's time to go."

"To go?" Piper holds her arms out and looks down at the shorty shorts and tank top she's wearing. "I thought you said I needed a whole new wardrobe because I look like a whore."

"That's not what I said and you know it." Tate pushes past us, ignoring Piper's continued argument. "I can't deal with her." He and Simon stalk down the hall, punching the button for the elevator.

For once, I'm irritated by Piper's argumentative nature. Normally I hope a little of it will wear off on me, but right now it's wasting time. "Myra called. We know where she is. It's time to go get her." I back away, ready to run as fast as I can. "You can stay here."

"No fucking way am I staying here." Piper grabs her own purse before running out of the room, leaving the door to close behind her. "I came all the way here to fuck some-body up. I'm not missing out on that chance."

The doors to the elevator are just opening when we get there and we all pile in, riding it down to the main floor before racing out into the parking lot. I ride in Tate's SUV again, but this time Christian is right beside me, sitting close as we pull away. Simon takes his truck, following behind us in what appears to be a perfectly orchestrated system. One it's clear they've used before.

"Where are we going?" Christian's palm rests on the flat of my back, smoothing slow circles against my skin through the fabric of my sundress.

"My father owns a cabin near Lake Greeson. About half a mile up the road from the cabin is a ravine. She's there." I struggle to sit still as Christian gives Tate directions, taking him straight to the location he must remember as well as I do.

It's only about twenty minutes away, but it feels like forever, every second ticking past agonizingly slow. Every minute might be the one they find her. Considering where she's at, *they* will include my father, and the possibility of him getting his hands on Myra right now is terrifying. Since I left, she's the only daughter he has for leverage. And he will do whatever it takes to keep her under his control.

Unfortunately for him, I'll do anything to get her away. *Have* done anything to get her away.

"We're almost there." Christian's presence and soothing voice are an anchor, the only thing keeping me from completely losing my mind as we slow down to safely navi-gate the winding roads. "It won't be long."

"It's already been long." The second Myra was married off to Matthias I knew I would have to leave alone. It's why I didn't leave the day I turned eighteen. Deep down I hoped something would happen and we could still go together, but as time went on I discovered not everyone was as comfortable walking away from everything they've known as I was.

Not that it was easy for me. I was terrified. But I was more terrified of staying. Of marrying a man whose presence disgusted me and being forced to service him in every way imaginable.

"I understand." Christian doesn't try to reassure me, just reminds me at least one person in this car does know what I've been through. Has been through it himself.

Piper twists in the front seat, reaching her hand back through the gap to grab mine, squeezing it tight. We've been friends since the day I moved to Memphis and answered her ad looking for a roommate, but until today she only knew bits and pieces of what my life was really like before we met. I know a lot of what I said on the ride here shocked her, and part of me wondered if it might make her look at me differently.

It didn't.

It did, however, piss her all the way off to discover exactly what I'd been told my place was in this world. And I'm pretty sure if she could figure out how to make it happen, Piper would be driving a bus through Mountain Oak with a megaphone right now, collecting any woman ready to walk away from the bullshit.

I hate that one of Rodney's people scared her today, but I'm so grateful she's here with me right now. Her bravery makes me feel brave. Like maybe I'd be right there beside her on that bus.

I squeeze her hand back, letting myself soak up her support. She's had my back from the beginning, helping me find a job, reaching out to her family for secondhand furniture so I could have a bed and a nightstand. Even now, her life has been turned upside down by me, and she's still right here at my side.

"Thank you for being here with me." I blink a few times at the burn of tears edging my eyes.

"Shut the fuck up. You are my best friend. I'm your ride or die." Piper responds in true Piper fashion, and I love her even more for the tiny bit of relief I feel as she breaks the tension with humor and sarcasm.

My laugh is half cackle, half sob, and I'm pretty sure a little snot comes out of my nose. "I don't know what that means."

"It means I will do anything for you." Piper turns serious, which is a relatively rare occurrence. "I got you."

I've felt alone my whole life. Spent so much time realizing how different I was from everyone around me. It was like I was the only one who hadn't swallowed the Kool-Aid, but still had to play along because I didn't want anyone watching too closely. So they wouldn't see when I finally made my move.

But Piper has always seen me. Always supported me and encouraged me to do everything I wanted.

Like find my sister and bring her where she belongs. Where she deserves to be.

"Turn off all the lights." Christian's command sends my stomach sinking, scaling away the temporary reprieve Piper's undying support offered. "Slow down just in case she comes to us."

Christian reaches between the seats, pointing to the gravel shoulder. "Pull over there and park."

"This isn't it." I sit up straighter, trying to get my bearings in a place that looks distinctly familiar, but still different than I remember. "I think it's farther up the road."

"It is." Christian turns to me. "But if they're out looking

for her, they'll hear us coming up the road. Our safest bet is to go get her on foot."

"Okay." It's risky. There's a chance that not only will Myra be caught, but I will too.

It's a risk I'm willing to take.

"Let's go get her then." Piper has her door open and I'm gripping the handle of mine when Christian grabs me.

"You two are staying here with Tate." His expression is serious in the darkness.

What? "But Myra—"

"Myra knows I'm coming for her. It will be fine." He leans closer, his voice low. "And I won't risk your safety. Not even for her."

My mouth opens but nothing comes out.

Because suddenly Christian's lips seal against mine in a kiss that catches me completely by surprise. His mouth is just like the rest of him. Strong and demanding, but oh so careful as it nips at mine in a way that threatens to make me forget about everything. Including the sister I'm here to save.

When he pulls away, I lean to follow him for as long as possible, keeping the connection until his hands come to my face, holding me still. His eyes lock onto mine. "I need you to promise me you'll stay here."

I start to offer the promise he wants but stop.

"I'll do my best."

18

CHRISTIAN

IT IS DARK as fuck out here.

I didn't realize how much I'd forgotten about my childhood, but apparently it's quite a bit, because I don't remember the nights out here ever being so fucking dark.

Simon stays close at my side, which is good, because right now it would be impossible to see him if we got separated. Even the dim light from the moon only allows me to see a few yards in front of me. Everything else is a blur of shadowy shapes that are impossible to decipher. And that doesn't bode well for our chances of finding Myra. I know she's out here somewhere, but I have no idea how in the hell we're going to narrow down her hiding spot. Even if we do, there's no way she'll be able to tell I'm the one closing in and not one of the other men currently hunting her down.

It's never easy to help a woman find freedom. Sometimes we're moving more than just her. Sometimes we end up having to deal with her abuser in more of a hands-on fashion. We've gotten them out of all kinds of situations and handled whatever came our way. But I've never had to hike through the woods at night, hoping I get my hands on her before her abusers do. Add on that this particular job hits a little closer to home than the rest, and my frustration level starts to climb quickly.

I have to find Myra. For Lydia. She'll never forgive herself if I don't.

And she might not ever forgive me.

Simon taps me on the shoulder, motioning for me to stop. We both go completely still, and a few seconds later I hear what he must have also heard.

I thought I knew the spot Lydia was explaining, but the breathy, almost whimpery sound is coming from a different direction than the one I'm headed. And much closer to where we parked than I expected. Maybe the pitch-black darkness isn't the only thing I forgot about my nights out at Lydia's father's lake house.

I nod, sticking close to Simon as he heads toward the sound, keeping my steps as quiet as possible as we move through the leaves and underbrush. It's slow going, and I'm just starting to give up hope when we hear the sound again. This time it's more of a snort. Maybe a huff of frustration.

I understand completely.

Simon and I move a little faster, pushing through the scrappy saplings and brushy shrubbery as fast as we dare.

The huff of breath comes again, this time so close we've got to be right on top of it.

"Myra." I whisper into the night, my voice as loud as I dare to make it. "It's Christian. My friend Simon and I are here to take you to your sister."

I hold my breath, hoping I haven't given away both our locations, and wait, listening for any sign of where she might be. But that breath explodes from my lungs when a large form suddenly materializes from the shadows. A huge buck jumps directly into our path, head down, antlers pointed our direction as he makes the huffing noise I believed was Myra.

"Oh shit." Simon's reaction is barely audible beside me, but at this point it doesn't really matter because the territorial, ticked-off deer is giving us away as he thrashes around, stomping one hoof against the patch of packed dirt between us. "What the hell do we do?"

"I would say we start by backing the fuck up." I slowly ease away from the challenging buck, scanning the pitch-black space around us for some semblance of protection. "The more distance we can put between us and him, the better off we'll be." I put both hands up, palms out, ready to do whatever I can to protect myself just in case. "We should probably split up too. He can't chase both of us, and maybe then we'll have some chance of finding Myra."

Simon nods. Jerking his head to the right. "I'll go this way."

"Good luck." It's the last thing I say before we each take off, forcing the buck to choose between us.

Our tactic is more successful than I hoped it would be. The sudden shift stuns the big animal enough that he stands there for a handful of seconds, giving us a head start. Unfortunately, he eventually decides he's still pissed off, and starts tearing through the trees, hot on my heels as I run for my life. The moment brings back a vague recollection of a diagram showing deer kill more people than sharks. I always thought it was a result of them jumping out in front of cars, but right now I'm questioning that assumption.

The quiet of the woods is now gone completely, replaced by chaos all around. Hopefully, it works in our favor and Myra takes advantage, getting herself to a spot where we can get her to safety.

But once again my hopes for a positive outcome sink

when I hear a voice in the distance. One that settles dread and rage in my gut.

"She's running. To the east."

I might not remember the darkness of the night, but I sure as hell remember the darkness of that man. Hearing the booming voice of Pastor Ansel Parks, Lydia and Myra's father, makes me reconsider my objective. Makes me weigh the benefits of changing my target. It's dark enough out here he would never see me coming. Wouldn't know I had him until it was too late. He would be wiped from the face of the earth, setting Lydia and Myra free of the fear they will always feel as long as he's breathing.

"I hear it too. I'm headed right for her."

The second voice halts any plan I might have formed, reminding me that while I might decide to start hunting them, they won't stop hunting Myra. And getting Myra out of here safely is the most important thing.

So even though I want to keep running, both away from the buck still hot on my trail, and toward the men who deserve every evil thing I could do to them, I stop. Holding perfectly still. Refusing to even breathe as the team of men tear through the woods like fucking elephants.

My intent was only to confuse them, but luckily, it also confuses the buck. After skidding to a stop, he lets out a wailing scream, and changes his own trajectory based on the sounds. I stay completely still as he jumps up a slope, zeroing in on the same target I just abandoned.

Hopefully he finds what he's looking for and the number of deer-related fatalities goes up by two.

Once I'm sure the buck is far enough away not to be pulled back my direction, I slink through the shadows, moving slow and silent as I try to regain my bearings. I scan my surroundings, hoping to see something familiar. A spark of recognition from the past I've spent so long trying to forget. Hell, I'd even take a case of déjà vu right now. Something to let me know I'm where I need to be.

But all I see is fucking trees.

So I do the only thing that makes sense, and resume my search, moving away from the continuing noise, hoping to simply put as much space as possible between me and the hunting party looking for Myra.

I smile as a deep voice hollers, the sound of surprise and fear echoing around me.

"What happened?" From the second man's question, it would seem my antlered friend crossed paths with Ansel. I hope his whole life flashes before his eyes, and he recognizes it won't be his maker he meets when his days are done. It's an unrealistic dream, but I can still hope. Especially since I'm pretty sure it would make him shit his pants.

Suddenly the clog of leaves and branches gives way, sending me stumbling out onto the gravel shoulder of the road we came in on. It's a frustrating discovery, but at least now I have some idea of my location. Since I'm pretty sure I haven't passed the ravine Lydia described, I head away from where we parked, easing into a jog as Lydia's dad and the man with him continue yelling. I make it about a hundred yards before I hear steps on the asphalt. I stop, sliding into the tree line as I wait to see who's heading my way.

The footsteps come closer and I nearly jump out of my skin when Simon moves in at my side, his hand resting on my shoulder the only thing keeping me from tumbling out in front of whoever is coming our direction.

The steps are awkward, a stumbling collection that makes me sure they belong to more than one person, but it's hard to tell if they're running or walking. A scuffing, sort of dragging sound, muddies any sort of steadiness there seems to be.

When three forms come into view my heart stutters to a stop.

"Christ." I run directly at the trio. "What in the fuck are you doing out of the car?"

"Did you not hear the screaming?" Lydia puts all her focus into providing support for the woman braced between her and Piper. A woman I'm sure I would recognize in better lighting. "I couldn't just sit there while she screamed."

We pause as the men yelling in the woods get closer, the sound louder with each passing second.

Simon rushes past me, quickly scooping Myra up. "We've got to move." He turns and races back in the direction of the SUV, holding Myra close.

I grab Lydia's hand, gripping it tight as I take off behind him, easily keeping pace with his longer legs since he's carrying Myra's added weight. But Lydia and I are the only ones keeping up. Piper starts to fall behind, clutching her side as she wheezes in the moonlight filtering in through the split the road makes in the trees. Turning to Lydia, I point at Simon and Myra. "Stay right behind them."

I pivot, planning to go back and grab Piper, but before I even let Lydia's hand go, a familiar form rushes from the trees. Bending at the waist, he plants his shoulder in Piper's middle before hauling her up off the ground and racing our direction. Tate passes me with Piper dangling upside down, arms flailing as she fights his hold. A sudden smack echoes through the night as his hand plants against her ass. "Hold still." He doesn't slow as she continues to rant, voice low but filled with an amount of venom that would terrify most men.

"I should have nuked your nuts when I had the chance."

I pull Lydia faster, since we're now bringing up the rear, and when she starts to lag I pause just long enough to throw her over my shoulder. I know it's not the most comfortable way to travel, but right now it's the fastest, and speed is critical.

I barely slow my steps when the SUV comes into view, dumping Lydia into the back next to where Simon is carefully sliding Myra into the seat, gently tucking her feet into the floorboard before giving her a final look and closing the door. The beam of a flashlight streaks across the night as he runs back to his truck.

"Shit." Her eyes are wide as the first of the men hunting her sister stumbles out into the roadway. "Hurry."

Tate drops Piper to her feet, keeping one arm around her waist and hauling her along with him as he gets into the driver's seat, leaving her tangled across his lap and the console as he starts the engine and cranks the wheel as far as it will go, making a U-turn. The tires up the passenger's side run off the pavement and onto the grassy shoulder, bouncing us all around the interior as he floors the gas.

Myra clings to Lydia, sobbing as we fly down the pavement, Simon following right behind us.

Other than the soft sounds of Myra's cries, everyone is quiet as we speed down the dark roads, making sure our path to the hotel is convoluted and difficult to follow. It takes twice as long to get back as it did to reach our destination, but it's worth the extra effort to ensure no one is tailing us. We've worked too hard and come too far to risk whatever altercation might follow.

But when we pull into the parking lot, Myra starts to tremble, holding Lydia in a white-knuckled grip as she begins to plead. "I thought we were leaving. I thought we were getting out of Arkansas. You said you lived in

Memphis. I thought that was where we were going tonight."

Lydia pulls her sister close, smoothing down her matted hair as she turns to me, expression full of uncertainty. "I'm not sure—"

"I'll go get our bags. Give me just a few minutes and we'll drive back to Memphis tonight. You ride with Tate." I know what it feels like to need to put as much distance between this place and you as possible. I felt that way the night they kicked me out, and I feel that way again right now. So as much as I hate having to separate from Lydia, I know it's what's best. "I'll be right behind you."

Lydia's gaze is uncertain as it lands on my friend, one of the two men I trust more than anyone else in the world.

Tate must notice her apprehension too, because the second we step out of the SUV, he tosses me his keys. "I'll take your car." His eyes drag to where Piper is now climbing into the back seat beside Myra. "I'm sure they'd much rather ride with you."

I hand him my keys before tucking his into my pocket. "I appreciate it."

Tate shrugs. "After the day I've had, I could use some fucking silence."

Simon joins us as we head into the hotel, quickly collecting everything from our respective rooms before hauling it out and loading it into the cars. The whole process takes under fifteen minutes, and soon we're pulling back onto the highway, and I'm once again putting Mountain Oak in my rearview mirror.

Only this time, I'm not alone. This time I'm paying them back just a little for all they've done.

We're barely thirty minutes into the drive before two of the three women sandwiched together in the back seat are asleep. Myra's head is on Lydia's shoulder, her mouth slack even as she continues to take shuddering breaths. Piper's slumped against the door, head cushioned against her purse as she softly snores.

But Lydia is wide-awake. Her eyes meet mine in the rearview mirror and she gives me a soft smile. "Thank you."

"You don't have to thank me." I itch to pull her close. To have her body against mine. To comfort her the way I know she needs. "I'll come back here whenever you want to clear out women who decide to leave this godforsaken place."

Lydia's soft smile lifts a little more. "Hopefully I can take you up on that."

19

LYDIA

I THOUGHT I would feel better once Myra was safe, but right now I think I might feel worse.

She seems so different from the sister I remember—the woman who was happy and sweet and kind. But maybe I should have expected that. Maybe I should have known Myra would have to completely change before she'd be ready to do what it takes to leave the IGL. I should be happy for her. Glad she finally found the strength to break away. But right now, laying in Christian's bed beside her, I feel like I'm staring at a stranger.

Myra sleeps soundly beside me, wearing a pair of my pajamas and missing three quarters of the hair she possessed two hours ago. It was the first thing she did when we got to Christian's house, hacking at her butt-length hair with a pair of kitchen scissors, cropping it just above her shoulders before throwing the remnants in the trash. It was a tangible cut, one that symbolized her commitment to separating from what is now her past. I still can't help but worry it's a little premature. It took me months to chop off my own ass-length locks, and she did it so quickly I worry it was a knee-jerk reaction she might regret.

It makes me worry *all* of this is a knee-jerk reaction she might regret.

I give the sister I no longer know one last look before carefully slipping from between the sheets. The upstairs is quiet as I creep out of the bedroom, so I'm assuming Piper is just as asleep in the spare bedroom as Myra is in Christian's bed. It leaves me as the only ghost to haunt the halls. And it turns out to be a pretty lonely venture.

I quietly creep down the stairs, looking for the only person who might understand how I'm feeling, and find him in his office. The long line of Christian's mostly naked frame stretches uncomfortably across the sofa parked against one wall. His eyes are closed, but there's nothing relaxed about his face. The dark slashes of his brows are pinched tightly together and his lips are pressed into a flat frown. He's still the most handsome man I've ever seen, and I'm not going to miss out on the opportunity to appreciate what I couldn't before.

I've technically seen Christian fully naked, though it was at a moment I couldn't really take in the full extent of his form. Which is a shame. Because it is beautiful.

He's solid muscle, with broad shoulders and long limbs. The office isn't as dark as his room was thanks to the glow of the streetlights peeking through the wood blinds covering the window, and it casts shadows that seem to etch out every muscle. The contrast of light and dark plays across his skin, making him look both dangerous and ethereal.

Which is surprisingly fitting.

"Are you coming in or did you just want to stare at me?" One of Christian's eyes squints open and the hardness from his face disappears as he gives me a little smile. "Because if you're here for a show I can certainly make it a much more interesting experience."

My mind conjures up the image of Christian in his shower, one big hand gripping the length of his cock as water trails down his tanned skin. My eyes snap to the front of his boxer briefs where the shadows outline the object of my more recent fantasies. I swallow hard.

I came down here thinking I wanted to discuss my fears that Myra might change her mind, but that plan shifts like sand, running through my fingers until all I hold is the possibility that maybe Myra's not the one reacting to freedom in an unexpected way.

Maybe I am.

I take a tiny step into the room, finding it surprisingly easy to push myself forward. "How would you do that?"

Like cutting my hair, sex, and all it entails, wasn't something I immediately jumped into when I left the IGL. Both terrified me, merely the thought of them overwhelming me to the point I couldn't really consider either for months. Even when I did finally decide to tackle the first of my fears, I cut my hair in tiny increments, scissoring away a little bit more every month.

I approached sex in a similar manner. I started out with the basics, familiarizing myself with anatomy that was completely foreign to me before slowly expanding my understanding until I didn't panic watching porn.

Maybe I still panicked a little.

So, while I am familiar with the ins and outs of sexual intercourse, pun intended, I'm not as well-versed in the variations it offers as most women my age would be.

And I'm so tired of being different. Of holding back. Of being afraid.

"I guess it depends." Christian shifts on the couch,

working his big body into a sit, feet on the floor as he studies me. "Do you still feel the same way you did at the hotel?"

I swallow hard, nervous excitement flipping my belly as I recall the filthy words he said to me. The possibilities he proposed. "Yes."

I want him to touch me. I want to touch him. I don't, however, have enough faith in myself to believe I could be the one to initiate either of those.

Christian's eyes study me in the dusky darkness. "Are you sure? You spent an awful lot of your life not being in charge."

I understand what he's saying, and I get it, but I'm looking at this in a different way. "But if I'm the one allowing you to take the reins, doesn't that mean I'm also the one who is ultimately in charge?"

Yes, Christian will be the driving force in anything phys-ical happening between us, but I gave him the keys. In my mind that puts me at the top of the hierarchy. It's a place I've never been before and is almost as motivating as finally feeling free.

Christian's eyes move over my face like he's still not quite sure he believes I know what I'm doing. "You can change your mind anytime you want."

"I know that." Yet another indicator I'm the one with the power here, not him.

Christian slowly stands up, tall, powerful, strong, and solid. He prowls toward me, and all I feel is excitement. Anticipation.

"What will you say if you change your mind?"

"I'll tell you to stop." It's a pretty simple answer. One I offer easily.

"And you feel confident you can do that? Tell me to stop

without worrying I'll be upset? Without feeling like you can't speak up?"

It's a good question, and more valid than I'd like. It also tells me Christian might be paying more attention to me than I thought.

I don't answer him right away. I want to be honest. For him. For myself. Because he's right. If I don't feel like I can tell him to stop then all my belief about my own power in the situation is wrong.

But this is Christian. The man who saved me. The man who saved my sister. I trust him. Honestly, I trust him more than I trust myself. Especially where sex is concerned.

So I nod. "Yes."

And I know that if I ever do tell him to stop, he will listen. Without anger. Without frustration. Without judgment.

He might be the only person I can say that about. And the realization tells me everything I need to know about whether or not I'm doing the right thing.

Not that I was actually questioning it.

Christian slowly circles me, his gaze pinning me in place as he moves around where I stand. "Then say it now. Tell me to stop."

I tip my head, meeting his stare. "No."

His brows lift, like I've surprised him. "No?"

"No." I almost smile because I'm shocked at how saying that one word is making me feel. "I don't want you to stop."

He circles at my back and I have to turn my head in the opposite direction to regain eye contact, but when I do I'm rewarded with a devilishly sexy smirk. "I think you like telling me *no*, Lydia."

I lift one shoulder in a little shrug because apparently my bravery has limits.

Christian moves to the door, quietly closing it before flipping the lock. "As much as I want you to get enjoyment out of telling me *no*, I have to admit I'm much more interested in hearing you say *yes*."

So am I, but again my bravery is faltering, so I just watch him as he comes back my way, closing the gap between us in long, heart stopping strides.

I expect him to stand in front of me, but instead Christian circles me again, bringing me right back to feeling like Little Red Riding Hood as the wolf decides where to taste her first.

"Did you ever think of me, Lydia?" Christian's voice is soft as the front of his body brushes against the back of mine, teasing me with a barely-there touch. "Or did you forget me as soon as I was gone?"

I lick my suddenly dry lips, deciding how much to give away. I don't know the way real interactions between men and women work. I only learned about things like playing hard to get and flirting after spending two decades being taught nothing more than my father would choose the man I would marry and then he would dictate every choice in my life from that point on. I had no say in the matter. There would never be playing hard to get or flirting. It simply wasn't an option.

I was taught to be sweet and agreeable, so with only those options to fall back on, I decide to tell the truth, hoping Christian won't dig deeper. "I thought of you."

Maybe he'll leave it at that. Maybe he won't ask about all the ways I thought of him over the years.

"Did you wonder what I was doing? Where I was at?" His hands brush against my hips, curving around the tiny bit of fullness they've developed now that I can eat what I want.

I shake my head. "No." I thought I'd known where he

went. It never occurred to me that *everything* I'd been told was lies. Only most of it.

"Did you think about what happened when we were kids?" Christian's fingers slowly gather the cotton fabric of the oversized T-shirt I stole from his drawer and wore to bed. "Was that what you thought of?"

I shake my head again, nervous and afraid and excited as I wait to see what will happen next.

Christian leans closer, his breath warm against my skin as his lips slide along the column of my neck. "Then tell me what you did think about."

I close my eyes, rocking my head to the side, lost in the feel of him against me. The slow drag of his mouth. The heat of his hands. "I thought about what might have happened if you hadn't left."

Christian's hands still where they rest against my waist. "And what did you imagine would have happened if I hadn't left?"

I'm not willing to sum up the extent of that for him. Not right now. I don't want to take the time and I don't want to spend this moment going back. "You were the only man I knew that I wanted to imagine touching me."

I expect him to pick up where he left off, but Christian doesn't move. "Is that what you still want, Lydia? For me to touch you?"

I feel like the answer is obvious. Especially considering less than twenty-four hours ago I climbed into his bed and rubbed myself all over him looking for relief. But I don't say that. Instead I accidentally make a sound.

Christian chuckles, the deep resonance of it sending a shiver down my spine. "Did you just scoff at me?"

He doesn't seem bothered by my irritation. In fact he seems amused, and his lack of frustration or anger is enough to loosen my lips just a little. "I think you already know the answer to that question."

Christian chuckles again, his voice warm and rich. "Fair enough." One of his hands flattens against my belly before sliding lower to tease along the waistband of my panties. "Then I'll ask a question I don't know the answer to." He pushes into the soft cotton. "Are you wet for me?"

It's another question I don't answer. Before I even have a chance, Christian slides his fingers between my legs, slicking along my folds, the glide of his skin against mine offering up the answer he's seeking. My knees buckle as he brushes my clit, but I don't come close to falling. He bands one arm tight around my middle, pinning me against him as he continues proving just how inadequate my imagination is.

"You *are* wet." He presses deeper, moving closer to my core before teasing at the opening of my body. "Is this what happened when you thought of me, Lydia? Did your pussy get wet and aching?"

I can't bring myself to say *yes*. Can't admit something I've been taught to be ashamed of even though I know it's all bullshit.

Thankfully, Christian doesn't seem to expect me to answer. His smooth, seductive voice keeps whispering in my ear as his fingers glide against me. "I bet you did, didn't you? You laid there at night thinking of me. Believing it would be a sin to touch yourself." The pressure against my core increases and a second later one of his fingers dips inside me, making me gasp. "Fuck, you're tight." Christian groans as the finger he has impaled in my body slides free before easing back in. "And so goddamn wet for me."

The feel of being penetrated is completely foreign, but not unpleasant. It doesn't carry the same zing of sensation I get when he touches my clit, but maybe I can see how being filled like this might be just as satisfying.

Not that satisfaction is necessarily all I'm looking for tonight. Tonight I want more from him.

Going back to Mountain Oak made me realize I might have gotten away, but I'm nowhere near free. And knowing a part of what they put on me still lingers makes me sick.

"Christian." I gasp as his finger drives into me again, offering a taste of what I'm about to propose. "I want you."

Christian stops moving, his big body going completely still. So still, I'm not sure he's even breathing. "I don't think I heard you right."

I squeeze my eyes shut, skin heating at the thought of having to say it again. "I want to have sex." I nearly choke on the word but manage to keep going. "With you." I try to suck in a breath and fail. "Right now."

Purity was one of the most important pieces of the foundation my old life was built upon and there's no way to tear that house down with it in place, so I want it gone. I want to be completely free from every rule and limitation they gave me.

Christian's hand slips from my body, sliding free of my panties, leaving me feeling empty and embarrassed.

And sends me falling back on my old ways. "I'm sorry. I thought—"

"You thought I just wanted to fuck you?" There's a surprising amount of sharpness in his voice and it spins me around to face him.

"No." I meet his hard gaze. "That's not what I thought at all." I don't know exactly how to explain everything tonight made me realize. "I just—" I sniff as humiliation starts to sink in. "I don't want to be anything like they wanted me to be." They could have caught me. Kept me locked up the same way they did Myra. Tried to break me so my father could marry me off to a man who would rut against me like I was nothing but a warm hole for him to use as he pleased. "And you're the only person I trust to help me do that."

Christian backs away from me, easing down onto the couch, his dark eyes watching me intently. "You make it sound like I'd be doing you a favor."

If that's how he wants to look at it. "You would."

Christian is silent for a second before he slowly shakes his head. "Fucking isn't a favor, Lydia." He leans forward, bracing his elbows on his knees, gaze so intense it makes me want to squirm. "If you fuck me it's going to be because you can't stand not to."

It's not far off from how I feel now. Between the still throbbing ache left from his skilled fingers and the desperate need for liberation, I feel like I'm on the edge. "Then let's do it."

Christian huffs out a breath that almost sounds amused as he leans back again, draping one long arm over the back of the sofa. "I'll make you a deal." He relaxes against the cushions, looking a little too certain he knows how this is going to go. "If you make it happen, you can do whatever you want to me."

20

CHRISTIAN

I DON'T EXPECT to see Lydia again tonight. When her eyes widened and she rushed from the room, I knew I'd done the right thing. As much as I might want everything she's offering, she's simply not ready.

I scrub one hand down my face and shove the other past the elastic of my underwear to adjust my still raging hard-on. I was just drifting off to sleep when she crept into my office, and now I'm too restless to consider lying back down.

I could continue to stare at the ceiling with an aching cock, or I can actually make good use of the time and do something productive. I lean forward, planning to go to my desk and get a little work done, get my mind off of what didn't happen, while I wait for dawn.

"Where are you going?"

I glance up to find Lydia standing in the still open doorway of my office, eyes filled with uncertainty.

An uncertainty I now share.

"Nowhere." I lean back, attempting to look more relaxed than I am. "I wasn't expecting you to come back."

And now that she has, my body is fully invested in the

reasons behind her return, urging me to do exactly as she's asked and claim control of the situation. To give her all she's asking me for.

But I have to be careful with her. Lydia's more hesitant than her friend or sister, so even though she claims to be ready to throw all the caution she holds close to the wind, I need to be sure she means it.

Lydia's eyes slowly move over where I'm sitting, stopping to fix on where my cock stands at full tilt, stretching the limits of my boxer briefs. She stares at it, unblinking, the silence stretching out between us until I can't stand it anymore. "Is there something specific you want to see, Sweetheart?"

Her eyes flick to meet mine before dropping back down to fix on my dick, which is only getting harder at her unabashed attention. She licks her lips, the motion, and the suggestion it offers, making it jerk in response.

Lydia's breath rushes free, eyes widening. "Oh."

Her surprise just reinforces how innocent she really is. And the deepest, darkest parts of me can't help but love it. No one's touched her but me. No one's tasted her but me. No one's felt her come undone but me.

She's mine and mine alone.

Lydia's lips rub together, eyes still glued to where my erection stabs toward the ceiling. "I didn't know they could move like that."

I force myself to stay still, trying my damndest to remember she's not like most women. "I would guess there's a lot you don't know."

Lydia frowns, her chin lifting the tiniest bit. "I've watched porn."

That's an interesting development.

Now I'm picturing my sweet, soft Lydia tucked into her

bed at night, watching all the ways people can fuck on the tiny screen of her cell phone, driven by curiosity but still too afraid to take care of her own needs. "But you've never touched yourself?"

She shakes her head.

"Because you were worried you wouldn't like it, right?" I understand the fear. After being told sex was only something she was meant to endure, it isn't surprising she might be afraid that was true. "Are you still worried?"

Lydia finally drags her eyes back up to mine and shakes her head. "No." She opens her mouth to say more, but then hesitates, sealing her lips together.

"Say it." I want her to know she can tell me anything. Everything.

Lydia licks her lips again, shifting on her feet. "I like when you touch me."

"Good." I tip my head toward the door. "Then lock us in and come over here so I can touch you."

I expect her to do as I ask. She's back at my door for a reason and I'm happy to accommodate her need. More than happy. Eager might be a better word for how I'm feeling.

But Lydia doesn't budge from her spot. "I didn't come here for touching." She lifts one hand, showing me the small foil packet she has gripped in her fingers. "I came here so you could set me free."

Once again Lydia has surprised me. Proved she is so much more than she seems. And as much as I want to be the one to save her, I can't. So I shake my head. "Fucking me won't free you, Lydia."

Her fingers move over the condom in her hand, tracing the edges. "What if I want to do it anyway?" She turns away without waiting for my answer, silently closing the door and locking it. Then she faces me, steps slow and steady as she comes my way. "You said I could have anything I wanted from you, but I was the one who had to take it. Did you change your mind?"

Did I? I should. "No. I didn't change my mind." I fight for calm as she stops in front of me. "I just don't want you to do anything you'll regret."

Lydia meets my gaze. "I won't."

I stretch my arms along the back of the sofa, lifting my hands toward the ceiling. "Then do your worst."

I still don't entirely believe she'll follow through, but my cock has complete faith in her, and it's straining for any attention she's willing to offer. So much so that when she reaches for the waistband of my underwear it flexes again, almost as if fighting its way free.

Lydia pauses, her eyes lifting to my face. "Can I touch you?"

My hips twitch with the need to flex, to shove myself into her waiting palm, but somehow I manage to stay still. "It'll be hard to accomplish what you want without touching me."

Lydia pulls her hand back and I nearly groan in unmet need at the withdrawal. Her expression is so sweet and filled with concern as she studies my face. "We don't have to do this if you don't want to."

The situation is almost amusing. Somehow I've managed to get myself in a position where a beautiful, sweet, kind, sneakily defiant woman wants to fuck me and is worried I don't want her hands on me. But I'm happy to straighten things out for her.

"Lydia, I would have fucked you the first night you walked into this room." I grab my underwear, yanking it away from my body before working it down my thighs. "I've thought about fucking you every waking minute since then."

I kick the briefs away, leaning back again. "My desire to fuck you is not what I'm questioning."

"Oh." Lydia curls her hand into a fist, holding it suspended in the air between us. "What are you questioning?"

"Your motives."

Lydia's eyes narrow. "Do you usually question a woman's motives when she wants to sleep with you?"

I know where she's going with this, and I'm glad. I shake my head. "No."

Her lips press into a barely perceptible frown before evening out, reminding me she's been trained for years to hide how she really feels. It backs up the point I'm about to make.

Lydia's spine straightens the tiniest bit. "So you're treating me differently."

"You are different." I won't deny it. "I protected you when you were little. I'm still protecting you now. Even from me." I lift one finger and direct it her way. "And even from you."

Her expression softens. "You can't protect me from the whole world, Christian."

Bet. "I can try."

Lydia's hand drops, grip loosening. "Fine." The fingers she almost touched me with trail up the outside of her thigh, dragging the hem of her borrowed T-shirt higher. "But I don't need to be protected from you." She hooks her thumb into the waistband of her panties, dragging them down her thighs until they're loose enough to fall to the floor. She steps forward, leaning close as one knee presses into the sofa beside me. "You are the only person who has ever wanted me safe." Her other leg wedges against the leather as she straddles my lap, hands going to the couch back for leverage

225

as she slowly lowers her body against mine. "So if you think for a second I will ever believe you'll hurt me, then you are very wrong."

I hiss as the slick heat of her body brushes against my cock. "I shouldn't do this, Lydia." It's a reality I've tried to avoid. To ignore. To pretend doesn't exist. "I shouldn't want to touch you the way I do."

I should still look at her the way I always did before. But Lydia is no more that sheltered little girl than I am a young kid who believes he can change the world. We've both grown up. Both become more but still so much the same.

"Why not?" Lydia's palm flattens against the center of my chest, moving over my skin. "I want to touch you." Her hand slides lower, surprisingly confident as it slips between our bodies to grip the base of my cock.

It's a touch that breaks me. Severs the ties I've tried to keep in place. I fist my hand in her hair, dragging her lips to mine.

I should kiss her sweetly. Gently. I can't.

The need to drink her in is too great. And the sweet taste of her lips only makes me greedy for more. I sweep my tongue into her mouth as I plant my other hand against her ass and drag her against me.

Lydia makes a soft sound that sets my already heated blood on fire, and I thrust up against her, eager to hear it again. The line of my cock slicks through her heated folds, mimicking the act she claims to be ready for. Part of me expects her to shy away at some point. To be scandalized by the reality of what she's asking for. But Lydia meets me every step of the way.

Her tongue toys with mine, movements soft but unhesitating. Her hips mimic the action I initiated, sliding her body against mine, the liquid heat of her cunt growing wetter with each pass. She pauses and my heart stops.

This is it. She's reached the limit I knew would come.

Lydia's eyes meet mine and I wait for her apology. Her embarrassment.

Instead, her hand catches mine, pressing the foil-wrapped condom into my palm. "Put that on." Then she captures the bottom of her nightshirt and sweeps it over her head, fully bearing her body to me for the first time.

"You are really testing my commitment to doing the right thing, Sweetheart." Her body is soft and curved, tits full and sloped with large brown nipples I can already feel pulling tight under my tongue. Never in my life would I have believed I possess this much restraint, because it is taking everything I have to not pull her forward so I can suck one of those perfect nipples into my mouth.

"I think we must have different opinions on what the right thing is." Lydia's eyes slide shut as she drags her cunt against my cock again. "Because I don't think what I'm asking you for is wrong." Her lids lift, dark eyes meeting mine. "Do you?"

Getting caught between right and wrong has been the story of my life, and my definitions of both have changed more times than I can count. Most people think killing is wrong, but sometimes it's the rightest thing you can do.

The lines between the two aren't as definite as most people think, and right now I'm caught in the blur. "What you're asking for isn't wrong, but I don't know if it's right of me to give it to you."

Lydia goes still above me, the tip of her chin the only indication she's about to fuck my whole world up. "Does that mean you would rather someone else be the one to give it to me?"

The sound that comes out of me is feral and a little unhinged. "I will rip the arms off anyone else who tries to touch you."

A breath rushes out between Lydia's lips as her pupils dilate. "Oh." She rolls her hips again, leaning closer to me, bringing those perfect tits close to my face. "You would do that?"

I don't know how to handle her reaction to this. Hell, I can't believe I even said it. But saying it isn't the biggest problem I have. The biggest problem I have is I meant it. The thought of another man touching what's in front of me makes me absolutely fucking insane.

"I would. And that's exactly why I shouldn't give you what you want. Because once I do, there won't be any going back." I wrap one arm around her back, hauling her body closer so I can nuzzle the valley between her tits, hoping it will take a little of the edge off my need. "So if you just want to do this with me because it will make you feel like you finally left it all behind you, I'm not the man for the job."

I'm not here for a quick fuck with her. That's not what I want from Lydia. I want it all. Everything she has to give. And I want to offer her the same in return.

Lydia brings her hand to my head, fingers tangling in my hair as she continues to grind against me. "What does that mean, there's no going back?"

Lydia's not running from the room, which encourages me. Gives me hope I will finally have everything I've wanted. I've watched, envious, as so many of my brothers fell, dropping one by one into a happiness I've never had.

Now I know how fucking insane they went trying to get it.

"It means from then on you sleep in my bed, with me,

every night." I slide my hand between her thighs, finding the hard nub of her clit and rubbing it gently. "It means when you ache you come to me so I can give you what you need."

Lydia's head falls forward on a gasp. "If you're trying to deter me you're not doing a very good job."

Is that what I'm trying to do? I'm not so sure it is anymore.

I pull my hand from her pussy, gritting my teeth at the soft sound of protest she makes. I hold the condom up between us. "Then decide what you want."

I expect her to think it over. To weigh the options in front of her.

That's not what happens.

Lydia snags the packet from my hand and tears it open, sliding the rubber free as she leans back. Then her hands are on me, urgent and determined. But, unsurprisingly, her skills at putting a condom on are lacking. She makes a frustrated sound as she fights to get it in place.

I swipe her hands away, fisting the protection into place.

She gives me a sweet little smile. "Thank you."

"Don't thank me yet." I grip her hips, sinking my fingers into the softness there as I pull her back over me, notching the head of my dick against her before sliding my thumb against her clit as I nose along the swell of one tit, working my way toward a nipple. "Your turn, Sweetheart. Do your worst."

21

LYDIA

PART OF ME can't believe I'm here.

Part of me can't believe it took me so long.

Physical intimacy was one of the things that intrigued me most when I finally found myself in the real world. I expected it would be something I would jump into with both feet but, like cutting my hair, that isn't how it worked out. And right now, I'm glad.

Because I can't imagine doing this with anyone else but Christian. Not just because of how he looks, though that is definitely a perk. It's his hesitancy that lets me know this is exactly what I want to do and exactly who I want to do it with.

He's still worried about what's best for me, and after spending the majority of my life surrounded by men who only worried about what was best for them, I'm starting to get a little addicted to being the one put first. So addicted, I've managed to not only sneak a condom from Piper's purse but also muster up the courage to come all the way back down here and use it.

Or at least I plan to use it. I'm currently adjusting to the sensation of something so thick pressing up against a part of me that suddenly feels very small.

"Relax." Christian's mouth latches on to my nipple, the pull of his lips shooting a wickedly sinful sensation straight between my thighs to amplify the ache there.

It's an ache I'm very familiar with, but tonight I'm noticing an aspect of it I haven't before. An emptiness. I feel almost hollow. It's strange and surprisingly unexpected given all I know about the mechanics of this particular act. Obviously I knew penetration must feel good, but I didn't expect to crave it like this.

To *need* it.

Christian's mouth draws at me again, but this time his tongue flicks against my nipple, adding another level of sensation. It feels unbearably good and compounds everything happening between my legs.

Without meaning to, I bear down against him, seeking relief. I inhale sharply as his body stretches mine, caught between an odd combination of discomfort and relief.

And I want more.

I blow out the breath I've been holding, forcing my muscles to stop contracting, and press down again, working more of him into me.

Christian's mouth slips from my breast as he hisses between his teeth.

I freeze. "What's wrong?" I glance down, worried I've done something terrible like bent him in half, but everything looks right. Fascinatingly right. Right enough I watch as I sink a little lower, eyes glued to where our bodies meet.

"Fucking hell." Christian's hands grip my hips tighter, not trying to shove me onto him, just holding. "You're fucking killing me, Sweetheart."

I glance up, looking over his strained expression. "Am I hurting you? Am I too tight?"

I don't know if that's a thing, but maybe it is. Maybe I should have moved past my discomfort and touched myself. Used the vibrator Piper bought me instead of leaving it in its box and hiding it away in a drawer.

"Not too tight." Christian releases my hips and fists one hand into my hair, pulling my mouth to his in a hard kiss that drives my aching need higher and sends me sinking deeper over him as his lips drag across my jaw. "Just so fucking sweet I can hardly stand it."

For some reason his words don't sit right.

"I don't want to be sweet." I drag in a breath and sink the rest of the way down, completely impaling myself even though it's slightly uncomfortable. "I want to be sexy."

I've been sweet. Way longer than I should have. I may not ever leave that part of me behind completely, but now I want to be more. I want to be the kind of woman Christian wouldn't question when she's offering herself up. But to do that I have to get past the overwhelming fullness stretching my insides to their limits.

I pull in a steadying breath before rocking forward, mimicking the motion I've witnessed during shame-filled nights in the comfort of my own bed. But I don't feel ashamed right now. As I sink back over Christian, watching him as his expression tightens and his nostrils flare, I feel powerful.

Just as in control as I should want to be.

I rest my hands on his shoulders, using them for leverage as I work to find a rhythm. The pinching stretch subsides a little more with each move of my body, only to be replaced by a familiar ache. I move faster, trying to ease it. Trying to soothe the throb pulsing deeper and deeper. But no matter what I do, no matter how I move, there's no relief.

"Christian—" I almost sob his name as frustration makes it more and more difficult to chase down that feeling he creates so easily. "Help me."

The words are barely out of my mouth when the whole world tilts and I suddenly find my back against the plush rug softening the hardwood of Christian's office. I gasp, shocked at the sudden and marked change.

"Legs wide, Sweetheart." Christian catches me behind one knee, pushing it out in the most exposing and suggestive way. A way that also brings his body flush against mine. I shove my other leg out the same way, spreading wide for him as he slowly starts to thrust.

Where my own movements were focused only on the task of penetration, Christian's hips work in a way that rubs parts of me with shocking accuracy. Each roll of his body into mine is also against mine, teasing my clit with pressure and friction that offers blessed relief.

"That's what you needed, wasn't it?" Christian's fingers lace with mine, lifting my hands over my head as he continues to fuck me.

"Yes." It barely sounds like a word, more like a moan, as he dips his head to suck at my nipple. I buck against him, but the press of his weight keeps the movement from being more than a wiggle.

And I like that too. I like that I'm pinned down. I don't have to worry about how to touch him. How to move. How to act. I don't have to try to pretend to be something I'm not.

I can just be.

Christian's mouth pulls from my nipple, teeth dragging gently across my flesh. His forehead comes to rest against mine, putting us palm to palm, face to face, and body to body. For the first time the moment feels intimate. Like this is about more than just sex. More than just freedom. More than the past and more than what we used to be.

Like maybe it's about what we could become.

It makes me consider that maybe I've been wrong about a lot of things. Who I thought I should be. What I thought I should want. How I thought I should live.

Christian's thumbs stroke against mine, eyes locked on my face as everything inside me begins to crumble.

I wasn't failing. Wasn't wasting the life I finally had. I was simply trying to be what I'm not.

Unfortunately, I'm not completely sure what I am.

Christian tucks his chin, eyes focusing between our bodies. "Look at how well you take me." One of his hands pulls free of mine and curves around my breast, fingers rolling the nipple as he drives into me a little harder. "How perfect my cock fits your sweet little cunt."

I'm not sure how it happens but suddenly my hand is gripping Christian's face, dragging his eyes back to mine. "I'm not sweet."

I'm frustrated. Confused. Caught between what I should be and what I am. And for the first time in my life, I'm not worried a man will be mad at me for what I've said. Not because I no longer care what men think, but because I know this particular man well enough that the smirk he shoots my way is completely unsurprising.

"You are sweet, Lydia." He adjusts his body, pressing his pelvis tight to mine as he drives into me harder, each thrust rubbing my clit in a way I can't ignore. "You're also sexy as hell." He grips my ass with his free hand, angling my hips up so there's no escaping the maddening friction, and within seconds I start to come.

And it's nothing like the other two orgasms I've had. This one is consuming. Possesses me in a way I can't explain and might not survive. It claims my body and maybe even my soul, stealing all thought and reasoning, leaving nothing but a whimpering, writhing mess.

Christian buries his body into mine, reaching deeper than ever before as he shudders against me, breath ragged and choppy as he goes still.

I blink, unable to really process what just happened. Between the sex and the revelation, my brain is filled to capacity.

But then Christian leans close, his lips brushing against my ear as he adds a little more to my poor flooded mind.

"And now you're all mine."

"LYDIA."

I jerk awake, detangling myself from Christian as I work my way upright at the sound of my sister's voice.

Christian groans as I roll off of him, sliding from the couch to the floor, my butt dropping against the area rug while my legs stay draped across the sofa.

"Myra's awake." I manage to get to my feet, straightening the fabric of my sleep shirt as I hurry toward the office door.

Christian is right behind me as I rush out into the entryway, glancing up the staircase, expecting to see my sister at the top of it. But the only person standing at the top of the stairs is Piper, and she looks half asleep.

I glance around, uncertain where Myra might be.

A banging noise in the kitchen clues me in, and I head in her direction. She sounds upset. Like the reality of what happened last night is finally sinking in. I want to be there for her. To help her through the process of—

I stop short when I see my sister in Christian's kitchen, fingers stabbing at his high-end espresso machine. "Fucking, crazy ass—" Myra swings around to face me, blowing out a dramatic breath as she thumbs over one shoulder. "How in the hell do you use this thing?"

If I was surprised by how Myra was acting last night, today I'm absolutely flabbergasted. "I don't know."

Her eyes move from me to where Christian stands at my side and then back again. "Did you stop drinking coffee?"

"No." Her confusion is confusing me. "This is Christian's house."

Myra's lips flatten as she gives me a side-eyed look. "Yeah. I figured that, but I assumed you lived with him."

Christian moves between us, his big, mostly naked body blocking my view of my sister. "It seems complicated, but it's not." He grabs a little lever on the top of the machine and twists it open. The entire top hatch lifts up in a coordinated move that sends a metal pod dropping into a hidden well. "It's kinda like a Keurig." He glances at Myra. "Have you used a Keurig before?"

She makes a face at him. "The IGL only likes to pretend it's the fifties when women are concerned. They're happily integrated into modern society on most things."

"I'll take that as a yes." Christian opens the cabinet above the machine, revealing stacks of cardboard sleeves. Each one is torn open at the end to reveal more of the metal pods. "Pick your poison."

Myra ponders for a second before snagging a pale purple tinted option. "Do you have milk to froth?"

"Dairy and almond." Christian leans back, crossing his

arms as he props one hip against the counter. "Does that change your choice?"

"Nope. Confirms it." Myra leans closer to the machine, peering at it before dropping the disc into the well that automatically vacated upon opening. "Now I just close it?"

Christian reaches out, pushing down the hatch before sliding the lever into place. "Close it and then press the flashing button."

Myra does as he instructs and offers him a smile. "Thanks." Her smile slips a little. "And thank you for coming to get me. I don't think there are a lot of people who would've done that."

I cringe inwardly because it's more than she might think. Being reminded of Rodney, and all that happened because I brought him into my life, dampens my mood instantly.

"That's not something you have to thank me for." Christian's eyes come to me. "I'm gonna go take a shower." He pushes off the counter, giving me a smoldering look as he passes, one that makes me think the ache I woke up with between my thighs isn't as bad as I initially thought.

Unfortunately, Christian and I are nowhere near alone right now, and I have important things to deal with.

Like what in the hell is going on with Myra.

Last night she was a mess. A sobbing, shaking mess. Right until we crossed into Tennessee. And then it was like someone flipped a switch. A switch that still seems to be in the same position this morning.

Myra stares into the coffee cup balanced on the platform of the machine. As it continues to brew, she leans down and inhales against the steam rippling up. "God I've missed coffee."

"Missed coffee?"

Myra's lip curls. "I haven't had it since they moved me

out to that fucking cabin." She pulls the mug from the maker as soon as it's done brewing, setting it on the counter before going to the fridge. "They literally took away anything they knew made me happy." She grabs the milk and pulls it out. "Including toilet paper."

"Why didn't you just act like you were sorry? I could have gotten to you sooner. They would've let you go back home."

Myra pours milk into the silver pitcher beside the coffee maker, pressing the lid into place before surveying the buttons across the front and making her selection. "Because fuck them, that's why."

I've never heard my sister say a single cuss word, let alone five over the span of a few minutes. I completely believed Myra would come out of the IGL worse off than I was. That she would struggle to break away from our old beliefs and teachings.

But that doesn't seem to be the case.

When the milk is finished frothing, Myra pours it into her cup before taking a long sip, moaning as she swallows it down. "That is so fucking good." She opens her eyes, giving me a smile. "I think I want to go get my hair done today." She reaches up with one hand to ruffle her self-induced haircut as she takes another swallow of coffee. "I want it shorter and highlighted." Her eyes widen. "Do you think I can get my makeup done too?"

"Maybe? It might take a few days to get an appointment with somebody good though." She's really jumping in with both feet, and I'm not sure how to handle it. "I can try to even it out a little for you until then."

Myra shrugs. "I'll just pull it up. If we can't go to the salon then maybe we can go shopping for new clothes." She downs a little more coffee. "Does Christian have a fire pit? I want to burn the ones I had on last night."

My head is spinning. Trying to keep up with her right now is making me feel off balance.

And ashamed.

I didn't go through half of what Myra went through, and acclimating to my new life has taken me a year. I've struggled every step of the way, and here she is running into it head on. Determined and unafraid.

"We can definitely go shopping. But we'll have to pace ourselves. I don't want to blow through my savings too fast." I've been pinching pennies in the hope Myra would join me, so I'm somewhat prepared to take care of her, but not if she's going to want regular salon visits and a brand-new wardrobe.

Myra's brows pinch together. "I would never expect for you to pay for that, Lyd."

"Well someone has to pay for it, and you don't have a job yet."

Myra's lips curve into a slow smile. "Do you think I didn't prepare for this?" She comes closer, leaning against the island between us. "I have thought about this day for three years. I knew the second our piece of shit father promised me to Matthias I was getting the fuck out of there one day." Her smile fades. "But I'm not sure Memphis is far enough away for me."

22

CHRISTIAN

I STAND ON my stoop, a little surprised to see the men crowding my doorstep.

My hair's still wet from the shower I rushed through and, since Myra was monopolizing my coffee maker, I haven't got a lick of caffeine in my veins. I am most definitely not prepared for what I think I'm about to face.

"Hey." I lean against the casing, trying to look casual and relaxed while doing my best to block my unexpected visitors' view into my house. "Everything okay?"

I get together with my whole family once a month. My brothers bring their wives and kids and we all eat food and talk and laugh, just like millions of other families around the world. The only difference is it's not DNA that connects us. And while I normally enjoy spending time with my brothers, this particular visit doesn't feel like a social call.

Evan's expression is serious as he looks me over. "You got something you want to tell us?"

The fact that Tate and Simon aren't part of this group is telling, and it makes me think these men already know more than they're letting on. But my best bet is to continue to play stupid until I know exactly why they're here.

"No." I shake my head, offering a shrug. "Everything's fine."

Cody stands just behind Evan, his long hair looking a little wilder this morning than normal. I'm willing to bet his daughter has already had her hands in it, using him as her own real life Barbie doll. "Is that really how this is going to be?" His expression is disappointed. "You're gonna start keeping secrets from us?"

I was hopeful they wouldn't dig too deeply into the incident with Rodney. That they wouldn't trace the connection back beyond what I'd offered.

I should've known better.

Shaun's scowl makes it clear it's not disappointment he's feeling. "If you're fucking around in some shit, we need to know about it. We have wives and kids to protect."

I rake one hand through my wet hair, aggravated. Tate, Simon, and I have managed to do what we do right under their noses for years, but the second I get attached, I fuck it all up.

That doesn't mean I'm not ready to give in. Not yet. What we do is too important, and if my brothers find out, they'll want it to stop. And I can't blame them. Like Shaun said, they have wives and kids to protect.

That's why we kept it from them. Why we've been so careful, pretending like what they don't know won't hurt them. But there's no way I can continue to claim that's true. Not with three women in my house who prove what you don't know absolutely can hurt you.

Still, the thought of confessing to my brothers after all this time is difficult to stomach, so instead, I double down.

"We took care of Rodney. No one's going to find him.

Even if they do, they won't be able to prove we're responsible."

"We're not here because of Rodney and you know it." Shaun is the bulkiest of my brothers, and right now he looks dangerously close to putting all that size to good use. "Who's in your house right now?"

I should spill my guts. Tell them everything.

But I can't. Not without talking to Simon and Tate. I'm not the only one who's been going behind our family's back. I don't mind risking my own skin, but I won't out Tate and Simon.

Besides, we were able to get Myra out without being seen in a way that any of us could be connected. Just like ninety percent of the jobs we do. The chances of her husband or her father figuring out she's here are slim to none. There's no possible way any of that could come back on me or them.

"Piper and Lydia are here."

Evan takes a breath and blows it back out. "I thought we were a fucking family, man." He huffs out a bitter sounding laugh. "I thought we were all in this together."

"We saw the other woman." Niko, the youngest of our group, stands propped against one of the pillars I've been meaning to paint, looking slightly less upset than everyone else. "Brooklyn and Kaylee were playing in the yard when she came outside this morning."

Fuck.

Last night was so chaotic, between the late trip back from Arkansas and the even later visit Lydia made to my office, I didn't have time to make sure Myra knew to stay in the house. I didn't really think I'd need to tell her though. I expected her to spend most of the day in bed, not fighting with my coffee maker and chopping off her hair.

I also figured I would hear the security alarm ping when a door was opened, but I must have been sleeping deeper than normal with Lydia draped across me.

"That's Lydia's sister, Myra." I hope the explanation is enough to keep me from having to admit anything more. "They wanted to be together."

It's not an outright lie. They did want to be together. So much so, Lydia was willing to pay a man like Rodney to make it happen.

Butch, the only one of us who doesn't live in the little neighborhood we've carved out, eyes me with suspicion. "Where's she from?"

"Arkansas." I can't stretch that truth so I keep it simple.

"That's where you're from." Butch continues to watch me a little too closely. "Seems like an odd coincidence."

They all assumed I was helping Lydia because I was interested in her, and I let them believe it. I knew they would understand since so many of them had similar situations when they met the women who are now their wives. But it seems like, for whatever reason, my brothers weren't willing to accept my explanation and decided to dig a little deeper.

"Lydia and I knew each other when we were younger." I choose my words carefully, trying to walk a line I'm not even sure exists anymore. "Our paths crossed again."

Butch doesn't let up. "Just by chance?" He shakes his head. "I don't think that's what really happened." He continues on, making it clear that, despite lurking at the edge of the group, he's the actual ringleader of this confrontation. "I think you've been up to something. I think while we were all getting our shit together, you and Tate and Simon kept fucking around."

I'm surprised at the venom in his words, especially considering, unlike the rest of the men on this porch, Butch doesn't have a wife or children to worry about. Hell, he doesn't even live on the same street as everyone else. And it didn't particularly bother me until now. "I guess you would know since you've been so involved with the rest of us over the past few years."

I didn't take it personally when Butch started coming around less and less, but right now I am. Because he doesn't get to have it both ways.

"I've got a fucking life now." He gestures around him. "We all do. Because we've moved on from the shit we used to do."

I don't like what he's insinuating. My hands might not be completely clean, but they're sure as hell not covered in the same shit they used to be. "So have I."

I've got a business and a home. Hell, I've even got a well-known band that could book to play every weekend. And I don't deal in the shit we all used to. I don't sell drugs. I don't fight for the sake of fighting. I don't go out of my way to break the law.

"We deserve to know what you're doing, Preacher." Evan's use of the nickname I used to go by makes me straighten. It makes it clear he still thinks I'm what I used to be: A delinquent. Filled with rage and lacking control. Out to fuck over everyone I can because of how badly fucked over I was myself.

"So that's how it is, *Tracker*?" I hold his gaze, throwing his own nickname back in his face.

We all had them. They were bestowed by the man who pulled us from the gutters, claiming to offer a better life. Technically, he did. We had a place to live. Cars and bikes and as much food as we could eat. A family tied together by fate and suffering.

But he was using us. Manipulating me and my brothers for his own personal gain.

The day we decided to break away from him everything changed. Our lives. Our dreams. Our futures.

I don't like being taken back to the past.

Evan sighs, looking guilty. "I shouldn't have said that. It was out of line." He moves closer, reaching out to rest one hand on my shoulder. "We know you're not like you used to be, but we also know something's going on. And I think we deserve to hear the truth from you."

I rub my head, squeezing at the tension making it ache. He's right. Tate, Simon, and I kept what we were doing quiet because we were afraid our brothers wouldn't approve. That they would demand we stop.

And maybe that was wrong. But it would be just as wrong for me to spill the truth without Simon and Tate here.

"Let me get my shit together and we can talk about it tonight."

Butch scoffs, clearly unhappy with the timeline of my offer, but Evan nods. "We'll be back at eight."

I nod, even though it feels like the clock on life as I know it is ticking, counting down to a shift I'm not sure I want to face.

My brothers leave, heading down the stairs before dissipating in the direction of their homes. I watch them go for a second before closing the door and turning around to find Lydia standing right behind me, her dark eyes wide.

"Is everything okay?"

I don't want her to worry about me. She's got enough on her plate. But the concern on her face still hits me in a way I like a little too much.

I glance around, looking for any sign of her sister or

Piper before pulling Lydia close. "Nothing's wrong. My brothers just came to see how I was."

This morning should have gone differently than it has. Hell, last night should have gone differently than it did. Lydia's first time shouldn't have been on the couch. She shouldn't have slept in my office, and she sure as hell shouldn't have been woken up the way she was.

"Is everything okay with you?" I can't stop myself from asking. Part of me is still worried she'll regret the decisions she made. Or, that I was simply nothing more than a Band-Aid she wanted to rip off before chucking in the trash.

Normally, fucking a woman and walking away wouldn't bother me. I've had my fair share of casual encounters both parties recognized would never go beyond the bedroom. But that's not what I'm looking for now. And that's sure as hell not what I'm looking for with Lydia. But she's young. She hasn't had the opportunity to experience sex, or anything else that comes with a relationship, in just about any capacity. Expecting her to give up the chance to explore all that was withheld from her would be unfair.

No matter how much I might want it.

Lydia wraps her arms around me, pressing the side of her face against my chest. "No. Everything's not okay."

It takes everything I have not to react. Not to drag her back into my office and show her just how good it could be between us. "What's wrong?"

"Myra doesn't want to stay in Memphis. She says it's not far enough away from Mountain Oak. That she'll always worry they'll be able to find her here."

I relax a little, relieved Lydia's not upset about last night, regretting what happened between us. "Where does she want to go?"

Lydia sighs, stepping out of my embrace. "That's part of

the problem. She's all over the place right now. She's cutting her hair and wants to go buy a whole bunch of clothes." She leans in, lowering her voice. "Do you know she stole money from Matthias?" She shakes her head like she can't believe it. "She's been collecting it ever since my dad made her marry him."

I'm actually pretty impressed by this, but Lydia definitely wouldn't want to hear that right now. "It probably made her feel like she had a plan. It gave her a sense of control and a reason to keep going."

Lydia doesn't seem comforted by the possibility. Her brows pinch together, the line between them firming. "But what would've happened if he caught her? If he figured out what she was doing?"

"Something bad." I'm not going to argue with her on this, because she's right. "Situations like this are tricky, Lydia. So much can go wrong. That's why I have to be so careful."

Lydia studies my face for a second before looking toward the front porch. "Your brothers don't know you do this, do they?"

I was hoping she hadn't heard the full conversation, but obviously she was standing behind me for longer than I thought. "No. They don't."

"Why not?" She seems genuinely curious. Interested in knowing more about my life.

And I want to tell her, but I haven't lived the kind of life a reasonable person wouldn't judge me for.

"I didn't think they would agree with the choices I was making." I want to offer her an explanation, but I also don't want to change the way she looks at me. I know she's seen what I'm capable of first-hand, but situations like that haven't always been as warranted or excusable.

"They wouldn't want you to help abused women?" There's an edge to her voice that tells me I'm not the one she's considering judging, and I don't want her looking at my brothers badly. They've always had my back. They're good men, and it wasn't the saving women part that concerned me.

"No, but I was concerned they would question my means." Early on, we didn't know what we know now. Over the years we've made a lot of mistakes. Mistakes that resulted in certain, necessary, eliminations.

Lydia holds my gaze. "Then they don't know what it's like to be abused."

I think about the men who were just on my doorstep. Of the lives they've led. "They do."

Lydia gives me a soft smile. "Then maybe you're not giving them enough credit." Her fingers brush mine for a scant second before she turns to go to the stairs, stealing the connection I desperately need and changing the subject. "I need to get ready for work."

I follow behind her, unable to let her get too far away. "You're working today?" I'm surprised, no, shocked, that she's awake, let alone planning to take on a shift at The Cellar.

"I have to. I'm on the schedule and since we're not in Arkansas I don't feel right calling in or trying to find someone to cover my shift." She continues up the stairs. "Piper's off though, so she'll be here to keep Myra entertained."

I chase after her, crowding Lydia on the landing. "Do you really think I'm going to stay here while you go out alone?" I catch her by the hand, pulling her body back against mine. "I meant what I said last night, Lydia. You're mine. It's my job to protect you. That means for now, I go where you go." I lean close, sliding my hand down to palm the swell of her ass, pulling her against the rapidly thickening line of my cock. I need to know she's still in the same place she was last night. I need to hear it from her lips or I'm going to go fucking crazy. Especially now that I might lose my family in the blink of an eye. "Are you regretting your decision yet?"

Her eyes lift to mine, lips parted as her skin flushes a pretty pink. "No." Her mouth slowly pulls into a small, slightly mischievous smile. "But you might soon."

23

LYDIA

I HOLD MY breath, ear pressed to the wood door of Christian's office, eyes closed as I strain to make out the words being said inside.

It's a tactic I should probably be ashamed of, but it was a necessary part of the life I used to live. Women weren't a part of major conversations. We were told it was because we wouldn't understand them anyway, but I always knew it was because they wanted to keep us as in the dark as possible. Knowledge is power, and like every other opportunity to possess some of my own, this too was withheld from me.

Not that I think Christian is necessarily withholding this from me. However, I'm also not confident he'll share the specifics of it. Specifics I deserve to know since I'm pretty sure I'm the reason he's in that room with nine other men right now.

At least part of the reason.

I haven't been able to hear everything, but the bits and pieces I've been able to make out, along with what I overheard on the porch this morning, are enough to put together what's happening. The men who filed into Christian's house one by one as soon as we got back from my shift at The Cellar are upset they weren't informed about what Christian, Simon, and Tate have been doing. Which is kind of crazy to me since they didn't seem bothered when we showed up with a dead body.

The voices on the other side of the door quiet and a soft scuffling tells me they're on the move.

I turn, racing past the stairs and down the main hall into the kitchen, hiding in the shadows as the men file out through the front door one by one, just like they came in. I expect Simon and Tate to linger, but they too head out into the night.

To be fair, they probably didn't have much left to say to each other.

As promised, Christian went with me to work today, camping out at the same table his friend Damien occupied not so long ago. But he didn't stay alone for long. Soon Tate and Simon joined him and they spent most of the afternoon in a hushed, serious-looking conversation.

Yet another one I can't help but feel I had a part in causing.

The house goes quiet, and I lean just enough so I can peek around the edge of the wall. Christian is still standing at the door, his back to me, shoulders slumped. He looks defeated. Broken down in a way that makes me think maybe I didn't pick up as much of the conversation in his office as I thought.

Sure, his brothers seemed upset, but more disappointed than anything. I know what yelling sounds like, even through a door, and no one yelled during their conversation. Voices stayed calm and even.

He starts to turn and I quickly tuck myself back into the darkness of the kitchen, holding my breath.

"Lydia. I know you're there."

I cringe in the darkness, skin heating with shame and guilt. Slowly, I step from the shadows, worrying my lower lip between my teeth as I wait for him to reprimand me. To show his anger.

Instead Christian holds one hand out. "Come on."

I blink, not sure how to react. I was ready to spit out an apology, but instead find myself silently walking down the hall, bare feet barely a whisper across the hardwood. When I'm close enough I reach out, letting him take my hand in his, still unsure how this will play out.

Christian leads me into his office, closing the door and locking it before walking to his desk, dropping into his seat and pulling me into his lap. He nuzzles my neck, breathing deep as he holds me close.

"I'm sorry you couldn't be in the room. My brothers deserved to hear the truth from me and Tate and Simon without feeling like they had to temper their reactions."

I press my lips together, fighting the pleased smile trying to take over my expression at an inappropriate moment. "You would've wanted me there otherwise?"

Christian curves one hand around my head, tucking it against his shoulder. "Of course. But for purely selfish reasons."

I try to figure out what he's saying, but I can't really begin to guess. It's another frustrating aspect of being so separated from the rest of the world my whole life. I'm not particularly great at reading between the lines of a conversation. But I want to understand, so I ask, "What does that mean?"

"It means I would've felt a hell of a lot better having that conversation with you right here." His other hand settles on the side of my ass, pulling me closer. "Like this."

A hint of the guilt I felt before creeps back. I've been so focused on how Christian makes me feel that I haven't once considered how I might make him feel. All I've thought about is myself. What he can do for me. What he could bring to my life. My own needs and wants and satisfaction.

And it feels dangerously close to how the men who used to control my life behaved. It was wrong of them and it's wrong of me.

I shift around on his lap, straightening as I pull from his hold, ready to right the wrong I've accidentally allowed. The man holding me so tenderly deserves so much more than I've offered.

So I'm going to offer more.

Luckily, the thought of offering is much easier to handle than the thought of requesting. It's something I might have been ashamed of before, but not now.

Not with Christian.

His brows pinch together in concern as I move away. "Where are you going?"

"Nowhere." I slide free, sinking to the floor between his knees, letting my hands trail down his chest before anchoring at the waistband of his blue jeans, making my intention pretty clear.

At least, I think it does.

"What are you doing, Lydia?" Christian's voice is husky as he watches me.

"I don't know." I offer up the kind of honesty I've only felt comfortable giving him. Christian understands. Knows what I've been through. He won't judge me for knowing what I would like to do, but not being entirely sure how to go about it.

I fumble around with the button of his fly, shocked at how difficult it is to undo pants in the opposite direction.

Somehow I manage to get it loose before raking the zipper down and spreading the fly open to reveal the reaching line of his cock.

The urge to feel embarrassed—to stop in my tracks—is strong. It's happened to me before. Over my hair. Over my clothes. Over makeup and just about everything else imaginable. I was scared of feeling ashamed. Of feeling like I was breaking the rules even though I am now the maker of the rules.

But I don't want to feel ashamed about what happens between me and Christian. I'm tired of letting my past define me.

So I reach for the waistband of his boxer briefs, stretching them as much as I can to free his dick without causing any sort of tension or discomfort.

I start to lean in, but Christian's voice stops me.

"Lydia." One of his fingers presses against my chin, tipping my face up until my eyes meet his. "Are you planning to suck my cock?"

I lick my lips, already feeling a familiar ache building between my thighs. "Yes." I expect him to let me go. To be thrilled at this development.

But Christian's finger stays firmly planted on my chin. "Why?"

My list of reasons is long. Too long to offer up right now without delaying my plans, so I settle on the simplest one. "Because I want to."

Christian stares at me, finger keeping me in place as his hazel gaze holds mine.

Last night he argued with me, seemed convinced I didn't know what I wanted. Made me work harder than I ever thought possible for an act I was led to believe men took at every opportunity.

Not this man. And that only makes me want this more.

Christian's finger slowly slides, tracing up the line of my jaw. "Do you know how to suck a cock?"

The right answer seems like it would be no, but it's not a completely honest answer. And at this point I'm pretty confident my perception of right and wrong are still very skewed, so I decide to go with the truth yet again. "I've watched videos."

Christian's finger stops and his nostrils flare. "Videos of women sucking cock?"

I nod, eyes dipping down to where his straining length juts high and proud inches from my face. I lick my lips again, anticipation keeping me eager. I want to do this right. I want Christian to see he doesn't have to protect me from myself. That I know what I want and I'm not afraid to take it.

Even if sometimes it seems that way.

"Did you like watching those videos?" Christian's hand starts to move again, his touch sliding up into my hair.

"Yes." I don't feel wanton or sinful admitting it. Not to him. "But not as much as I like the thought of doing it to you."

Christian's hand fists into the hair at my nape, fingers twining as they pull tight. "Show me how much you like the thought of sucking my cock."

I don't hesitate. I'm afraid he'll change his mind. Go back to worrying I don't completely understand the ramifications of what I'm doing.

I absolutely do.

I rock forward, lining my lips up with the flared head. I open my mouth and flick my tongue against the tip of it, raising my eyes to his face so I can watch his reaction. I've seen how this is done, but I'm not confident enough to blindly trust my abilities, so my only option is to hope I can figure out what he likes based on his reactions.

To my surprise, Christian's focus is locked on where my tongue touches the heat of his silky-smooth skin, jaw locked tight as I tease against it. There's definitely intensity there, but not the blissful expression of pure pleasure I'm hoping to achieve, so I part my lips more, opening my jaw wider so I can take him into my mouth.

I expect it to feel like an invasion. Uncomfortable, especially as his rigid shaft glides over my tongue, sliding deeper. But I don't seem to be thinking about the stretch of my lips or the hint of a gag that happens when he bumps the back of my tongue.

All I can think about is the sound Christian makes. The deep growl of a groan that comes through his lips as he watches me swallow him down.

His hand tightens in my hair, like he can't stop hanging onto me as I find my footing, working my mouth over him with slow, deep passes.

My spit makes his skin slick, easing the way, making it possible for me to take more and more of him with every bob of my head. At some point, it becomes a challenge. Seeing how much of him I can push between my lips. How tight I can make his fingers pull my hair. How fast I can make him breathe. How hard I can make his cock jerk.

I know I believed I was doing this for him, but somehow it's starting to become for my benefit too. Because for the first time in my life I feel powerful.

This man, who is capable of unimaginable things, is at my mercy.

It's a heady feeling, one I already want more of.

I watch Christian's face as I sink over him yet again, but this time I hollow my cheeks, sucking as I pull back.

The sound that comes from him is inhuman and feral and it shoots straight down to the ache throbbing in my pussy. I press my hand between my thighs, trying to ease the suffering, but I'm still not bold enough to take my pleasure into my own hands. The pressure of my palm makes me whimper with unmet need, and the sound resonates in my mouth.

The hand Christian has in my hair grips so tight it almost hurts as he pulls me away so fast a string of saliva continues to connect us. His thumb comes to slide along my lower lip, wiping away the wetness collected there. "Stand up."

His command pulls my nipples tight and has my thighs pressing together. I liked being in control, but maybe not quite as much as I like Christian being in control. He knows what he's doing. He knows how to satisfy both of us.

And ultimately I know he would stop all this if I asked him to.

So I stand, continuing to watch him as I move, drinking in every expression, every sound, every breath.

Christian tips his head toward the shorts and T-shirt I changed into after work. "Take it all off."

He's the only man I've ever been naked in front of, and surprisingly it didn't feel strange last night. Actually, it made me feel a whole lot like I do now. Powerful.

Because the way he looks at me makes me feel like I matter. Like he wants me as much as I want him.

So I strip down, shimmying out of my shorts and panties before dragging the T-shirt over my head, dropping it to the floor along with my bra.

I hold my breath, knowing he's going to touch me. Knowing he's going to make me feel so good.

Christian nods toward his desk. "Bend over."

Those filthy words he said to me in the hotel have been marching through my brain like a never-ending parade, so the demand makes me flush with heat. It also makes me do as he asks. I turn, facing the wide expanse of smooth wood and slowly lower my upper half to the surface. It's cold against my nipples and cheek as I turn my face so I can continue to watch him.

Christian studies me, his gaze dark and languid as it drifts over my bent body. He slowly rolls his office chair until he's positioned directly behind me. When his fingers slick along my slit, I gasp.

And my knees buckle.

"Hands on the edge. Hold on." The words are barely out of Christian's mouth before he strokes my clit, splitting two fingers around it to tease up both sides.

I flail around to get my arms in place, barely managing to wrap my fingers over the edge as he continues teasing me with a remarkably accurate touch, giving my already throbbing clit a few teasing touches before moving away. I gasp as his teasing finger eases into my body with a slow stroke.

"Are you sore?" The question is surprisingly gentle given the harshness of his previous requests.

I shake my head, the motion stunted by my position. "No."

"Good." A drawer pulls out beside me as Christian gets to his feet. A condom wrapper falls to the desk beside me a second before his big body blankets mine, his weight pinning me in place. The prod of his hard length teases against me as he sucks at the spot where my shoulder meets my neck.

I instinctively try to push back against him, seeking out the same full feeling I craved last night, but I can barely move, so all I manage to do is grunt in frustration.

Christian chuckles, his breath warm against my skin. "Greedy girl."

Is that what I am? Maybe.

And maybe I'm a little proud of it.

Proud I'm finally starting to take what I want. What I deserve.

The air rushes from my lungs as the head of his cock fits into place and his hips rock, giving me the tiniest bit of what I'm craving. "Christian." I sound whiny, desperate. "Please."

"Shhh." His lips move against my ear as his hand slides around to the front of my body where it hangs off the edge. "I'll take care of you, Lydia. I promise." His fingers find my clit, expertly stroking with a steady touch that makes my legs start to shake.

And then he pushes into me, the stretch of his cock and the slide of his fingers already too much to bear. I barely have time to take a breath before I'm coming, gripping the edge of his desk as I rock back against him, taking everything I can.

Then I collapse against the wood, panting and boneless.

Christian slides from my body, still just as hard as before.

I turn, craning my neck as I try to regain my bearings while he peels the empty condom free and tosses it in the trash.

"Wait." I straighten, keeping one hand braced on the desk as I move just in case my legs decide to give out. "You didn't—" My tongue ties, caught on a word I didn't know existed until I was twenty.

Christian pulls his underwear back into place, but leaves his pants undone, looping one arm around my waist to pull me close. His lips whisper across mine. "That's not what this was about."

That was what it was *supposed* to be about. I was going to

offer him the same pleasure he's offered me. Prove I'm not just here to take from him. "But—"

Christian nips at my lower lip, sucking it between his teeth before letting it free. "No buts."

He pulls away, grabbing a box depicting a handheld air pump from behind his desk and passing it to me before picking up a larger box and carrying it to the center of the room. "Now help me set up our air mattress."

24

CHRISTIAN

"COMFORTABLE?"

Lydia's limbs are heavy where they drape across my chest and legs, effectively answering the question I couldn't stop myself from asking.

I want her to be happy here. I want her to be happy with me. I want her to see what's between us the same way I do.

I want her to know this is something real. Something that doesn't come along every day. I would know. I've been watching it happen to my brothers over and over, waiting years for the day it would happen for me.

And now it has.

"It's not as soft as your bed, but I guess it's better than the twin I have in my apartment, so I'm not going to complain." Her reply lacks a little of the enthusiasm I was hoping for.

I tip my head, looking down at where her face is pressed against my chest and find her grinning up at me. "You need to make it more obvious when you're giving me shit."

"Wouldn't that defeat the purpose?" She cuddles a little closer, obviously pleased with herself.

I stroke down the arm she has draped across my middle, closing my eyes to savor this moment. "Not my purpose." I tuck the blankets around her, making sure she's well covered as the air conditioning kicks on, blowing from the floor vent right next to us. "Did you hear everything you wanted to earlier?"

Lydia's quiet for a minute, her silence making me peek her way again. Her expression is somber. "I'm sorry. I just —" She pauses, lips pinched. "I had to be sneaky for a long time. It was the only way to know what was going on and keep them from knowing what I was thinking of doing. Otherwise I would've ended up just like Myra."

The reminder of how her life could have been sits hard and heavy in my gut. And it's far more powerful than the guilt I'm feeling over admitting to my brothers what Simon, Tate, and I have kept from them.

I want to feel bad about it. And I do. But I would feel worse about not helping all the women we've saved over the years.

Women like Lydia and Myra and Stella, the owner of The Cellar.

"Do you feel like you have to be that way with me?" I understand why Lydia is the way she is, but it directly impacts my ability to keep her safe. She's said one thing to my face and done something completely different on more than one occasion, and I can't allow it to continue going forward. Not when Rodney's associates are still looking for him. Still trying to figure out where he's at and what led to his disappearance.

"No, but it's not easy to stop." Lydia's sighs. "Lots of things aren't easy to stop."

"Like what?" I want to understand her. Know her inside and out. I crave that connection. That closeness. Been waiting for it my whole fucking life. And it only got worse the more it was paraded in front of me. I was happy for my brothers, but I wanted to be happy for myself too.

"Like everything." One graceful hand catches a strand of her hair twisting it around a finger. "I thought I would get away and everything would be different, but it wasn't. I wasn't part of the IGL anymore, but I was still so afraid of doing something wrong. Of blatantly going against what they wanted me to think and do. It felt like I was going to get in trouble. Like they were going to catch me even though no one was here to see what I was doing."

"For twenty years you had to watch everything you said and did to avoid being punished. Twenty years of trauma doesn't just go away." I know. I've been fighting my own. Doing everything I can to convince myself I'm better than they claimed I was, even though I proved them right for a lot of years.

Lydia's eyes lift, her head shifting against the bare skin of my chest as she looks up at me. "Is that what you think it is? Trauma?"

"You were threatened every day of your life, Lydia. Told if you didn't act the right way, say the right things, wear the right clothes, you were going to burn for an eternity." I pull her a little closer, trying to smother away the anger brewing inside me. "If that's not trauma, I don't know what is."

Lydia's eyes stay on my face for a second as her lips press together. "Why did you leave? If it wasn't to go be a preacher, then what was it?"

"I was competition." Going back to that time isn't as painful as it used to be, but it still stings. "And they knew I didn't think like they did. They knew I wouldn't continue to perpetuate the same fucked-up ideas they rely on."

Up until that day, I was young and stupid enough to

believe I could change things. That once I became a man I could show everyone around me how wrong they had it. But that went against their agenda, and there was no way Ansel Parks was going to let that happen.

"Your father came to my father and told him I couldn't be around your family anymore because I was a bad influence. I'd told your brother I didn't think the way they treated women was right. I'd seen what it did to my mother and my older sister and I knew how fucked-up it was. I thought Jeremiah could help change things with me, but it turned out that wasn't what he wanted."

Jeremiah's betrayal was the worst part of the whole thing. Realizing someone I thought was my friend would throw me under the bus so easily nearly broke me. Made it hard for me to really trust anyone for a long time.

Hell, maybe it still does.

Lydia's sweet and soft expression goes stony, her eyes narrowing at me in the shadowy darkness of my office. "I wish I could say I'm surprised, but I'm not." Her lip curls. "He's just like my father."

I already had my suspicions about who put their hands on Lydia when they started to notice she was pulling away, but her reaction confirms it. "He should probably hope our paths don't cross. Because I have a few scores to settle with him."

Lydia's chin tips up a little more, hinting at the defiant spirit I know she carries. "Me too."

I love seeing the fight in her—especially since she's worked so hard to keep it hidden from everyone else—but the thought of Lydia putting herself in a dangerous situation steals any enjoyment I might have. "I don't want you trying to take them on, Lydia. Them, or anyone else. That's my job."

I expect her to agree, but Lydia barely shakes her head, rocking her cheek against my pec. "I can't make that promise."

It's the honesty I've been hoping for, asked for, but it is not what I want to hear. And unfortunately, I can't argue with her, because I don't want her to go back to shutting me out. To telling me what I want to hear in spite of her actual plans. "We'll cross that bridge when we come to it."

Lydia's lips pull into a slow smile. "I vote we burn that bridge when we come to it."

A laugh springs free at the unexpected vitriol in her tone. "I think I like this ruthless side of you. It's sexy as hell."

Lydia's expression morphs into surprise. "Sexy?"

"That's not saying as much as you think it is considering I think everything you do is sexy." From the second she walked into my office, I've been hooked. Unable to think about anything but her. The woman she is now. The strength she carries. The drive. How far she's come from that scared little girl I once knew, but still manages to carry the same sweetness in spite of everything.

I tuck her head into my shoulder, smoothing down the soft strands of her hair as I close my eyes. "Now you and your sexy ass need to go to sleep."

THE SECURITY ALERT of my front gate unlocking wakes me. It's not the alarm, which means whoever opened it has the code, so I'm not overly concerned.

But I'm also not unconcerned.

I hold my breath as I slide away from Lydia's warm body, easing myself to the edge of the air mattress we slept on before working to my feet, being careful not to shift the bed too much. She's had a rough week and needs to sleep.

Unfortunately, the second I stand, Lydia's eyes fly open on a sharp inhale as she sits up, looking disheveled and disoriented. "What's wrong?"

I start to tell her it's nothing, but that doesn't seem right. I want her to be honest with me. I should be honest with her too. "Someone opened the front gate."

"Oh." She blinks, eyes widening. "*Oh*." Her limbs flail around as she tosses the covers back and wrestles her way off the constantly shifting bed, losing her balance and dropping back down. "I think I hate this thing." She slides to her knees before standing, giving up on pushing her way out as she continues to grumble. "It's fine as long as you don't try to move, I guess."

I feel the sudden urge to smile. I'm used to waking up alone. Spending my mornings in silence as I drink coffee and get a little work done.

But silence is overrated when the alternative is a rumpled Lydia sporting bedhead and a grumpy frown.

"Not a morning person?" I grab my discarded pair of pants and pull them on as I make my way to the door.

"No." She yawns, one hand going to the mess of her hair. "Not at all."

I unlock the office door and crack it open, making sure neither of my other two houseguests are waiting in the hall. All clear, so Myra and Piper must still be asleep, which I'm grateful for.

I'm positive they know where Lydia is spending her nights, but I'm not quite sure she's ready to fess up to it just yet.

I step out, using my body to keep Lydia blocked into the office as I peer toward the narrow windows flanking the front door. The etched glass blurs everything on the other side, but there's no mistaking what I'm seeing.

"Who are all those people?" Lydia grips my arm, holding tight as she leans around me to get a look.

I swallow hard. "My family." I take a deep breath just as the knock comes. "You might want to brace yourself."

I should have known this moment was coming. Should have guessed this would be the outcome of the conversation I had with my brothers last night.

Lydia's hand stays on my arm as I go to the door, unlocking the deadbolt before opening it wide to reveal the crowd of smiling faces.

Jill, the matriarch of our mismatched crew, beams, her focus entirely fixed on the woman still mostly hidden behind me. "Good morning." She shoves the covered dish in her hand out. "We brought you breakfast." Her eyes slide my way, narrowing into a glare I knew was coming. "Since we can't rely on Christian to take care of the things he's supposed to."

I step back, not by choice, as Jill shoulders her way past me, the collection of women occupying my porch filing in right behind her. My brothers' wives aren't shy and they certainly won't leave one woman, let alone three, thinking they're not part of the group. So, whether Lydia's ready for it or not, she's about to be claimed.

"How did you sleep, honey?" Jill reaches out to pat Lydia's shoulder, expression full of motherly concern and care. "This house only has two beds. Where in the world does he have you sleeping?"

Lydia freezes up, a conflicting combination of forced politeness and horror caught on her face.

I step between them. "Give her a little room."

I love Jill. I understand where she's coming from and

who she is. But I also understand where Lydia's coming from and who *she* is, and right now she's afraid. Afraid of judgment. Maybe still a little afraid of eternal damnation.

I loop one arm around Lydia's waist, tucking her into my side as I keep myself between her and the rest of the group, watching as they mill around my house like they own it. "Make yourselves at home."

"We plan to." Jill continues to lead the pack, heading straight down the main hall that leads to the back portion of my house. Her daughter, Kerri, is right behind her, carrying a dish of her own. Felicity and Shelly walk side-by-side, both of them smiling wide as they pass. Carly, Josie, and Hope bring up the rear. They're the ones I think Lydia will get along with the best. They're a little calmer than everyone else. Quieter. They've been through similar experiences and I think she'll feel understood by them.

As long as she's willing to peel herself away from my side. And right now that doesn't seem like it's going to happen anytime soon.

I watch as the women my brothers love, along with one of their mothers, take over my kitchen and dining room, filling my house with noise and chaos. Chaos that's compounded less than a minute later when Piper and Myra rush down the stairs, looking for the source of the commotion they heard all the way on the second floor.

Piper blinks hard, wiping at the outer corner of one eye as she frowns at the commotion. "What the fuck? Who in the hell has a party at eight in the morning?"

"There you are." Jill comes right for Piper, reaching out to her the same way she did Lydia. "You must be Lydia's sweet friend." She pulls Piper into a tight hug. "I have heard so much about you."

Piper's eyes are wide, her body stiff as she looks my way. "From who?"

Jill leans back, wiggling her eyebrows. "That's for me to know and you to find out." Then she boops Piper on the end of her nose before turning her attention to Myra. Her expression softens. "And you're Myra, Lydia's sister." She pulls Myra into the same hug she offered Piper, squeezing her tight. "How are you, honey? Are you doing okay?"

Myra seems less caught off guard by Jill. She hugs her back, squeezing tight. "I'm good." Her eyes drift to the island where Kerri, Shelly, and Felicity are popping open a bottle of champagne. "But I will be better once I have some of whatever they're making."

She and Jill walk arm in arm to where my sisters-in-law are mixing up mimosas, filling every glass and coffee cup I own and passing them out.

Piper's brows slowly lift as she turns my way. "Maybe I don't mind your family's parties." She sidles up to the counter, snagging a drink poured into a coffee mug emblazoned with the logo of my company.

Lydia keeps one hand tangled in my belt loop as she watches, pinching her lower lip between her teeth.

I lean into her ear, keeping my words just between us. "What's wrong?"

Lydia's eyes hang on the scene a second longer before coming to mine. "I just don't understand how this is so easy for Myra and it's been so hard for me."

"Just because it looks easy, doesn't mean it really is." I don't want Myra to have a hard time, but I also won't have Lydia thinking she's not been successful. That she's lived her life incorrectly in Memphis.

Some people are careful and cautious and some people

dive into shit with both feet. The people who are careful and cautious face problems as they come. The people who jump in with both feet deal with problems when they can't avoid them any longer. The family I've made for myself is large and filled with all kinds of people. People like Piper. People like Myra.

And definitely people like Lydia.

I tip my head to the three women standing together at the outskirts of the group, smiling as they watch the louder women entertain everyone. "Let's go talk to the women I think you'll feel most comfortable with."

Lydia's lips press into a thin line, expression uncertain. "I'm starting to think I may not be comfortable around anybody."

"You're comfortable around Piper." I give her a grin. "You're comfortable around me."

"That's different."

I lift my brows, surprised. "Why is that?"

Lydia's lips finally soften, twisting into a little bit of a smile. "You guys didn't give me any other option."

25

I DON'T KNOW how to act. I've never been in a room full
of women speaking so freely. Or so loudly. It's nice to see but
is completely overwhelming and makes me want to shrink
back. Hide myself away so they won't notice how out of my
element I am.

Seeing my sister and my best friend acting right at home
in this situation makes me feel even more out of place. Even
more disappointed in myself for failing to figure out how to
insert myself into the real world.

Christian has assured me no one in this room will judge
me or question the way I act, but I can't help feeling like
they are. Just for the exact opposite reason of why I used to
be afraid I was being judged.

"You okay?" One of the women Christian parked me
next to leans my way, her smile soft. "I know this can be a
lot."

I take a sip of the spiked orange juice in my hand,
smiling back as I nod. "I'm good."

The woman sitting on my left snorts softly. "You don't
have to say that." She tucks a strand of her light brown bob

behind one ear. "I'm frequently not okay at these things, so I definitely won't judge you if you're not." She seems to ponder it for a second. "Actually, I might feel better if the volume is a little too much for you. I won't feel as guilty about the earplugs I've been considering buying."

Her honesty makes me feel a little more comfortable. It's the same reason I'm so close with Piper. She calls it like it is. Speaks her truth every time she opens her mouth. I've never felt like she was manipulating me or trying to trick me in any way, and it made me feel comfortable. Safe.

And now I feel guilty I didn't offer up honesty myself. "It is a little loud." I glance at the blonde woman sitting to my right. "And unexpected."

The blonde nods. "If it makes you feel any better, you do sort of get used to it." She reaches one hand out. "I'm Hope. Niko's my husband. We live next door to the old firehouse."

I take her hand, glad when she doesn't squeeze it to death. "I'm Lydia."

The woman on my left lowers her voice as she leans in. "I'm Carly. I'm with Levi, the one with all the colorful tattoos on his arms." Her lips curve in a little smile. "He looks scary but he's really a teddy bear."

I return her smile like I know who she's talking about, but I don't know if I could identify a single one of the brothers in a lineup outside of Christian, Simon, and Tate who I already knew. Maybe Damien since he scared the shit out of me and then sat at one of my tables for three hours.

I've seen all of them a couple of times, but the first involved an attempted abduction and a dead body, and the second was last night as they quickly filed into Christian's office. I definitely don't remember tattoo or attitude specifics.

Carly turns to the group in front of us and motions at

the older woman in the room. "That's Jill. She was married to the asshole who brought all of the brothers together." Her smile slips for just a second as an unidentifiable emotion passes over her pretty features. It's gone just as quickly and she goes back to her task, pointing finger moving to the younger woman standing at Jill's side. "That's Kerri. She's Jill's daughter and my half-sister. She's married to Evan, the guy with the uncolored full tattoos."

I turn toward Carly, my brain struggling to do the genetic math. "Half-sister? Does that mean your father—"

Carly's lips flatten. "My father was a piece of shit who abused my mother, cheated on his wife, and took advantage of broken little boys." Her nostrils flare. "Luckily he's where he belongs."

My brain scrambles through everything Christian told me about the man who called himself King and I suddenly understand why I'm sitting where I am. My eyes drift to where Christian stands in the kitchen, looking over the man who never seems to stop looking out for me.

Carly continues down the line of women, pointing out Shelly, who's married to the enormous man named Shaun. Felicity's married to the long-haired guy named Cody who runs the warehouse we brought Rodney and his car to. The final woman in the trio joining me on Christian's couch is Josie. She's married to Damien, my friendly, neighborhood stalker.

"We'll leave it at that." Carly drops her hand, blowing out a breath. "I can introduce you to everybody's kids later. If I do that now your head will explode."

"I think my head is already exploding." I take another sip of my mimosa, swallowing it down in the hopes it might help me relax a little.

I'm used to being around large groups of people. My

family was decently sized. Besides Myra and Jeremiah, I have three additional older brothers. We did a huge amount within the church since my father was the pastor, but all those gatherings looked entirely different from this one. Those, just like everything else, were focused on the men. Feeding them. Listening to them talk.

Then the women cleaned up the mess.

Right now I'm seeing the complete opposite. Christian is doing his best to control the fallout dropping around him, wiping up spills, taking out the trash when one can fills, and juggling dirty dishes. The craziest part of it is he doesn't seem bothered by it at all. If anything he seems almost—

Happy.

Hope gives me a little bump, pulling my gaze away from where Christian is forearm deep in a sink full of soapy water, scrubbing through glasses as he jokes with Kerri. "So you and Christian, huh?"

As if he hears her words, Christian turns, giving me a heated glance that curls my toes and makes my thighs press together as thoughts of his desk hijack my brain.

Carly leans into my ear, eyes on Christian. "Are you on the pill? Because if not, he might have just gotten you pregnant."

My face is suddenly very hot. A little bit because I'm embarrassed I've never even considered birth control, and a little bit because now I'm imagining what it would take for Christian to actually get me pregnant. After only two penetrative interactions with him, I'm already jonesing for a third. One that's mutually fulfilling.

"We just—" I don't know how to explain the situation I'm in, so I stop there.

But Carly doesn't seem bothered by my inability to sum up what Christian and I are. She waves my hesitation off.

"Don't worry about explaining it to us. We know exactly how these guys work. One minute you're out living your life —doing your thing, following your plans and dreams—and the next you've been wifed-up by a gorgeous man with a snake tattooed on his dick."

My head snaps her way in surprise. "A what?"

Carly nods. "A snake." Her eyes are wide as she leans in. "And I was practically a virgin when we got together, so you can imagine my surprise when that's what jumped out at me."

I rub my lips together, more interested in the other part of what she's saying than whatever's tattooed on her husband's privates. "You were a virgin?"

"Not technically, but about as close as you could get without actually being one." Her expression turns sad. "I was raised to believe good girls didn't have sex and that being good was the most important thing, so I had a lot of baggage as far as physical intimacy was concerned."

I hang on her every word, suddenly feeling like maybe I will fit in here. Like maybe I can be understood. "How did you get past it?"

"Finding a man who is very, very good at it got me over the initial hump." She smiles, lifting one shoulder and letting it drop. "But the shame still tries to linger. I'm not sure it's something you ever completely forget, so I just keep reminding myself having sex doesn't make me bad. Nothing really makes a person bad, as long as their motives are good."

The way she says the last part is different, and it sits with me. I've worked so hard to move forward, scared of judgment even though I didn't dish out any of my own. Piper's brought men home before, spent one night with them and never saw them again. I never thought she was bad or wrong.

I witnessed Christian do something most people would consider the ultimate sin, but he did it to protect me. To save me from a man who was going to do horrific things to me. My eyes once again find where he stands at the sink, smiling at Jill as she pats him on the back, whatever made her glare at him earlier already forgotten. I would never consider him bad.

So maybe my perceptions of good and bad need a little fine-tuning. Maybe I need to give myself a little more grace than I have been.

Hope leans into my side. "Tell me about your sister. What's she like?"

I force my eyes away from Christian to where Myra is standing with the two loudest women in the group, smiling and laughing like she's known them her whole life. "She's brave."

At first it was jarring to see how ready Myra is to move forward. It made me question her. Question myself.

But now it gives me hope. Because if she's brave—if she's moving forward—then maybe I can be too.

"YOU LOOK LIKE you need a nap." Christian pulls me close the second the door closes behind our unexpected guests, breathing against my hair as one hand palms my ass through the shorts I slept in. "Maybe we should go lay down."

"I can't." I groan, dreading going into work for the first time ever. "I have to work." I would much rather partake in whatever he's proposing, but my shift at The Cellar won't wait.

"I guess we're going to work then." Christian drapes one arm over my shoulders, walking with me to the stairs.

I peek at him from the corner of my eye. "I'm not sure you should come with me."

Christian's expression turns serious. "We've talked about this, Lydia. I'm not leaving your side until—"

"I know, but I don't know if my boss will appreciate you sitting there my whole shift." I've worked hard to prove hiring me was a good decision and I don't want to undo all that effort. Especially not when I'm close to getting bumped to a better schedule.

"Stella?" Christian grins, relaxing again at my side. "You don't have to worry about her. I'm allowed to sit in her bar all day every day if I want."

The cocky edge of his words makes me smile back. "Because you bring in so many customers when you play?"

Christian's face hardens, smile gone completely. "No. Because I helped get her away from her abusive ex-husband."

I stop, standing halfway up the stairs as I stare at him. "You helped Stella?" The owner of The Cellar is not the kind of woman I would have ever expected to be trapped in a relationship. Abused. She's so confident. So strong. So capable.

"I know what you're thinking." Christian's voice is soft. "It can happen to anybody, Lydia."

I don't know if that makes me feel better or worse. "I'm glad you helped her."

"Me too. She's done a lot with her life." Christian urges me to continue up the stairs, leading me into his bedroom.

"So don't worry about what Stella thinks. And you can pretend I'm not even there."

Right. Like that will be simple to accomplish. I've never been good at ignoring Christian. Not as a little girl who was openly fascinated, and definitely not now that I'm a grown woman who knows exactly what he's capable of.

But Christian can't follow me to work forever. "What happens when you have to go back to your job?"

"When I have to go back to work we figure something else out." He says it like it's a simple solution. Like it's any solution at all.

"But—"

Christian presses one finger to my lips, cutting my argument off. "You will always be protected, Lydia. In case you didn't notice, my brothers' wives have decided you're part of the family, and we protect our family." His eyes fix on mine. "Always."

That's not what family has meant to me. My father was never interested in protecting me. I was simply a tool he could utilize for his own gain. Whether it was cooking, cleaning, or making connections by marrying me off, his motives were never about what was best for me. And they certainly weren't for my safety.

That makes it difficult to wrap my head around what he's suggesting. "So if something happened to Carly, and her husband wasn't there, you would—" The words trail off as I imagine all Christian's done to keep me safe.

"I would do whatever it took to protect her and I can promise Levi would do whatever it took to protect you." His hands move to my hair, stroking down the strands before he curves them against my face. He drops his forehead down to rest against mine, eyes closing. "I should have trusted them more. I should have told them what Simon, Tate, and I have been doing."

The vulnerability in his confession shocks me. I close my eyes, letting the moment sink in. Absorbing all the emotion it carries. Because in this moment, Christian is looking to me for support. Admitting what he perceives as a failure and treating me like what I think and what I say matters.

It's what I've longed for my whole life. The opportunity to be an equal. A partner. Respected. Appreciated. Cherished.

"You were afraid they would tell you it was wrong." I slide my hands along his arms, wanting to soothe the turmoil I know he's feeling.

"I never told Myra I was leaving. I was afraid she would try to talk me out of it even though I knew it was the right thing to do. I was hoping I would break free and then I could tell her how wonderful it is and convince her to join me." I open my eyes, meeting Christian's. "But I should have told her. Should've known she would have come with me even though she'd already been married off."

I pause, struggling with the full impact of what might have been. "She might have actually helped me handle it better than I did." I glance over at the neatly made bed and immaculate space surrounding it. "But it was difficult to know who I could trust and who I couldn't, especially after what happened with my brother." I manage a little smile. "But now I know."

Christian smiles back at me, his thumb stroking over my cheek "I hope so." He leans close, and my eyes flutter closed, waiting for the brush of his mouth against mine.

"Hey, Lydia." Piper comes banging out of the spare bedroom down the hall, looking completely unfazed at seeing me tangled in Christians arms. "Stella just called. She bumped me to the early shift today, so it looks like we're going to be bar buddies again." She yawns, the sound long and loud. "I was really looking forward to getting a nap in before my late shift too."

I start to step away from Christian—the urge to separate my body from his strong—but I fuse my feet to the floor. No one cares if I touch him. If he touches me. I deserve to do the things I want without old fears and lingering threats continuing to control me. "At least now you'll get off early. You might even be able to go to bed at a reasonable time."

Piper's lip curls, lifting one side of her nose with it. "Gross. Bedtimes are for losers."

Christian chuckles, sliding one of his hands down my back. "Bedtimes are for people over thirty. Just wait. It's coming for you."

Piper makes a disgusted sound. "Not gonna happen. I'm a night owl." She tips her head to the side, eyes narrowing in consideration. "Unless Jill shows up again with mimosas. I could be bribed out of bed for that." She straightens, pointing in my direction. "Go get ready. We've got a bar to tend."

I turn to Christian as she disappears into the bedroom. "Looks like you'll have more than just me to babysit tonight."

Christian's eyes drift down the hall before coming back to me. "Go take a shower. I'm going to call in reinforcements."

26

CHRISTIAN

"LAST NIGHT WENT better than I expected." Tate tips back the beer in his hand, swallowing down a mouthful before continuing. "I wasn't sure how everyone would take it."

"I'm not sure it went over as well as you think it did." I lean back in my chair, glancing across the bar to where Lydia is lining a tray full of drinks in front of a table of girls wearing cowboy boots and hats. "Jill showed up at my house this morning at the ass crack of dawn with all the wives." I sip at the drink I've been nursing for an hour. "She didn't seem too thrilled with me."

"Was she pissed?" Simon leans closer, resting his forearm against the table we've been sitting at all afternoon. "Or was she disappointed in you?"

I wince at the memory of the look Jill gave me. "Definitely the second one."

"Ouch." Tate shoots me a grin. "Makes me glad I didn't have a reason for her to show up at my house."

Simon holds his beer out, tipping it against Tate's. "Amen to that."

They're both celebrating their singledom, but I don't miss the way they watch when Lydia comes to our table, her hand resting on my shoulder as she checks in on us. They might not be willing to admit it, but they are just as lonely as I was. Hell, Simon might be even worse.

He spends most of his time on the road, hauling his camper from worksite to worksite. Chasing the highest paying jobs available across the country before coasting back into town for a quick check-in and a gig or two.

The table falls quiet for a minute. After a few seconds of silence Tate meets my gaze. "Have we heard anything from The Horsemen?"

I shake my head. "Cody called earlier and said he reached out to a few of his old contacts. Said to keep them in the loop if anything interesting was going on."

I've put my brothers in an awkward position. Because of me, we're standing with one foot edging toward a grave we buried years ago. We worked hard to leave our old—less legal—lives behind us, and I dug them up and pulled them front and center. Not only that, I delivered an entirely new problem to our doorstep, one that outed the secret life Simon, Tate, and I have been leading.

Simon works his jaw from side to side, tapping one finger against the table. "I talked to Evan." His eyes lift to me before moving to Tate. "He asked if we might want to all sit down together and talk about the possibility of continuing on with what we're doing."

I'm stunned. Sure, none of my brothers seemed livid last night when we fessed up to helping women escape abusive situations by any means necessary, but I sure as hell didn't expect them to want to keep it going. Actually, I've been assuming the opposite. That Myra would be the last woman we'd be able to save. That my brothers would decide the risk wasn't worth the reward and our trio would be shut down.

I look from Tate to Simon. "How do you feel about that?"

The thought of stopping was almost unbearable to consider. Doing what I did kept me from wallowing in the pain of the loss of my sister. The realization that I played a part in her death. Punishing all the men I could since no one punished the man who hurt her.

"I think it's worth considering." Tate turns to me. "I assume I know your answer?"

Loud voices drag my attention away, pushing me to my feet before I even identify the source. The Cellar is surprisingly busy for an afternoon, so there's a decent number of people blocking my path as I push my way toward the bar with Tate and Simon following right behind me. I see a flash of dark tattoos and hear a feminine grunt that turns my blood cold.

I move faster, knocking a couple of college aged guys out of my way as someone groans, and an odd snapping sound cuts through the air.

By the time I break the edge of the crowd, the heavily tattooed man is flat on the floor, body twitching. Piper stands over him, a triumphant smirk on her lips. "I told you to get your fucking hands off her." She swipes across her face with one forearm, pushing at the mess of tangled hair sticking to her sweaty skin. The taser I told her not to carry is clutched tight in one hand as she glares down at the incapacitated man, her shoulders heaving as she tries to catch her breath.

I push Simon in her direction, not wanting to leave Piper to fend for herself, but also needing to get my hands on Lydia. To see that she's safe. But the crowd of people in the bar cinches in, hoping to get a look at the source of the commotion, making it a difficult task. With each second that passes my pulse speeds faster and fear turns to anger.

I should have kept my eyes on her. Should have sat closer. Shouldn't have allowed myself to get distracted by the conversation I was having. Should have—

The door leading to the back hallway opens, catching my eye. Lydia steps out, carrying a box. Her eyes widen as they sweep across the scene in front of her.

I shove through the crowd, the air rushing from my lungs when I reach her side. I snag the box from her hands, balancing it in one arm as I use the other to pull her against me. I've never felt so relieved in my life. Those few seconds of not knowing where she was, thinking maybe someone managed to drag her away in the chaos, were unbearable.

"What happened?" Lydia sticks close to me as she surveys the bar. "Is everything okay?"

"Not that guy's nuts." Piper strides in our direction with Tate close on her heels, carrying her weapon of choice.

Lydia presses her lips together, shaking her head. "I told you he was going to be a problem." Her flattened mouth tips into a frown. "I didn't like the way he was talking to his girl-friend. He would lower his voice when I walked past, but he didn't know I have years of watching men abuse women under my belt, and I knew exactly what he was doing."

"Well he found out exactly what I did." Piper looks pleased with herself. "I think for a second he thought I was going to hit on him." She snorts. "Like I just go around trying to put my hand on a strange dude's junk." She makes a face. "I wouldn't touch that one with a ten-foot pole." Her head tips to one side. "Might with a baseball bat though."

A decade ago I might've been shocked to discover women like Piper existed, but not now. Now, a few of my brothers are married to women with strikingly similar personalities, so her confidence and brash attitude don't surprise me at all. If anything, they make me like her even more because I see them for what they are: a shield she uses to protect an unexpectedly tender heart. At least that's the case with the women I know like her.

The swinging door beside me shoves open and a familiar face rushes out. Stella looks directly at me. "What in the hell happened?"

I hold up my free hand, taking it off Lydia for only a second. "Wasn't me."

Stella's focus swings to the next most likely cause. Piper beams at her, smile wide. "The prick at table ten wound up like he was going to backhand his girlfriend after berating her for twenty minutes straight."

Stella's head tips back, face pointing toward the ceiling as she slowly inhales. "Please tell me you did not take that fucking taser to a customer's scrotum."

Piper deflates a little. "What did you want me to do? Just let him hit her?" She crosses her arms, posture going stiff. "He might get away with that shit at home, but not when I'm standing there."

"This is my business, Piper." Stella seems more resigned than angry. "I am responsible for what you do and that means it's my ass on the line right now, not yours."

Piper's shoulders slump. "But I'm the one who did it. Not you."

Stella reaches out to pat Piper's arm, her own soft heart showing for just a second. "I don't think what you did was wrong, but sometimes the world looks at things differently." Her eyes snap to the entrance as the door opens. "Especially in a legal sense."

The next hour is a blur of cops and statements and feeling a little too close to both for comfort. As a rule, I generally try to stay as far from the police as possible, especially given my past endeavors, but there's no escaping them tonight. At least this time I'm nothing more than a witness.

Stella ends up closing the bar early, locking the doors once the tasered man has been hauled away and the cops clear out.

Unfortunately, they don't clear out alone, and Lydia and I end up at the station, waiting while they decide what to do with Piper.

It's well after midnight by the time we get home, and all three of us are exhausted. Piper's high wore off hours ago and her steps drag as we make our way from the detached garage behind my house to the back door. Lydia leans against me as I unlock the door, the security alarm beeping as it opens. Piper trudges in behind us, going straight down the hall toward the stairs. "I'm going to bed." She pauses, looking back our way. "I'm really sorry."

Lydia shakes her head. "You don't have anything to be sorry for. That guy deserved everything he got."

Piper gives Lydia a sad smile. "I'm not so sure the police will feel the same way." Her smile falters. "Or Stella." She turns away, disappearing up the stairs, leaving Lydia and I alone in the kitchen.

But we're not alone for long. The knob on the back door jiggles and I spin that way just as Myra knocks on the glass between us. She gives me a wave.

I flip the lock and open the door. "Where in the hell did you come from?"

"I was across the street talking to Felicity." She closes and locks the door, the alarm beeping as it resets.

I point toward the front of the house. "I didn't hear the gate alarm."

Myra waves me off. "I don't use the gate. I can never remember the code."

I'm starting to realize Myra learned a lot of tricks in her time, figuring out ways to get around locks and alarms. Whether they're put in place for control or protection is irrelevant to her. "Then how did you get into the yard?"

"I jumped the fence." She lifts one leg, kicking it out to the side in demonstration. "And it's way easier to do when you're not wearing a dress that goes down to your ankles."

Myra's obviously not worried about her husband or father coming to find her, but those aren't the only men I'm currently concerned might show up on my doorstep. I still haven't heard a peep from Rodney's friends since one of them tried to knock down Piper and Lydia's door. And it's starting to worry me. They aren't patient men. It's been too quiet for too long. Something is coming soon.

"You need to be careful." It's a blanket statement. One that doesn't give away too much information, but hopefully it's enough to make her a little more cautious. Myra still doesn't know the lengths Lydia was willing to go to for her, and I'm not going to be the one to offer that information up. At least not yet.

Myra stands a little taller, much more blatant in her defiance than Lydia is. "I'm done living the life someone else wants me to live, and that means I'm done letting them control me in any way. She pulls an item from the hidden pocket in her borrowed leggings. "And if anybody tries to grab me, they will regret it."

I don't need to ask where she got the taser, I already know.

But that is another conversation I'm leaving until tomorrow. I'm exhausted. Lydia is exhausted.

And I want her all to myself after having to share her attention all day.

"We're going to bed." I gesture at the kitchen lights. "Can you take care of these when you come up?"

"Sure." Myra reaches out to stop me before I get very far. "Thank you for letting me stay here. I really do appreciate it."

I didn't know Myra as well as I knew Lydia. Looking back, maybe it's because she's always been as independent as she seems to be now. But I still know what she's been through, and regardless of how it seems to have affected her or not, I recognize the difficulties she's faced. "You can stay here's long as you like."

Myra glances at Lydia before refocusing on me. "Okay." There's an offness in her tone, but it's one more thing I'm not fucking dealing with right now. I'm maxed out, so I just nod before directing Lydia toward the stairs.

Her eyes jump to mine in surprise when we start up them. "Where are we going?"

"Jill and the rest of her group were nice enough to handle a furniture delivery today." We reach the top of the stairs and I point at the room at the end of the hall. "Now there's another bedroom set up next to Piper's. It's got a brand-new bed, an attached bathroom, and a television. They helped Myra get all settled in, so the master bedroom is now ours."

Lydia's brows lift. "Ours?"

"Are you going to pretend you forgot what I said?" I pull her into my bedroom, *our* bedroom, shutting the door and locking us in. "Because I'm positive you know exactly what I mean."

I'm not a kid anymore. Haven't been for a long time. I grew up fast, but it took me longer than most to really grasp what I wanted from my life. Maybe because for so many years I expected I would have to settle for what I got instead of chasing after what I wanted. But then the lives of the men around me started to change and I began to hope I could have more.

I could have this.

Someone who understands me. Knows my past. What's turned me into the man I am. I struggled to believe I'd be able to find a woman who wouldn't judge me for the things I've done, but I have. Lydia's seen the best and the worst I have to offer, and she embraces all of it.

The only problem is I don't know if Lydia is in the same place I am. If she wants the same things. Myra clearly wants to spread her wings and fly. Maybe Lydia does too.

I meet her gaze, my stomach turning at the possibility. "If this isn't what you want, you need to speak up now."

Lydia licks her lips before rubbing them together. "And what exactly does *this* mean?"

"You and me. Together." I lace my fingers with hers, lifting them to my lips. "I want you living here with me. I want you in my bed at night. I want you to be mine and I want to be yours." She needs to know this isn't a one-way deal. That I'm not planning to take anything I'm not willing to offer.

Lydia is quiet for a minute, eyes staying on my face. "Okay."

I like that she's agreeing, but I know her well enough not to take it at face value. "Do you mean that, or are you just telling me what you think I want to hear?"

Lydia smiles, the expression bright as it blooms across her face. "I feel like maybe you've got me figured out." Her eyes drop to my chest as she lifts one hand to toy with the fabric of my shirt. "And, I do really mean it." She pauses, expression thoughtful. "Since I moved to Memphis, I've felt like I haven't been doing the things I should. I wasn't dating. I wasn't partying. I wasn't running wild the way I expected I would." Her eyes come to mine. "I felt bad about it for a long time, but I finally understand I genuinely don't want to do any of those things. And I'm done feeling like that makes me a failure."

My lips twitch with the urge to smile. I'm so fucking proud of her and so goddamned relieved. "So what I'm hearing is you're willing to settle for me so you can avoid all the dating and partying."

Lydia nods, her expression solemn. "Yes, but I'm sure I'll be able to cope with it somehow."

"Cope? I'll show you cope." I loop her arm behind my head, bending over to press my shoulder into her belly before standing up, carrying her down the hall and across our room as she squeals, to deposit her right in the center of my bed.

The bed I might never let her leave.

Lydia cackles as I drop her down onto the sheets, her head tipped back as she laughs. "It's a sacrifice, but someone has to make it."

The lightness of her words eases a little of the tightness still weighing on my chest. I crawl over her body and nose along her neck, breathing deep as I savor the moment. "I appreciate the selflessness you're showing."

Lydia loops her arms around my neck as her knees bracket my hips, allowing my body to settle between her thighs. "I guess it won't be so bad now that I don't have to sleep on that air mattress." She traces one finger along my chin, her dark eyes moving over my face. "You know, you grew up to be really handsome."

"Did I?" I catch the tip of her finger between my teeth,

raking gently across her skin before setting it free. "Tell me more."

Lydia tilts her head to one side. "I guess you're a pretty good singer too." She tries to flatten out her smile, but it keeps sneaking through.

"You're talking an awful lot about shit that doesn't really matter." I skim one hand along her belly, teasing under the hem of her shirt to stroke over her soft skin.

"I would say there's a whole lot of women here in Memphis who would argue that your looks and voice matter a hell of a lot." Her lower lip pushes out the tiniest bit. "I saw all the panties that landed at your feet when you played the other night."

"Are you jealous, Lydia?" I drag my hand higher, sliding my fingers over the band of her bra. "Because if you remember, I only asked one woman to come home with me that night." I nip at the line of her jaw before leaning into her ear. "And she turned me down."

Lydia sucks in a breath as I drag my thumb across her nipple, teasing it through the thin fabric of her bra. "Knowing what I know now, that might have been the wrong decision."

I smile against her skin as I work her shirt up her body. I want to feel her. I want to taste her. I want Lydia to see how good it will be being mine. "I'm happy to know you've learned from your mistakes."

"Me too." Lydia lifts her arms over her head and it's the only encouragement I need. I drag her t-shirt free then make quick work of the rest of her clothing, sending it over the edge of the bed, running my mouth over all the skin I've exposed.

Lydia grabs at my shirt as I lick along the line of her

collarbone, yanking at the fabric. "Why do you always keep so many clothes on?"

I chuckle as she tangles me in the neckline, strangling me a little. "Always?" I lean back before she cuts off enough air to steal a few of the brain cells I can't afford to lose, yanking the garment free. "You're being pretty broad with that word." I push up to my knees, keeping my eyes on hers as I unfasten my belt, dragging it free of the loops before tossing it away. "Because I'm pretty sure I remember being completely naked the night you worked that pretty little pussy onto my cock."

Lydia's eyes drop to the front of my pants, locking in place as I unbutton my jeans and drag down the zipper. "But you kept your pants on last night."

"So I'm fifty-fifty." I shove at my pants, pushing them down my hips, cock springing free, hard and eager. I smirk as I kick the jeans away. "Now I'm two out of three."

Lydia continues staring at my dick, eyes widening. "Are you keeping track?"

"I am now." I slide over her, dragging my body against hers until our faces are lined up. "Can't have you being the only one who knows our statistics."

Lydia laughs again. It should be so out of place, but it's fucking perfect.

She's perfect.

This is perfect.

I catch her lips with mine, stealing that smile for myself as I rock against the heat of her body, dragging my cock along her slit.

The mood between us shifts on a dime and Lydia widens her knees, opening her body up to mine. Her hands flutter over my chest, their touch soft and fleeting, as if she can't decide where to put them.

I snag one, dragging it back to rest it on my ass, pressing it into my body as I rock against her again. Her free hand locks onto my other ass cheek, fingers digging in as she pulls me in again, sliding my cock along her hot, slick cunt.

"Christian I want—" She stops short of making a request.

And I'm not pushing her tonight, so I decide to finish it for her. "You want me to fuck you?"

"Yes." The word is breathy, like she's relieved.

"Were you worried I didn't know what you wanted, Lydia?" I reach for my nightstand, grabbing a condom while keeping my mouth against her ear. "You should know me better than that." I drag my lips down her neck, nipping at her soft skin as I work the condom into place.

I planned to take my time with her the first time she was in my bed, but the way she's digging her heels and hands into my backside, fighting to get me where she wants me, makes it clear she's not on the same page. And that's fine. Because we have all the time in the world to fuck every way there is.

Lydia won't just be in my bed tonight and tomorrow, but the next night too. And the night after that.

And every night beyond.

I tease the tip of my cock against her clit, rubbing back and forth until my sweet, soft Lydia sinks her nails into my skin and growls out a handful of words that steal any sanity I might still possess. "Fuck me now."

I drag my dick lower, positioning it before sinking into the heat of her welcoming body with a ragged groan. I bracket her throat with one hand, tipping her head to the side as I pull back and thrust again. "What was that you said?"

Lydia only whimpers in response, her hands still gripping my ass as I set an unforgiving pace. One that has her so wet our bodies make sloppy sounds as they slide together, her hips meeting each thrust I make.

"I think you like asking for what you want from me, don't you?" I grit my teeth as the moment threatens to overwhelm me. Threatens to take me out before we've even really started.

Something tells me I might need to get used to it.

From day one I've been at her mercy. She's been the only thing I can focus on. The only thing I care about.

The only thing that matters.

Lydia's lids lift, her eyes meeting mine as I rock into her willing body, each stroke more difficult to sustain than the last. I can't look away. Can't make myself break the connection we have. I need it. Crave it. Will do anything to keep it. Beg. Borrow.

Kill.

Lydia whimpers, gripping me tighter. "Christian." Her heels dig into the backs of my thighs as her hips rock, trying to get closer, reminding me she needs more.

But I want her to say it. I want her to know she can ask me for anything. *Demand* anything.

I catch one of her legs behind the knee, pushing it out to the side as I change the angle of my body to tease her with what she's aching for. "Tell me what you want, Lydia."

She whines, writhing under me in an attempt to obtain what she's seeking without having to actually ask. So I grip her hip, pinning it in place, holding her hooded gaze. "Say it." I punctuate the demand with a slow thrust, dragging my body against hers as I move.

Lydia lets out a low moan, shuddering as I grind against her clit. "Please."

"So fucking sweet." I lean down to nip her lower lip.

"But you don't have to use that word with me, Lydia. Not ever." I go still, balls deep in the hot, tight well of her cunt. "What do you want? I want to hear it."

She whimpers, still fighting the hold I have on her hip. After a few fruitless seconds, she glares at me. Eyes narrowed, nostrils flared. "I want to come."

I smile, proud and amused and fucking turned on as hell. "Good girl."

I release her hip and catch her hand, lacing our fingers together as I press it into the mattress above her head, my hips working in those long, dragging thrusts she loves so much. I barely make it thirty seconds before my balls are pulling tight and the base of my spine is aching with the need to come. Being with Lydia is like nothing else, and it tests my stamina in the best of ways.

With her it's not just about getting off, seeking a needed release. I don't want to be released. I want to be tied. Dragged closer. Pulled in and attached. Connected in more than just a physical way.

And that changes everything. In good ways and bad.

Lydia's legs jerk where they're wedged against my hips, flexing tight as her breath hitches and her hand grips mine, sending relief flooding through me. She's close. I just have to make it a little longer.

But I can't.

I'm fighting a losing battle and a split second later my cock swells as the climax I've been trying to delay edges closer. It takes all the focus I have to keep my pace instead of pistoning into her warmth and riding out the wave threatening to drown me.

But then my sweet, soft Lydia growls out one, blessed word.

"Harder."

It breaks me, snaps my control and resolve, unleashing what I've tried desperately to contain.

With a ragged groan I pin her body to mine, chasing the bliss I never expected would be mine as she clings to me, her body locked tight as the clench of her cunt fists around me in the most perfect fucking grip I've ever felt.

It's the same hold she has on the rest of me, and God help anyone who tries to take her from me.

Because I will willingly go to the depths of hell to bring her back.

27

LYDIA

WAKING UP IN Christian's bed should be strange. Technically, I've woken up with him a few mornings in a row now, but this is the first time it's in his bed. In his room. It's different, but not weird. It feels oddly normal. Comfortable.

Mostly.

Unfortunately, even though I generally wake up grumpy and groggy, I can't make myself sleep in. So, even though it's barely past six, I'm wide awake and in desperate need of a trip to the bathroom.

I wiggle my way free of the heavy arm draped at my waist, and I'm a little surprised when Christian barely stirs. He's probably exhausted. Technically, I am too. But twenty years of getting up at dawn has basically programmed me to wake up without an alarm, so I slide out of bed and make my way to the large bathroom I think is now also mine.

I've been in it before, but this time it seems different. Probably because I'm looking at it as more than just a place I'm visiting. Now it's a place I'll be for a while.

Maybe forever.

The possibility isn't as offensive as I always felt like it should be. When I moved to Memphis, I believed I should start an entirely different life. One completely free of any of the old limitations put on me by cowardly men. But that's not what happened.

Creating a new life also meant creating a new me, and that's where I stumbled. I ended up spending a year feeling guilty and ashamed, thinking I was failing to move forward. Believing I was still caught in my past. But now I'm not so sure that was really it.

Maybe I genuinely want many of the things I felt like I should be rebuking. Maybe I don't want to date around. Maybe I don't want to spend nights at the club and mornings nursing a hangover. Maybe I'm more like the woman I was taught to be than I initially wanted to admit.

Maybe I really do want to get married and be a mom and cook dinner and do the laundry—I just don't want it forced down my throat. I want to do it because that's what I choose. Because it's what I want.

And I want to do it with a man who sees me as an equal instead of another possession. A man like Christian.

I do my business, brushing my teeth and fluffing my hair, smiling a little at the hickey hidden just below the neckline of Christian's company T-shirt I wore as a nightgown.

Last night was—not what I believed sex could ever be. It was hot. It was exciting. It was intense.

It was also fun. Liberating in a way I never imagined sex could be. The experience was amazing.

And enlightening.

It's added yet another piece to the puzzle I've been trying to put together for the past year, filling in enough of the spaces I'm finally starting to feel like I can see who I really am and what I really want. The life I want to live.

And I definitely want Christian to be a part of it.

I open the bathroom door, peeking out, hoping he's awake. I pout a little when I see he's still completely sacked out, face slack with sleep.

I guess if this is my home now, I can go downstairs and make some coffee. Have some breakfast. Get comfortable in a house that already feels safe and warm and inviting.

Tiptoeing across the thick carpet, I quietly open the door and creep out into the hallway. Once downstairs, my bare feet move silently over the hardwood of the main floor as I pad into the kitchen. I brew myself up a cup of coffee, following the directions Christian gave Myra yesterday, then dig through the refrigerator, figuring out what I want to eat. It's a pretty simple process considering everyone left the remnants of yesterday's impromptu breakfast party. I zero in on Jill's egg bake and Carly's French toast casserole—which her husband apparently made—and scoop some of each onto a plate, setting it in the microwave to cook.

Grabbing the plate right before the timer beeps, I sit down on a stool at the island and dig in, scrolling through my phone. I smile when I notice I have quite a few new friend requests from the same women responsible for my morning meal. I accept all of them and spend a little time being nosy, poking through photos of Christian's brothers and their families.

With breakfast devoured and the dishes loaded into the dishwasher, I'm just wiping down the counter when Piper comes in. I glance at the clock on the microwave, a little shocked. "What are you doing awake?"

She shuffles to the stool I just vacated, sliding into the seat before catching her face in her hands. The motion squishes her cheeks, pursing out her lips and distorting her words. "I can't sleep." She sighs. "I think Stella's going to fire me."

"Did she say that?" I'm a little concerned myself, not because I believe our boss genuinely wants to fire Piper, but because she might not have much of a choice. Technically the guy Piper stunned didn't put his hands on anyone, so she's caught in a gray area. Lots of things could go either way, including her lack of an arrest record and her long-term career prospects.

"No, but she seemed pretty upset." Piper snags my coffee cup and peeks inside, frowning when she finds it empty. "I don't know what I'll do if she fires me. Bartending is all I've ever done. Plus, how do I explain that my last job canned me because I tased a customer in the crotch?"

"Hopefully the fact that they didn't officially charge you with anything will be helpful." I snag a new coffee cup and load it onto the machine, dropping in a pod before setting it to brew. "Maybe this will all blow over and everything will go back to normal."

Almost everything. I don't want to kick Piper while she's down, so I decide not to mention Christian wants me to move in with him.

Actually, it wasn't so much a request as it was him more or less saying I *will* be living with him. And I don't particularly want to disagree with his demand. It's one of many things I'm finally willing to admit I actually enjoy.

I like how decisive he is. I like that he knows what he wants and isn't afraid to voice it. It's making me feel a little more confident about admitting my own desires. My own wants.

While also finally admitting to the things I don't.

"I hope that's what happens." Piper gives me a weak smile.

I'm not used to seeing my friend down like this. She's always happy. Always upbeat. Always positive and looking at the bright side. This melancholy bothers me and I want to fix it. To help her the way she's helped me.

I finish mixing up her coffee before sliding in front of her. "Let's go do something fun today. Maybe we can go shopping or go out to lunch."

Piper shrugs. "Sure." She takes a sip of her coffee, closing her eyes as she swallows it down. "That's really good. Christian has a better coffee maker than we do." She opens her eyes and looks at me. "I guess it won't be so bad if Stella fires me. I'll just move in here with you and use his good coffee maker."

It's not a completely terrible thought, and somehow I don't think Christian would mind if Piper hung around for a while. "Everything has a silver lining."

I glance toward the hall. "I should see if Myra wants to come with us. She mentioned she wanted to get some new clothes."

"I'm willing to bet she'll say yes. She seems ready to move on with her life." Piper takes another sip of her coffee. "I was surprised she was already out of bed when I got up."

I snap my head in Piper's direction. "What do you mean she was out of bed?"

Piper's coffee cup hovers in front of her lips, suspended in place. "Her bed was made when I got up this morning. I figured you'd already talked to her and she was across the street hanging out with one of the girls."

I shake my head. "I haven't seen her." I'm glad Myra is acclimating so well, especially now that I'm not as actively comparing our lives, but I don't like that she's going out alone without telling anyone where she's at. "I'll be right back."

Piper slides from her stool. "I'm not just going to sit here while you guys get to hang out and have fun." She carries her coffee cup with her as we move to the front of the house.

I unlock the front door and open it, security system beeping as I step out onto the porch I found scary not so long ago. Granted, it's currently well-lit instead of dark and shadowy, but even at night Christian's home no longer intimidates me the way it once did.

The ivy still needs to go though.

Piper follows me down the stairs, drinking her coffee as we make our way along the sidewalk in our bare feet and pajamas. I'm relieved to see Myra headed our way. She smiles brightly, offering up a wave. "Good morning."

I unlock the gate, punching in the passcode before pulling it open and stepping out onto the sidewalk. "Where were you?"

Myra crosses the street, looking so unlike the sister I grew up with in one of Piper's borrowed sundresses and a pair of wedge sandals. She sighs loudly. "I can't seem to stop waking up at five in the morning. Felicity told me she's always up at five with her daughter, so I went over to have coffee with her."

"I guess it's good you guys can keep each other company then." I'm really glad Myra is making friends, but she's acting like everything that happened to her is done and over with. And maybe it is.

Maybe Rodney's friends will figure he met an early and deserved demise and go on with their lives. Maybe her divorce will be quick and easy and painless. Maybe her transition into the normal world will be seamless and satisfying.

But what if it's not?

"I wish you would leave me a note or something. So I

know where you are." I reach for her as she steps up onto the sidewalk, grabbing her hand with mine. "I worry about you. I just want to be sure—"

The sound of an engine revving catches my attention.

Myra, Piper, and I all turn at the same time to look down the street as a large, black SUV barrels toward us.

Myra's hand tightens in mine and her skin goes pale. "Run."

I turn, fully intending to race back through the gate and lock it behind us, but I only make it a few steps.

The SUV screeches to a stop only a few feet away and the doors fly open. The faces of the men who jump out are devastatingly familiar and send my stomach sinking.

Hard hands grab me with enough force to leave bruises, dragging me toward the open doors of the vehicle. I try to dig my bare feet into the cement, but they fail to find purchase, the rough texture peeling away the skin of my soles as my brother drags me away.

I glance over as Myra screams, the sound cut short when Matthias backhands her across the face. He hits her with enough force that her body slumps, crumpling toward the ground. He picks her up, all but throwing her into the same back seat I'm being stuffed into.

To her credit, Piper doesn't go down without a fight. Some people are all bark and no bite, but she isn't afraid to sink her teeth in. Literally. She swings her coffee cup, the ceramic shattering when it hits its mark, dumping the caramel-colored liquid into my father's hair and down his pristine white shirt. When that's not enough to secure her freedom, she clamps down on his arm, face scrunched up with the force she's using as he howls in pain, trying to shake her free.

Some other time it might be a satisfying thing to witness,

but right now I'm just terrified. Afraid for my sister. Afraid for Piper. Afraid for myself.

And all I can think about is the warning Christian gave me about what happens when women return to abusive men.

About how dangerous it can be.

I can only imagine it's even worse when that dangerous man hunts a woman down and drags her into his car kicking and screaming.

Along with two somewhat innocent bystanders.

Unfortunately, despite her best efforts, Piper ends up thrown across the back seat along with me and Myra, the three of us squeezed in between my brother and my brother-in-law. My father climbs back into the driver's seat, huffing and puffing. There's blood running down his arm from where Piper did her best to take a chunk out, and a sheen of sweat glistens across his face from the first effort he's put into much of anything besides furthering his own ambitions.

But technically that's probably what this is too. He certainly didn't come to get Myra because he misses her and loves her and wants what's best for her.

The soles of my feet sting and feel a little sticky against the mat beneath them, making me cringe at the damage I did trying to avoid landing exactly where I am. But it's nothing compared to what happened to Myra. She's conscious, but her eyes are glazed and unfocused and her head keeps lolling back and forth as the car races away. Hopefully it's just shock, but, either way, any hope of escape rests squarely on my and Piper's shoulders.

Unfortunately my partner in crime is new to this particular game.

Piper shifts around beside me, smacking at my brother

as he tries to keep her pinned in place. "Get your goddamn hands off me you creep."

I brace, preparing for what I know is happening next, hating I can't warn her fast enough so at least she'll know it's coming.

My brother slaps her across the face, the sound echoing through the interior of the SUV. Then he leans in, nose almost touching Piper's. "Don't take the Lord's name in vain."

I want to grab her. Tell her to shut up. To play along. To be sweet. But I don't have the chance. In true Piper fashion, she winds up and lands a right hook in the center of his face, swinging her body as much as the confined space will allow. And obviously it's enough, because when it connects it makes a sickening crunching sound and blood shoots from both of his nostrils.

It's a deserved hit, but nowhere near as satisfying as the look of shock on his face. My brother has lived a life filled with agreeable women, so being faced with one who's not afraid of him must be one heck of a mind fuck.

"Keep them in line. If you can't control a woman, how are you supposed to lead a church?" My father starts spewing the nonsense fed to me for breakfast, lunch, and dinner my whole life. And somehow it flips a switch.

Maybe it's knowing Piper has my back. Maybe it's knowing if Myra was coherent she would too. Or maybe I just want to make sure Christian's proud of me when he saves me. Because I know without a shadow of a doubt he *will* save me. He always has. He always will.

So I turn to my piece of shit brother-in-law and swing an elbow, catching him right in the cheekbone. I was worried the lack of wiggle room would work against me, but it actually ends up being pretty damn beneficial. Piper and I are significantly smaller than our adversaries, which means we get more momentum going. And when my brother-in-law manages to recover and tries to grab me, I'm able to get one leg up and kick, catching him in the forearm hard enough to slam his fist back against the window.

He yelps, face crumpled in pain, confirming that kicking is a great option. So I do it again, this time thrusting my scuffed and bleeding bare foot right at the center of his chest, using as much force as I can muster up.

I hear a scuffle beside me, but I'm twisted in my seat with my back to Piper, so all I can do is tell myself she's probably managing to accomplish twice what I am. And it seems like I'm accomplishing quite a bit because Matthias is clutching his chest and struggling to take a breath. I take advantage of his temporary incapacitation and knock the heel of my hand at his nose, just like I learned in the single self-defense class Piper dragged me to.

It's barely connected when the SUV jerks to one side, jumping up over a curb as my father spins in his seat, spittle flying from his mouth as he recites some sort of scripture meant to scare and intimidate me into submission.

It won't work. Not just because I refuse to let him intimidate me, but also because I can't seem to hear anything. There's screaming and yelling and tires screeching and someone honking and it's all muddled together in one overwhelming cacophony that makes it impossible to decipher any one sound.

Until the car bounces again and comes to a sudden and violent stop.

Then everything gets very quiet. And very, very dark.

28

CHRISTIAN

I ROLL OVER in bed, disappointed Lydia managed to peel her body from mine during the night. I reach for her, intending to drag her back against me so I can finish waking up holding her close—and maybe with my hand between her thighs—but my reaching arm only meets empty sheets.

Squinting my eyes open to glare at the spot beside me, I sit up and press my palm into the still slightly warm bedding. She hasn't been gone long, but that doesn't make me feel any better. She shouldn't be gone at all.

I kick away the blankets and get up, making a quick trip to the bathroom before pulling on a pair of jeans and a T-shirt. It's not only Lydia and me in my house for now, so retrieving her in just my underwear isn't an option.

Just as I finish pulling my T-shirt into place, the security system beeps, making the short alert it offers when one of the outside doors is opened and closed. I groan. If Jill has shown up again to steal more of my time with Lydia I'm going to—

I'm not going to do shit. I'm going to let her love Lydia the way she deserves to be loved. Her own mother was always entirely focused on seeing to her ass of a father's needs, so I can't imagine Lydia's ever had someone like Jill around to take care of her. If Jill's smiling face greets me, I'll suck it up and wait my turn.

Impatiently.

I open the bedroom door and start down the stairs, expecting the sound of female voices to carry through the hall, but my house is eerily silent. Too quiet considering I have at least three women under my roof.

Reaching the bottom of the stairs, I shove my feet into the pair of boots next to the door, glancing around as I tie the laces, just in case she ventured across the street to one of my brothers' homes. "Lydia?" I listen for a response before calling for her sister even though I doubt it was Myra who set the alarm off. She's learned to be sneaky as hell. "Myra?"

Nothing.

The windows flanking the front door only offer a blurry view of the street outside, so I go to the door and pull it open, not even noticing the beep of the security system this time. Because all my focus goes to an expensive SUV pulled up in front of my house. The tinted windows offer no hint of who is inside. But I don't need to see their faces to know who's got enough balls to show up on my doorstep thinking they can take what belongs to me.

I race down the steps and along the neglected sidewalk, scaling the fence like Myra does to avoid wasting time, but I'm still not fast enough. The SUV is pulling away before my feet hit the cement, tires squealing against the asphalt like they think they'll be able to move fast enough to escape me.

They won't.

I stand in place for just a second, watching the retreating vehicle long enough that whoever's looking in the rearview mirror knows I've seen them. If they're smart they'll know I'm coming for them and rethink their plans. But smarts aren't what's gotten Ansel Parks where he is. All his power was gained through threats and intimidation, and he's about to discover they won't save his ass when I get my hands on him.

Even though it takes everything I have to pull my eyes from where I know Lydia is, I turn, jumping the fence and skipping the steps completely on my way back inside. I hit the panic button on my security system, setting off the alarm, letting it wail as I grab my cell phone and keys on the way out the back door. My phone's ringing before I'm in my car and I connect the call as I pull out of the garage.

"Please tell me Piper accidentally set your alarm off." Tate is out of breath on the other end of the line.

"A black SUV just pulled away from the front of my house and all three girls are gone." I speed through the gate as it opens, scanning the road and sidewalks to make sure they're clear of my nieces and nephews. "It's headed east. Brand-new Escalade with tinted windows." I hit the gas, revving the engine higher than normal to gain speed before I shift into the next gear. "And Arkansas plates."

Tate swears. "I don't know if that's the lesser of two evils or not." I hear an engine start on the other end of the line as he starts his own SUV. "I'm right behind you. I'll make sure Simon is right behind me."

The call disconnects and I drop my cell into the console, completely focused on the road in front of me as I watch for any sign of the SUV. I don't know how in the fuck Ansel found the girls' location, but he and whoever's with him are going to regret their decision to come to my front door.

I fly through a red light, clearing the intersection right as the only car headed my way lays on their horn like they think I give a shit. I don't even glance their way. I'm looking for one thing and one thing only. The SUV with Lydia inside of it.

A glance in my rearview mirror confirms Tate's already caught up with me, closing in fast. I wish his presence made me feel better, calmer, but right now the urge to cause pain is strong. The need to dish out retribution the way I know best is almost as consuming as the need to protect Lydia. Once I finally get my hands on the piece of shit men who tried to break Lydia, they'll be begging their God to take them.

I doubt he'll be interested in collecting.

A flash of brake lights up ahead catches my attention and sends my foot closer to the floor, pushing the limits of safety and sanity. I don't care. The only thing that matters is getting to her. Protecting her.

Proving I'm the same now as I was all those years ago, even if it's only in this small way.

Tate is right behind me as the Escalade comes into view, offering me a front row seat as it jumps the curb, bouncing across the sidewalk toward a steep hillside cutting down to a wet-weather creek bed.

My stomach drops as I watch, unable to tear my eyes away when the out-of-control vehicle starts to tip. There's no way for me to stop it. All I can do is stare helplessly, heart in my throat, as it starts to roll. It happens in slow motion, dragging out the worst moment of my life, forcing me to bear witness as the future I've finally started to weave unravels before my eyes.

I jerk to a stop, barely remembering to set the emergency break as I jump out. Tate's tires screech behind me as he comes to a similar stop and follows me down the hill. The SUV rests on its roof, wheels continuing to spin as I skid through the overgrowth, sliding my way toward Lydia, unsure of what I'm going to find.

She has to be alive. It's the only possibility I'm willing to consider.

If she's not...

Something hits the side window, planting against the tinted glass with a thud, stalling out my heart. Momentum carries me the rest of the way, slamming me into the side of the Escalade with enough force to make me see stars, but I don't stop. I yank at the handle of the door, but the panel is caved in and crumpled, making it impossible to open.

"Stand back." The voice on the other side is muffled, but the determination in it gives me hope.

I lean away just as something smashes into one corner, splitting the safety glass into a spiderweb of cracks. The hit is hard and effective and forces me a step back. Tate slides down the hill behind me, managing to stop within a foot of where I stand as the tempered glass shatters, stabbed through by some sort of metal rods. The bulk of the pieces drop to the grass but the edges remain in place, stuck to the film of tint still covering the space.

"Fucking fuck." A hand shoves at the black cling, tearing more away. Piper leans through the opening she's made, her face bloody and bruised, the headrest from one of the front seats gripped in her hands. "Get us the hell out of here."

Tate pushes past me, going straight for the handle I just wrestled unsuccessfully, but instead of simply yanking on it like I did, he leans in to open the lock then braces one foot against the side and wrestles it open, muscles straining as he fights the damaged door. To my relief it opens, protesting the whole way, and Piper tumbles out, looking a little beat up and mad as shit.

He scoops her up as I shove my way into the opening.

There's an unconscious man with a familiar face piled in my way so I grab him by the shirt and drag him free, rolling his soft, pasty body into the weeds before reaching in for the only thing I care about.

I grit my teeth at the trickle of blood sliding from Lydia's split lip as I carefully pull her from the wreckage. Her dark eyes are dazed and a little unfocused, but the smile she gives me is bright and clear.

I resist the urge to plant my boot into her brother's ribs as I pass him on my way up the hill, barely noticing Simon as he races past us to retrieve Myra, relieving me of that duty.

"I knew you were coming." Lydia loops her arms around my neck as I fight my way back up the incline, unwilling to put her down for even a second. "That's why I fought so hard. I wanted you to be proud of me when you got here." Her smile is a little lopsided, but still bright enough to ease some of the tension making it hard to breathe. "That and I knew Piper would be pissed if she was the only one throwing hands." Lydia's smile falters as she twists in my arms, eyes swinging across the landscape. "Where is Piper? Is she okay? She didn't get hurt breaking the window, did she?"

"Piper's with Tate." I should probably be worried about her too, but I'm not. She's not my priority right now and I know she's in good hands. Even if she doesn't realize it. "I'm sure she's okay."

Lydia lets out a little sigh, her smile coming back. "Good."

I hug her closer as I struggle to maintain my balance. "And I would have been proud of you no matter what happened."

Lydia curls closer. "I knew that, but I also wanted to be

proud of myself. I wanted to show them I wasn't just going to lay back and accept what they were doing." Her expression falls, lips flattening in disappointment. "I do kind of wish I was the one who got to break Jeremiah's nose though." She lifts one shoulder in a little shrug. "I guess all that matters is he found out not all women will put up with his shit. Hopefully it will make him rethink his life choices."

I doubt it, but I don't want to ruin this moment for Lydia. It's clear whatever happened in that SUV has left her feeling empowered and in control, and I won't take that from her. I won't let *anyone* take that from her. "He'll have plenty of time to think over lots of shit while he's in jail."

Lydia's eyes open wide, fixing on my face. "You think he'll go to jail for this?"

The possibility soothes an old ache I expected to carry forever. "Oh yeah. All three of those motherfuckers are going to jail." Members of the IGL rarely face the consequences of their actions, but there's no escaping this. I'll make sure of it.

"I don't think so." Lydia's lips press into a frown. "Matthias works in the prosecutor's office. That's why my dad married Myra off to him. He wanted to make sure he stayed in the church so they could use him to stay out of trouble."

I reach the top of the hill, my steps stalling out on the shoulder of the road. "Matthias is that well-connected?" In the fifteen years I've been out, I haven't spent too much time looking back—watching what the IGL was doing in my absence. It was too painful, especially after what happened to my sister.

The group had always been tight knit and members protected each other, which is how I assumed my sister's husband got away with what he did. He claimed what happened was an accident and everyone else backed him up, filling in any blanks until her death was explained away. It never occurred to me they might also have someone working within the system, but that explains why all my calls and pleas for justice were blown off and ignored.

Lydia's jaw goes slack, eyes wide and clear as they meet mine. "They can't hide this." Her hand grips the front of my shirt as the pitch of her voice rises in excitement. "They can't just make this go away."

I shake my head, smiling in spite of all that's happened in the past fifteen minutes. "No. They can't." I sag against my car, using it for support, keeping Lydia pinned to my chest as a level of relief I've never experienced steals my strength. "We've got cameras all over the street. Every bit of what happened is recorded."

There's no one here to lie for them. No one to cover their asses. It's finally time to pay for all they've done.

The sound of sirens carries through the air as Simon breaches the crest of the hill, carefully carrying a bruised and swollen Myra. Lydia straightens in my arms, focus snapping to her sister. I begrudgingly begin to set her down, knowing she'll want to make sure Myra's okay, but the second Lydia's foot touches the asphalt she cries out, her hold on me tightening as she gives me all her weight. "Shit. I forgot about my feet." She winces a little, curling one leg to take a peek at the sole of her foot. The skin is red and inflamed with lines of drying blood smeared across it.

"That looks like road rash." I straighten, glancing over the edge of the hill, questioning if I have enough time to make it down to get in a few good swings of my own before the cops arrive. But doing that would involve leaving Lydia's side, and apparently the thought of that carries more weight than whatever joy I would get out of knocking her brother and father's heads together.

"Here." Carefully balancing her weight, I wedge one leg under her ass so I can free up my hand enough to open the passenger's door and ease her into the seat before going back to dig my first-aid kit from the trunk. I kneel down in front of her, draping her feet over one bent knee as the first police cruiser arrives.

Lydia explains the situation to the collection of cops who continue to arrive as I clean her feet, doing my best to soothe her discomfort until the ambulance shows up. Unfortunately, Piper is in worse shape than Lydia, so when the medics arrive she's the one loaded into the back so her clearly broken ankle can be stabilized. I don't leave Lydia's side as she fills out statements and does her best to calm an inconsolable Myra. Once we can finally leave, I take both women to the hospital where Piper is being treated, insisting Lydia let them tend to her feet while we wait. Once she's bandaged up, we all pile into Piper's curtained-off room, waiting for orthopedics to set the broken bone of her ankle.

The day wears on and after one adorable but particularly large yawn, Lydia turns to me while Piper and Myra doze. "You don't have to stay. I can call you when we're done."

"Not happening." I hold out the bottle of water I've been forcing down her for the past hour.

She takes it from me and swallows down an obliging drink. "I'm serious. I know you can't be comfortable in that chair and—

I lean in, nose almost touching hers. "Sweetheart, you're going to be lucky if I let you out of my sight in the next six months."

29

LYDIA

"I'M SO SORRY. I just couldn't ignore the call." Myra sits on Christian's couch, wiping her eyes with the crumpled wad of tissues in her hand. "I thought it would be okay. I didn't think I was on the phone long enough for them to ping it."

I pull her into my side, squeezing her shoulders as I prop the side of my head against the top of hers. "It's not your fault. You haven't done anything wrong."

This is what I was expecting Myra's escape to be like. Me comforting her. Reassuring her. Helping her get over all that happened. Her carefree attitude definitely threw me off at first, but now I hate that it's been stolen from her. Hate that she now feels the same sort of guilt I struggled with for so long.

Myra takes a shuddering breath, the inhale hitching as she fights for air. "It is my fault though. I know better. I know how they are and I still turned on my phone." Her face crumples, fresh tears sliding from the corners of her eyes. "But I just couldn't leave them hanging. Not when they want so badly to get away."

Christian stands in the kitchen, watching where Myra, Piper, and I sit together on the sofa, banged up and exhausted, but safe and relatively whole.

It's more than I can say for the other three occupants of the car, and that makes me smile.

"I understand." I wipe at her wet cheeks. I don't point out that we could have gotten her a new phone. Could have switched over all the numbers and she'd have been able to contact anyone she wanted without fear of being discovered. It will only make Myra feel worse and remind her that no matter how much she wants to believe she's ready to jump into this world with both feet, the water might be a little deeper than she thought.

Christian studies me for a minute, his hand clenching into a fist at his side before he turns to where Tate and Simon stand with him, lowering his head and his voice as they have a conversation I know I'll hear about later. Christian won't hide anything from me. Whatever they're discussing, he will share it with me. Just like I'll explain everything Myra has confessed to me.

About how she wasn't the only woman ready to leave. About how she promised she would come back for the other women desperate to find freedom. And, because I know Christian, I know Myra won't be going back for them alone.

Piper nods off on my other side, her head dropping to the cushion as she dozes thanks to the lingering effects of twilight sedation and pain meds. Hopefully I can sleep soon too. It's nearly midnight and my head is starting to swim. Between talking to the police and our time at the hospital, we've lost the entire day to three men who don't deserve a second of our time.

I wish I could say they wouldn't get any more, but they will. Based on what we were told by the detective handling the case, there's a good chance the three of us will be testifying in court. I wish I could say I was excited for the opportunity to take down the three men who worked so hard to shut me up and steal my life, but honestly, I have better things to do.

Like go steal the rest of the women they're essentially holding captive.

I smooth down Myra's hair, trying to flatten the tangled mess. "Why don't you go take a shower? It'll make you feel better, I promise." A shower sounds heavenly, actually. Too bad my bandaged feet make that impossible. "Then get a good night's sleep and tomorrow we can figure out where we go from here."

Myra sniffles again, her watery eyes searching my face. "Please tell me you're not mad at me. I didn't mean to—"

"I'm not mad at you. Not even a little bit." I give her a soft smile. "I'm actually pretty proud."

Myra's puffy gaze moves to the men standing in the kitchen.

"They're not mad at you either. I promise." I'm actually pretty sure I already know what they're discussing, and it isn't how upset they are. "Everything is going to be okay."

It's the first time I've said it and meant it. Really believed things are going to be fine.

Sure, there are still some obstacles in the way, but after today I feel remarkably capable. Like I can handle whatever comes at me. That's probably because I know I won't be handling it alone, but still. I'm going to count it.

Myra presses her lips together, eyes remaining in the kitchen for a few seconds longer before she finally nods. "Okay." She smashes her ball of tissues against her face as she stands, wiping at the lingering wetness clinging to her flushed cheeks. "I'll see you in the morning."

"If you need me before then, you know where I'll be." I don't try to hide that I'll be sleeping in Christian's bed. I'm done pretending. Done feeling guilty for who I am and who I'm not.

Turning to Piper as Myra disappears down the hall, I look over my friend's injured form. She ended up getting the worst of it when the SUV crashed. Yet another thing I'm sure will dig at Myra. I reach out, intending to wake her so I can figure out how in the heck to get her to the second floor, but a deep voice stops me.

"I got her." Tate slowly moves in, carefully working one arm behind Piper's knees and one behind her back before gently lifting her off the couch to cradle her against his chest.

Piper barely stirs, her eyes fluttering open, lids heavy as she gazes at Tate. Her lips flatten into a frown. "You said I was fine." Her head drops to his shoulder, lids slipping closed again. "You're a fucking liar."

I could swear I catch the hint of a smile on Tate's mouth before it flattens out. He carefully navigates his way into the hall, angling his body to keep Piper's casted foot as far from the wall as possible.

Christian waits until they're gone before focusing on me. "What do you want to eat?"

My brain doesn't immediately recognize why he's asking, but my stomach does and growls loud enough I press one hand against it. "I don't think I've eaten today."

"I know you haven't because every time I tried to feed you at the hospital you swore you were fine." He opens the fridge and digs out a few foil-covered trays, reminding me that I have actually eaten, but not since breakfast. Which feels like forever ago. "And I was fine with that considering all they had to offer was shit from the vending machine, but now it's time for you to eat something."

I smile, finally willing to admit I don't hate a bossy man when the purpose for his bossiness is actually in my best interest. I came out of the IGL thinking I should never let a man tell me what to do, and feeling a little lost and ashamed because I don't actually hate being told what to do in certain situations. Specifically situations involving Christian.

I relax a little for the first time in hours, sinking deeper into the comfort of the sofa. Knowing he's got so much handled makes life a little less overwhelming. Makes figuring myself out a little less intimidating. "I'll eat whatever you put in front of me."

Christian's dark gaze fixes on mine. "Good girl."

My stomach flips the way it always does when he says those two magic words. I don't hate how free he is with praise, which makes me even more inclined to do what he says. Happily.

I stay on the couch while Christian warms up a couple plates of food. He brings them both to where I'm sitting, bandaged feet propped up on the ottoman, and settles one onto my lap before sitting beside me with the second. He flips on the television and we eat our late-night leftovers, laughing at an episode of some show where a woman moves in with three single guys. Despite the hilarity of the show, I yawn no fewer than ten times, and the minute the last bite has cleared my lips, Christian is collecting my dirty dishes and carrying them to the kitchen. He rinses them off and racks them into the dishwasher before scooping me up from the sofa.

"You really don't have to carry me around. My feet feel okay." They still sting a little, but it's nothing that should keep me from walking.

"Not happening. You've had a shitty day and there's no way I'm making you suffer more when there's something I can do to stop it." Christian moves down the hall, passing the front door as the alarm pings signaling the front gate's been opened.

"Maybe it's Tate and Simon going home." I yawn again, unable to stop myself.

"They left while we were eating." Christian's eyes narrow, jaw tight as two shadowy forms illuminate against the windows beside the front door. He glances around, going to the entry table and sliding my ass onto it before unlocking the door and opening it a crack. He seems to relax a little at the sight of whoever's on the other side and widens the opening, stepping back as Damien and the giant guy married to Shelly step in. They both glance my way, nodding in greeting.

Damien motions toward my feet. "How are you feeling?"

It's an interesting question. One I've been pondering most of the day. Technically, I was kidnapped. My feet burned like fire for the majority of the afternoon. My best friend broke her ankle and my sister is struggling with guilt and all it entails.

But I also never have to worry about my father again. I got Matthias back for some of what he's done to my family and what he helped do to victimize members of the IGL.

Today was definitely a mixed bag, but I feel like we came out on top. Like everything is going to be okay. And not just for us.

"I feel surprisingly good."

The big guy, Shaun, jerks his chin toward Christian's office. "We need to talk."

Christian studies Shaun cautiously as he comes my way, scooping me up from the table to deposit me in the chair behind his desk. He hovers while his brothers come in.

Neither one of them seem surprised that I'm a part of this conversation, and after meeting their wives, that makes sense to me. I can't imagine Shelly ever being okay with Shaun keeping her in the dark, and knowing Josie's history makes me sure Damien would never withhold information from her.

"We had some visitors while you were at the hospital." Shaun stands by the door, expression unreadable.

Christian goes completely still. "If you're about to tell me they came looking for Rodney today—"

"I don't think they're looking too hard for old Rodney." Damien smirks as he settles onto the sofa, stretching both arms across the back. "Seems like maybe Rodney was turning out to be more trouble than he was worth. His buddies didn't act super sorry to be rid of him."

I sit up straight, dread pooling in my belly. "They came here today?" I haven't been part of this family for very long, but I already feel surprisingly protective of them. They've all worked so hard to create the kind of safety and security they've never had before. The thought of being the one to steal that makes me sick to my stomach.

Damien points at Christian. "They wanted the money Lydia owes."

"Done." Christian doesn't hesitate.

"That's what I figured." Damien stands. "And why I went ahead and paid it."

My jaw drops open. Christian wanting to pay off my debt didn't surprise me, but Damien's willingness to put down that kind of cash without knowing the full situation is more than a little shocking. And solidifies all Christian has told me about the men he calls his brothers.

They really will do whatever it takes to protect me. To keep me just as safe as he does.

It makes my throat ache and my eyes burn. All I wanted was to get away from the men who only wanted to use me. Manipulate me. Take advantage of me. I never even considered I'd find a family that was the complete opposite of the one I was born into.

Christian moves behind the desk, flipping open one of the file size drawers that conceals a hidden safe. He quickly enters the passcode and opens it to reveal more money than I've ever seen in one place.

Grabbing a few stacks of hundreds, he holds them out to Damien. "Thank you for handling that for me." His eyes drift to where I sit. "For us."

Damien shrugs like it's no big deal. "You would've done it for me."

I feel like I should say something, but I'm struggling to come to terms with everything that's happening. I just started to wrap my head around the discovery that my father, Jeremiah, and Matthias were capable of doing much worse things than I expected in the name of power and control. Now I'm in a room with men who I *know* are capable of doing terrible things, but not for their own benefit.

It's a difficult dichotomy to rectify. I'm sure Christian and his brothers have done much worse than what my father and brother and brother-in-law did today, but the difference is stark. It's in the motives. The goals. Who gets hurt and who gets to gain. It's further proof that the limits of right and wrong, good and evil, are so much less black-and-white than I was taught to believe. The gray areas are almost everywhere, and I'm pretty sure I'm going to end up living in one myself.

"We'll get out of your way. We just wanted to be sure you knew what happened." Damien tucks the bills Christian gave him into one pocket of his expensive slacks. "I would also venture to guess we don't have anything to worry about as far as the whole Rodney situation is concerned." He glances at Shaun, lips twitching in a hint of a smile. "Someone made it real fucking clear they needed to stay as far from us as possible."

Shaun frowns, the expression consuming his entire face in a way that makes him look a little terrifying. "I haven't fucking forgot what they did to Shelly. They needed to know I'm still ready and willing to even out the universe."

My throat flexes, swallowing of its own accord because even I am a little scared of what exactly Shaun means by evening out the universe. And I didn't have any involvement in whatever he's talking about. But the murderous look on his face gives me hope that maybe they're right. Maybe this thing with Rodney is done.

But that seems awfully easy.

I stay put while Christian lets his brothers out, locking the door behind them before coming back to collect me, lifting me up out of the chair like he isn't just as exhausted as I am, and carrying me up the stairs to his room.

Our room.

He takes me straight into the bathroom, settling me on the side of the large garden tub before switching on the faucet.

I chew on my lower lip as the tub fills with warm water. Scrubbing away this mess of a day sounds glorious, but I'm struggling to get excited. My guilt over bringing Rodney's cohorts here looms thicker than the steam climbing toward the ceiling. "Do you really think they'll give up that easily?"

Christian reaches into the shower, collecting my shampoo, conditioner, and body wash. "I think it's possible."

I don't love that answer and it makes me ask a question I've been avoiding. "Did you and your brothers used to be like them?" I've been hesitant to ask up until now, but I want to really grasp the severity of the situation I got myself into. Got all of us into.

Christian lines my toiletries up along the ledge beside me, brows low as he considers. "In some ways, yes, but in some ways, no." He snags the washcloth from the cabinet, tossing it into the water as he comes to where I sit. "Arms up."

I lift my limbs, staying stretched as he peels my shirt over my head and tosses it into the garbage. "Hey."

"We don't keep clothes stained in someone else's blood, Lydia." Christian hooks his fingers into the waist of my cotton shorts. "Butt up."

I use my hands to leverage my rear end up enough that he can drag away the remainder of my garments, and only scoff a little when they go in the same can as my shirt.

Christian carefully helps me into the water, keeping my bandaged feet over the edge. Once I'm in place, he squeezes some body wash onto the cloth and begins to scrub my skin, his expression thoughtful. "We did a lot of the same illegal activities as The Horsemen. Sold drugs. Stole anything we could get our hands on. Whatever would make us quick cash." He rinses the cloth then uses it to wipe away the soapy residue. "We were like them, but they were never like us. They weren't a family. They fought with themselves as much as they fought with us, so no matter what they did they couldn't really compete because they were broken from the ground up." He slides the warm cloth over my chest, spending a little more time than necessary washing my breasts. "They tried to get it together for a little while a few years ago, but it didn't work and they started to go their separate ways. Rodney might have been one of the last real committed members left. Now that he's gone, hopefully everyone else will sort of fade away."

I watch him as he works on my legs, cleaning away any trace of what happened today. "Is that what you think will happen?"

Christian finishes washing my skin and moves to my head. "That's what I hope will happen." He motions for me to scoot forward. "Lean back so we can wash your hair."

I wiggle my butt across the slightly textured bottom of the tub and let him help me back into the water, the rumbly "good girl" he offers sending a jolt of heat straight through my insides. "What if it's not what happens?"

Christian's eyes hold mine as his strong fingers work through the tangle of my hair, separating the strands beneath the water. "Then I guess it's a good thing you have a family who can keep you safe."

EPILOGUE
CHRISTIAN

LYDIA GLANCES UP at the back door as Piper wobbles her way in. She looks over the new boot strapped to Piper's left foot and ankle. "Sexy."

Piper sticks her tongue out. "Shut up." She closes the door behind her, dropping her purse to the floor before hobbling her way to the kitchen island and sliding into one of the chairs. "If you think the boot is sexy, you should see what's underneath it." Her lip curls, nose wrinkling in the process. "My skin is peeling off everywhere and, based on the thickness and length of the hair growing on the lower portion of my shin, I'm pretty sure I might be part Sasquatch."

"Sasquatch, huh?" Lydia leans on the counter, propping her chin on one hand. "There's a place in West Virginia where you can go and stay at this bed-and-breakfast and hunt for Sasquatch." She wiggles her brows. "We should go. We might be able to find you a boyfriend."

"Gross." Piper shakes her head, looking disgusted. "I don't have time for a boyfriend." She turns her attention to where I stand at the stink. "Did you know your friend expects me to work forty freaking hours a week?"

"I have heard that rumor, yes." Between the testicle tasing incident and her broken ankle, Stella and Piper came to the joint conclusion that maybe continuing to work at The Cellar wasn't the best path forward, which left Lydia's friend a little devastated. Luckily, their lease on the townhouse they shared was practically up, so I offered to let her stay with us until she figured out what she wanted to do. Unfortunately, Piper hadn't given much consideration to her future, so coming up with a plan B was a slow and painful process. One that only ended when Tate accidentally mentioned he was in need of someone to help out at the front desk of his car shop.

I can't help but wonder if it wasn't as accidental as he made it seem.

Piper jumped on the opportunity, and for the past two weeks has been waking up early and getting to her new job on time, managing to make a career out of something she is hilariously skilled at: Driving Tate absolutely fucking crazy.

"At least everybody there likes to cook so there's always stuff to eat in the break room." Piper slumps down, folding her arms across the counter, letting her chin rest on top. "And Tate lets me go to the doctor whenever I have an appointment without having to find someone else to cover my shift."

"Do you have many more?" Lydia glances at the oven, grabbing a pair of hot mitts from the counter just as the timer starts to beep. "I thought they said the boot would be the last step."

"They did." Piper sighs. "But it seems like I have to wear the stupid thing for another six weeks to make sure everything is nice and healed." She straightens, holding her leg out, scowling at the medical grade brace strapped around her ankle. "It's just so ugly."

"Not as ugly as that broken bone was." Lydia pulls the giant dish of scalloped potatoes she's been working on all afternoon from the oven and slides them onto the counter. "I think if it had come through the skin I would have passed all the way out."

Piper goes a little pale, chin tucking like she's about to gag. "Stop. I can't even think about it." She glowers. "If I'd known your dumb-ass brother was gonna land his fat ass on my ankle when the car flipped over, I would've punched him again."

The reminder of where my former friend is going to be spending more than a few of his days always manages to lighten my mood. "I'm sure somebody will punch him in the face for you. Prison isn't a fun place for guys like him."

I can't help but smile at the thought of Jeremiah and his father facing down the general population while they wait for their court dates.

And it turns out they have plenty of them.

Once Ansel Parks wasn't around to rule with fear and threats, a whole lot of truths started being told. Truths that involved everything from conspiracy to money laundering to helping provide false alibis.

The last one is the one that interests me the most.

The prosecutor's office began looking into any case involving the IGL and started discovering some discrepancies. Crimes that were swept under the rug.

Like my sister's murder.

There's no guarantee they'll be able to make any charges stick, but for the first time I have hope her piece of shit husband will be held accountable, and that's enough for me right now.

Unfortunately, the prosecutor's office isn't the only place that's a mess because of Ansel and his son and son-in-law. Mountain Oak is crumbling fast, and more dangerous for women than ever as the men left scramble and fight for the power and control they've been built to believe is theirs.

"You're coming to dinner, right?" Lydia glances at Piper as she carefully wraps the potatoes with foil before zipping the dish into an insulated carrier while I collect our contribution to the dessert table.

Piper purses her lips like she's thinking it over, even though we all know she's not. She doesn't miss family dinner, but she likes to pretend she's undecided. Just in case the rug gets yanked out from under her.

My suspicions about Lydia's friend were right. All her bluster and aggression hide one of the most delicate hearts I've ever seen.

She's even worse than Shelly.

Piper sighs, continuing an act that is easy to see through. "I guess I could eat."

I take the potatoes from Lydia, carrying them with one hand and the brownies we baked in the other as we make our way out of the house and across the street to the converted firehouse where Cody and Felicity live.

Felicity opens the door as we file up the walk, her smile wide. "You have perfect timing." She steals the potatoes, lightening up my load. "Cody just fired up the grill."

I follow Piper and Lydia inside. The scent of food hangs in the air, along with the heavy drone of multiple conversations and rowdy kids. Myra waves from where she stands in the kitchen, helping Jill set up for our family dinner. It's an event that used to happen once a month but has recently become almost a weekly occurrence. And I'm not even a little mad about it. The girls need to feel supported and accepted, which is something my family's real good at.

Jill glances up as we walk in, immediately coming for the women at my side. Today she grabs Piper first, squeezing her in a tight hug. "How are you, honey?" She leans back, looking down at the new boot on Piper's foot. "Did everything go okay today at the doctor?"

Piper's lips pull into a small smile that she instantly flattens out. "I guess it went as well as it could have. I have to wear this ugly thing for six more weeks, but then I should be done."

"It's not that bad." Jill purses her lips, tapping one finger against her chin as she studies the boot. "I bet I know someone who could turn that thing into a work of art."

Piper snorts, rolling her eyes. "I'm pretty sure no one would ever call this thing a work of art no matter how much it's been bedazzled."

It's clear she thinks Jill is referring to Felicity's daughter and her penchant for gluing sequins and rhinestones to anything that holds still long enough—including a few pairs of my boots—but I know better. I see exactly what Jill's up to, and I'm pretty sure she's barking up the wrong tree.

Jill turns to Lydia, her expression soft as she pulls her in for the same tight hug she gave Piper. If I wasn't paying attention I might not notice she's careful to always rotate who she hugs first, but I don't miss anything that concerns Lydia. Thankfully she tolerates my hovering.

Might even like it a little.

Jill smooths Lydia's hair back from her face. "What about you, honey? How do you like working with Christian?"

Lydia sneaks a peek in my direction, and I know exactly

what she's thinking. "It's actually pretty great." Lydia smiles sweetly. "I think we're going to get a lot accomplished."

Jill pats her on the arm. "I bet you are. That boy's got a waiting list six months long. He needs all the help he can get."

I know Jill's proud of me, of the business I've built, but it's not what Lydia's talking about. While Lydia does seem to enjoy working with me and the rest of my team doing pre-construction demo in some of the nicest homes in Memphis, she enjoys our other job much more. The one we don't get paid for in cash.

What we do get is so much more valuable.

Jill moves down the line to focus on me. "And you've been working hard at more than just your day job, haven't you?" She grabs my face and hauls me down to plant a kiss on my cheek. "That front yard of yours is looking beautiful."

I chuckle. "It was mentioned that maybe I should stop putting that project off." I wrap one arm around Lydia's shoulders and pull her close, pressing a kiss to her temple just in case it's not already clear I'm teasing. "Apparently the outside of my house left a lot to be desired."

Piper snags a pretzel from one of the baskets on the island and pops it in her mouth. "It looked haunted." She thumbs over one shoulder in the direction of where Damien and Josie sit on the couch with Hope and Niko. "Especially when their cat comes over to mooch a snack."

Lydia grabs a pretzel of her own, crunching into it. "Poe is a sweet baby. He's allowed to come over for snacks when-ever he wants."

"Poe *is* a sweet baby, but hearing a creepy voice say *hello* as you walk from the garage to the back door in the dark is fucking terrifying when you don't know it's a cat meowing." Piper suddenly straightens, lips pressing together. She lowers her voice. "Did I just say fuck? I feel like I just accidentally said fuck."

Lydia scrunches up one side of her face in a wince. "I think it's a little too late to worry about it."

Piper's still acclimating to being around a family full of kids with eager ears and loose lips. She's managed to teach just about everyone capable of talking more than a few colorful words.

That includes some of my brothers.

The rest of the dinner passes like it normally does. Lydia has gotten more comfortable with everyone and even spends time chatting with Shelly and Felicity. She's no longer intimidated or overwhelmed and I love getting to see her bloom and grow.

Once everything is cleaned up we make our way back to my house, the four of us settling into my office just as Tate and Simon come through the front door.

Tate gives Piper a long glance, gaze lingering on her foot, but he doesn't ask how she is, confirming my suspicions that Jill is off the mark. His jaw is clenched as he turns to me. "What did you hear?"

"They're ready." Lydia is practically bouncing in her seat. I can feel the excitement radiating off her and I don't want anyone in this room to put a damper on it.

I stare Tate and Simon down, hoping they don't want to debate this. "The women have found a place to go and want our help getting there."

Simon's brows jump. "Really." He seems skeptical. "All five of them want to go to the same place?"

"Seven." Lydia sits perfectly straight in the chair behind my desk. As if she's daring anyone to tell her this isn't going to happen.

Tate's brows pinch together. "Seven, what?"

"There's not five, there's seven." Lydia lifts her chin, showing that hint of defiance she used to work so hard to hide. "One of the women has two little girls she's bringing with her."

"How's that going to work?" Simon pauses, like he's choosing his words carefully. "Won't her husband file kidnapping charges?"

"Her husband was one of the ones they arrested." Piper's voice is ice cold. "No one's bailing him out because they know he'll end up dead."

"She wants to file for divorce, but his parents are watching her like a hawk." Myra picks at one of her fingernails. "She has to be careful or she'll never get her girls out."

Tate glances at Simon before focusing on Lydia. "What's the plan?"

"We're going to go get them." She chews her lower lip, looking a little uncertain, and I can't blame her. I don't think Tate's going to be a big fan of what she says next. "Remember our initial plan when we went to get Myra?"

Tate's eyes roll Piper's way. She gives him a single-fingered wave. "Hey, husband."

He scrubs one hand down his face, rubbing at his eyes. "Shit."

"THAT WENT BETTER than I expected." Lydia follows me into our bedroom, closing the door. "I was a little worried Tate would refuse to help and we'd have to recruit one of your other brothers." Her lips twist to one side. "And I'm not sure which one of them would have been the next best option."

"None of them." I love my brothers and know they

would do anything they could to help us, but unless you've been part of the world we came from, it's hard to understand.

That's part of my concern when it comes to sending Piper in. Unfortunately, we don't have much of a choice. At least her healing foot will slow her down a little.

Lydia goes straight for the bathroom, switching on the shower. "I'm glad the girls are ready to go before we all have to go to court. Once that happens, Piper will be just as recognizable as we are." She turns just as I catch her, smiling as I pull her close. "What are you doing?"

"I like take-charge Lydia." I snag the hem of her shirt and lift. "You looked sexy as hell sitting behind my desk giving orders."

Lydia rolls her eyes. "I wasn't giving orders."

"You definitely were." I drag her T-shirt higher. "Which is good because we need you to give orders. You know how to escape that place better than anyone."

Instead of looking proud, Lydia looks a little sad. "I hope so. I really want to help those women get out of there."

"You will." I toss her shirt away and go to work on her shorts, flipping the button free before sending them sliding down her legs. "I promise."

I will move heaven and earth to help her get what she wants. To give her what she needs.

Lydia's eyes move over my face as she steps close, looping her arms around my neck. "Thank you."

"I should be thanking you." I slide my fingers over her cheek, relishing the moment. Enjoying finally having her to myself. Finally having the kind of closeness I never thought would be mine.

Her brows lift. "For what?"

I brush my lips over hers, peeling away her bra and panties. "For letting me fuck you in the shower."

Lydia gasps as my fingers find a nipple, teasing it to a tight peak. "You haven't done that."

"Yet." I tip my head toward the shower. "Get under the water."

Her eyes widen as a hint of pink creeps across her cheeks. Then she spins away, hurrying under the spray. I love how eager she is. How hungry she is for my touch.

I lean in, brushing her wet hair off her face. "Good girl."

Made in the USA
Las Vegas, NV
24 September 2023

78018758R00206